Based on a true story

Cry of

an

Osprey

Angie Vancise

Disclaimer

This is a work of fiction. Similarities to real people, places, or events are entirely coincidental.

CRY OF AN OSPREY

First edition. April 14, 2019.

ISBN: 978-1090238979

Written by Angie Vancise.

angievancise.com

angievanciseauthor@gmail.com

To my brother

"I love you and that is the beginning and end to everything.

F. Scott Fitzgerald

1

∾ℰ∾

BEN

July 2013

It was misty, the sun not up yet when I reached the shore. After placing my knapsack carefully on a rock, I stripped off my shorts and T-shirt and jumped in. The water of the bay was cold, only 65 degrees but normal for the island at this time of year. It felt bracing and familiar—yet unfamiliar. When I came up for air, I could smell cedar, algae, damp earth.

Usually I loved swimming naked, but today I felt strangely vulnerable. When I reached the large granite rock, I climbed on it and just stood there, shivering a little, gazing back toward the shore. For how long I'm not sure. It was just light enough that I could spot the place at the water's edge where Jax, Nikko, and I had posed when my camera's timer snapped that cherished picture.

I swore I heard Jax laugh.

I slipped into the water and swam back to shore, climbed out and quickly dried off after gently removing my towel from the knapsack. Drawing a deep breath, I thought about this island near Tobermory Harbour, how it had come to mean so much to my family, and to me. Ordinarily being on Flowerpot soothed me. But the sun, just coming up, was casting a sad yellow haze over the rough and rocky terrain and dulling the green of the trees. Georgian Bay, which a little later this morning would soon show off its Caribbean blues, was now an ominous grey fading out to a deep empty black.

As I pulled on my clothes, I squinted up at the small white lighthouse keeper's house. No one seemed to be up yet. I'd left Amelia and my kids in bed.

This was something I needed to do alone.

Picking up my knapsack, I headed for the main path, backtracking up past the house, continuing until I spotted the expansive maple tree. I climbed the eight-foot earthen cliff to another path, which brought me to a smooth flat rock set at a challenging 60-degree angle. If the incline wasn't daunting enough, the slippery algae made it more so. I remembered coaxing Jax that day. He'd laughed each time he slid back down: "See, I told you I couldn't do it." But he was always game for anything. Eventually he'd made it.

At the top of the rock, I slowed my pace, and reaching the oak tree where I was to turn left, I stopped for a moment.

My chest constricted, and I had to force myself to breathe. Finally, I pushed a branch out of the way, and there it was before me—the cliff, just visible in the mist.

I could hardly believe it had been nine months. So much had changed. For me, for all of us. It occurred to me that the island would be here long after all of us were gone.

The breeze was like an exhale, the leaves clicking like tiny maracas, as I stepped out onto the cliff top. A blue heron coasted toward the shoreline. I sat down slowly and dangled my legs off the edge, looking toward the horizon. The darkness of the bay seemed to go on forever.

I slipped the knapsack off my back and, hands trembling, rested it on the rock beside me.

2

AMELIA

October 21, 2012

I can't wake your brother up!" It was the way my Mom said it that made me fluff it off. She sounded confused, almost angry.

"What? What do you mean?" I said over the phone.

I was only half listening, wondering why I'd hit *snooze*, and how on earth I would ever get ready in time to get Dad to his appointment in Barrie for nine. It was a 45-minute drive and it was already eight. I would have to forego a shower—*damn*. I reached for my shirt and cradled the phone in my ear while putting my arm through a sleeve. The phone fell to the floor.

"Are you there? Did you hear me? What happened, where are you?"

I bent over and grabbed the phone again. "Sorry, Mom, I'm fine. Dropped the phone. I have to take Dad to this weird energy appointment for nine, and I slept in. I'm kind of stressed. We're going to be late—What's this about Jax? Another one of his exaggerated symptoms? Wait, I'm going to put you on speaker phone."

I placed the phone on the dresser and grabbed my pants.

"Rex went into Jax's room this morning and started barking at the side of his bed," Mom said. "When Bart went in to check on him and see what Rex was doing, he couldn't wake him up. We…we still can't."

I could hear a tightness in her voice, as if she was trying not to cry. In the background I heard Mom's boyfriend Bart shouting at Jax to wake up, then a ruckus like he might be shaking him. Mom had met Bart on a dating site that I'd set up for her. He wasn't the one I would have chosen, but that was a discussion for another time.

"Is he…is he…breathing?"

"Yes."

Relief.

"But he's not moving, and he's still not waking up."

My chest constricted.

"I heard him get up at six and go to the bathroom. He was stumbling and banging into the walls. I got up to help him. He took his blood pressure meds, then went back to bed. Now he's not responding…to anything. I don't know what to do!"

"What the hell is going on?"

My pants were on backwards. I dragged them off and turned them around. My shirt was wrinkled, and I noticed I'd grabbed two different coloured socks.

I was angered by the call and wasn't sure why. Jax was taking up a lot of attention from everyone lately, and I was already late.

"Mom, let me call Katie. I'll call you right back."

I threw my hair into a clip and dialled my stepsister. Katie was an Emerg nurse in Oshawa and would know what to do.

She answered on the first ring. The call was quick and to the point. I called Mom back.

"Don't you go in the ambulance with him, Mom. He's relying on us way too much lately. He needs to wake up without anyone there. Katie said this would be good for him, okay? Do you understand? She feels that he needs tough love right now."

Mom agreed. We said goodbye and I hung up the phone.

Holy, I was going to be late. Great, just what I needed: Dad on my back. *Shit…Dad. How would I tell him about Jax?* Dad had been saying for ages that there was more going on with my brother than we believed. *Was he right?*

Just last night we'd taken Jax to the Royal Victoria Hospital (RVH), Emergency Department in Barrie. He had visual problems, pressure at the base of his neck, high blood pressure. The doctor had said he was one hundred percent sure that Jax was fine, just suffering from anxiety.

So, what was this today?

And then that "fit," as Mom had called it on the way home after the hospital visit yesterday. His complexion had turned white, and his voice went funny, like low and droning. His entire body had spasmed, and he'd said, "I'm having a stroke!" He was shaky, and I had to help him into Mom's house after we arrived. Should I have taken him straight back to the Emerg then?

My anger and frustration began to fade, replaced by confusion. Fear. I took a deep breath, no longer worried about how late I was going to be for Dad. Questions battled in my mind. I thought of last night and how as I was leaving Mom's, I'd had the strongest urge to run over to the couch where Jax lay and hug him. I thought it would scare him, that he'd wonder why I was doing that. Do you think I'm going to die? would have been his first question, so I refrained. But I should have hugged him. He didn't want me to leave, begged me to stay. Now that I thought of it, he'd seemed a bit desperate, like he knew something. I remembered the ache in my gut as I left.

It was coming back.

They will get him to the hospital and all will be fine. He has to be okay.

But still, I had to call Fredrik, Jax's partner. He'd need time not only to absorb this but to arrange for a ride if necessary. He lived in Toronto, a couple of hours away, and didn't drive. While I was on the phone with him, Stu came into the room and stood by, listening to the conversation. We'd been married for twelve years. I recognized the veiled look on his face as worry. Fredrik said he'd get there as soon as he could.

I filled Stu in before leaving to get Dad. Although I told him I'd keep him posted, I hated rushing away. It was such a bomb to lay on Stu. He'd have the burden of telling Larissa, our daughter, after she'd come home after school. She and her Uncle Jax were close, she his only niece and often spoiled by him. I wasn't sure how she'd react. Fifteen was a confusing age for her: figuring out boys, friends, hormones, and trying to become her own person. I hated leaving before I could tell her about Jax myself. But, in truth, I didn't know much yet. Maybe everything would be okay. It had to be.

When I set off for Dad's condo—only a few minutes' drive away—the day was cold, damp, and grey. Typical for October. The sky looked angry. Maybe it didn't like the thought of winter either. The bright red, yellow, and orange leaves had mostly disappeared, leaving shriveled brown ones dangling until the wind blew them away onto their next journey. I smelled colder weather approaching.

Angie Vancise

A thick cloud hovered over the mountain, swallowing up its peak. Blue Mountain was my home, part of the Niagara Escarpment running 725 kilometres north from Niagara Falls to Tobermory in Ontario. Jax and I had learned to ski there as a kids. We'd gone for long family hikes on the trails through the forests. So many cherished memories--not just for me, but four generations of Vanbeermens who'd emigrated from Holland as farming settlers.

Pulling into Dad's condo, I wondered, should we have cancelled his appointment? *No… Jax would probably be awake and on the mend by the time we got back.*

I took a deep breath as I watched Dad walk toward the car, his cane in hand, a happy greeting on his face. He carried the cane more for confidence than balance.

"Hi, Sweetie, how are you?" he said opening the door. "Do you think this appointment is worth going to? Do you really think they're going to be able to help me?" He got in.

Gee, I wonder where Jax gets his worrying from?

Dad too had been dealing with health issues, and the doctors had prescribed so many meds. Heart meds, cholesterol meds, urine flow meds, stomach meds. His hands ached, his feet ached, and he suffered dizziness. Hence, the cane. His blood pressure was really low, and he'd lost a lot of weight. Side effects of his meds, or something else? We weren't sure, but I'd bet money on the side effects. Dad, however, was a strong believer in mainstream medicine, and trying to get him to look at anything else was like trying to straighten a warped door. His stepdaughter, Wendy, was a nurse who never thought outside the box. But a friend of his had told him about this energy-type treatment, whatever that meant.

Keeping my expression neutral, I said, "Hi, Dad, I'm not sure even what it is they'll do, but why not try anything."

I didn't want to look at him; he would instantly know something was wrong. Intimate conversation could be uncomfortable with him.

But today, he leaned over and kissed my cheek. Grabbing my hand, he said, "My darling daughter, at least I get to spend the rest of the day with my Sweetie."

He buckled his seatbelt. We began the 45-minute drive to Barrie, my mind in turmoil with thoughts of Jax.

Because of Jax's health problems over the past year, my brother had become reliant on family for almost all of his physical and emotional needs. His anxiety created additional problems that we found hard to believe existed. For example, we thought his vision problems resulted from him not breathing properly. He'd always been a worrier, *a mountains out of molehills* kind of guy. As a kid, he was an occasional worrier, but over the last year his worrying had amplified. When he looked through a screen, he'd say his vision was weird. Isn't everyone's? He was so uptight and hypersensitive that we didn't know what was real and what wasn't.

A year or so ago he was taken to the Collingwood General and Marine Hospital with alarmingly high blood pressure, 266/144. They rushed him through to a trauma bay. He lay on a gurney, dread in his eyes, staring at the monitor and asking us every five minutes, "What is my blood pressure now? Why isn't it going down? Do you think I have clogged arteries like Dad? Am I going to die? Am I having a heart attack?"

For the first time in forty-three years, seeing him in that trauma room, I was scared that I could lose my big brother. I had never before pictured my life without him. He was too big an energy to live without. I mean, we all knew we were going to die one day, but I'd always assumed we'd eventually become two old farts wreaking havoc on the nursing home.

As annoying as he could be, I loved him anyway. In fact, I needed him. I needed him for when we would lose our parents. I needed him for all the good and bad times I knew would be ahead. As my older brother, he'd been my strength growing up. He was lively and fun to be around, at least…until his recent setbacks.

I remember the room had smelled of latex and rubbing alcohol, with occasional whiffs of something unpleasant that I didn't want to think too much about. A nurse rushed by the door. I heard one kid vomiting, a woman was moaning, and the rest of the curtains were drawn. Ambulance gurneys were being pushed by with old and young lying on them.

Shaking my head, I'd said to him, "No, Jax, you aren't going to die, don't be silly."

I wondered if he could see how scared I was too. I reached over and put my hand on his, probably as much for me as for him.

"Then why do they have me in a trauma room? They must think I'm going to die."

He pushed himself up in the bed with his hands by his hips. He crooked his neck around to look at the monitor.

"Oh, for god's sake, they put you here because your blood pressure is really high, and they need to try to get it down. If you'd just calm down, maybe your blood pressure would too."

I was sure he made his blood pressure worse.

"And perhaps they had no other beds—did you ever think of that?"

Nothing calmed him.

After about six hours and two Ativans, the hospital released him with a blood pressure reading of 144/100. That was still high, but they advised him to go to his family doctor and to continue with Ativan, blood pressure pills, and some heart meds. My brother wouldn't admit that he didn't have a family doctor; he suffered a serious case of white-coat syndrome.

That next year, following that visit, had been hell for him and for all who knew him. My fun-loving, crazy brother became withdrawn and scared, not wanting to stray far from home or family. He stopped working and texted hourly. He'd asked repeatedly if he was dying, or why his blood pressure wouldn't go down; but when we suggested he go get checked, he'd only become more upset.

He'd finally found a family physician, but he couldn't seem to get his pressure below the 140/100 range or find the reason for the spike. All test results showed no blockages. The doctor labelled him anxious and chalked it up to that.

Two weeks ago, at Katie's wedding—and during my welcoming Mark into our family speech—Jax had collapsed to the floor. A later CT scan showed nothing, and his bloodwork was all normal. Again, the conclusion, 'It's just anxiety.'

And then, last night's race to Emerg. *What did it all mean?*

The trip to Barrie felt longer than usual.

I knew I had to find the courage to tell Dad about Mom's call regarding Jax. We were about halfway there when I'd found it.

At first, he didn't say anything. Glancing over, I saw the vein in his neck pulsing. His expression alternated between

14

confusion and anger. He'd been telling Jax to get more tests, that something else was wrong.

After a few minutes, he placed his fingers over the pulsing vein, coughed, then sputtered, "What the hell are we doing? What were you thinking? You should have told me this right away! Jax is in the hospital, and we are going to some stupid appointment that I'm sure won't do anything anyway." His voice grew louder. "Pull over and turn around, Amelia. We have to get to the hospital."

Feeling flushed, I pulled onto the shoulder, turned and headed back to Collingwood. I'd been trying to convince myself that Jax's condition couldn't be serious. I wanted to believe the paramedics would get him to wake up and he'd be fine. My thoughts were now racing, nausea setting in. Swallowing it back I focused on the road ahead.

Dad and I hadn't always had the relationship that we did now. And it was in times like these that I was reminded of the awkwardness still lurking between us.

The ride back felt even longer than the way down. Dad was quiet and just stared out the window clearing his throat and fiddling with his hands, picking at his cuticles.

I tried to make small talk, but he seemed uninterested in that.

I called Mom for an update, but nothing had changed. Jax was still in Collingwood, still unresponsive, still not waking up. I could hear Bart in the background repeating the same thing, 'It's not good, Amelia, it's not good.' Mom said the doctor thought Jax might have had a stroke. They might have to rush him to Sunnybrook in Toronto. But not yet. So maybe they were wrong…?

My brother wasn't making mountains out of molehills now. My fingers ached as I clenched the steering wheel tight. It was time to make some calls. This wasn't going to be easy in front of Dad. Unclenching my fingers, I pushed the buttons on the steering wheel to start Bluetooth and call my cousin Tom. He, Jax, and I had grown up together. Tom was two years younger than me, six years younger than Jax. We were like siblings, really. As kids, when Jax and I weren't at home, we were mostly at Tom's. Though he tried to hide his reaction, I could tell the news shocked Tom. He said he and my Uncle Arthur would meet us at the hospital. I called a couple of my close friends, but they were working. I left messages.

Katie said she'd leave Oshawa when she could after making arrangements for her three young children. Although she was two and a half hours away, somehow having her there would settle my stomach. I hoped she could make the arrangements as soon as possible. She was a stepsister from my mom's second marriage to a man who'd passed away from cancer years earlier. They weren't together that long, maybe five years, but Katie had immediately become family and had remained close to us. Besides maybe she could make some sense out of all of this.

During the calls, Dad kept clearing his throat and shaking his head, making me feel more uncomfortable and self-conscious. I didn't know what to say to help him or even if I could. Didn't he know that my own guilt was bad enough? He didn't need to make me feel worse.

I still hadn't heard from Ben, and I wondered if he'd received the message I'd left earlier. I sent him another text to make sure. I'd texted Stu to tell him there was no change but that I was worried and that we were on our way back to Collingwood.

Thirty minutes later, we pulled into the hospital parking lot. I dropped Dad off at the Emergency entrance. I noticed him using his cane to make his way to the bench in front of the door. Worried he was going to fall, I put the car in park got out and slipped my arm under his, guiding him to the seat. "Wait here— I'll be right back."

I parked the car, and as I got out, the cool dampness in the air went straight to my bones. I scanned the lot for Ben's truck. Not here yet. The last I'd heard from Fredrik he was still waiting on a ride up from Toronto. We agreed to text each other for updates.

Angie Vancise

It remained a dull October day. Dad looked much older sitting there on the bench, I thought as I walked over. The worry on his face created a lump in the pit of my stomach. I had the urge to run back to the car and drive away. I was afraid of what we were about to see, to find out.

I looked over at the helicopter pad. No helicopter. They hadn't air-lifted Jax to Toronto. Mom would have let me know that. What did that mean? Would it be good news or bad?

I joined Dad at the bench, hooked my arm through his again helping him up. Together we walked into a hell that no one expected that day.

3

BEN

October 21, 2012

I pulled into the parking lot on squealing tires and snapped off my seatbelt even before I stopped the truck. The northeastern wind slammed me the moment I opened the door and jumped out, ice pellets hitting my face like needles. The wind stank of dead worms and wet wood. The parking lot was slippery, but I ran in quick sprints with my head down and my hands in my pockets. The sky was ominously dark, I thought.

I stopped when I reached the main doors, captured inside my own fear, suddenly unable to breath. Hesitantly I stepped through the double doors that opened into a tiny vestibule.

The voice message from Amelia spun in my head, hardly comprehensible.

Angie Vancise

The vestibule led into a small room with a few plastic chairs and tables on one side. To the left was a glass partition behind which a woman was seated, *Cashier* written above her head. There was only a scattering of people in the room, one of them an elderly lady in a wheelchair with a volunteer standing behind her. The rest, I assumed, must be waiting to see a doctor, or waiting to see loved ones. There were two very pregnant women shuffling up and down the halls, grimaced faces. *In labour*. That scared me. I'd heard once that when a baby is born, someone dies.

Stop.

I pushed the thought away and looked toward the gift shop. A few people were there buying flowers or cards, one of them holding a balloon announcing IT'S A BOY.

Jax has been rushed to the Emerg at Collingwood General and Marine Hospital. Mom couldn't wake him up.

To my left a volunteer behind a small desk told a man what room his family member was in. *Couldn't wake him up. Emerg.* I was about to ask about Jax, when I realized that I wasn't in Emerg. What was I thinking? Dazed, I turned and walked back out the doors into the barrage of freezing rain and along the path to the proper entrance.

Ambulances were lined up in the bay, and when I entered, the waiting room was full of people—people I didn't know. Collingwood is a small town, and it's odd being in a

20

group anywhere and not seeing at least one familiar face. But I was relieved. I really didn't feel much like talking.

The message had come in from Amelia around 10 a.m. It was now two o'clock. I'd replayed it in my mind several times, hoping I'd heard wrong. I'd been in my workshop—an old barn I'd converted—building a custom railing for a home nearby. It wasn't until I headed into the house around noon to grab a bite for lunch that I saw I had a message.

They're rushing Jax to Emerg. He's still breathing but won't wake up. They tried several times, but nothing. If you get this message, please meet us at the hospital. We will be in Emerg.

I moved to the living room and sat on my sofa, dumbfounded. What could be wrong? Was this why he hadn't responded to my text the night before?

I had tried to get up several times to go to the hospital but couldn't seem to find the strength. Also, I didn't think it was my place to be there. When the shock dwindled, I bolted out the door. By that time there had been four more unanswered texts from Amelia, each sounding more urgent than the last.

I must have looked like I needed assistance, because a nurse rushed right over and asked if I was okay.

"I'm here to see Jax—Jaxon Vanbeermen. He was brought in a few hours ago."

"Are you related to Mr. Vanbeermen?" Her tone was gentle.

I knew that if I didn't lie, I wouldn't get in to see him.

I cleared my throat. "He's my partner," I said.

"Oh, let me take you to him right away. We usually only allow one person in, but under the circumstances we'll make an exception."

Under the circumstances. What did she mean?

I wondered whether Fredrik was in there with him. If so, I'd be caught in my lie. What I wanted was to be alone with Jax.

Fredrik had met him in Toronto a couple of years after I'd kicked Jax out. *I* was the one who'd let him go. I'd let someone else have him for ten years. Twelve years wasted, dating back to our breakup. All that time. *We could have been making memories.*

I had always tried to be respectful of their relationship. I knew Jax loved Fredrik, though I knew he loved me too. They lived together, bought a condo a couple of years back, sold it and bought a house on the Danforth in Toronto. Jax worked at a local car dealership in Collingwood and stayed with his sister, mom, or friends for part of the week, Toronto for the other when he had his days off. We had been making a point of getting together for dinner at least once a week since our second year apart. It had been too hard that first year, awkward, but it was even harder to stay apart. Jax would bring in dinner, and we'd catch up, always knowing that secretly we each wished for more.

Unlike me, Fredrik was comical and knew how to have a great time. Jax needed that. I had always been too tame for him. Fredrik was opposite to me in looks too with dark hair and being a bit shorter. His build was more like Jax's being that of average size. Something must have worked between them, they were together ten years. We'd only lasted four and a half years, not nearly enough time.

"His mom, dad, and sister are with him now," the nurse said, breaking into my thoughts. "Follow me."

The Emergency entrance wasn't all that different from the main one, apart from the dozens of chairs for waiting patients. The triage nurse sat right in front of the entrance with about eight more chairs opposite her for new arrivals. There were two sanitizer stations within ten feet of the door. I automatically placed my hand underneath the closest one and massaged the gel liquid over my hands.

The nurse guided me toward two large wooden doors that only opened with a key tag. They led us straight into a spacious room sectioned off into tiny spaces, blue curtains pulled across the entrance to most of them. Nurses and other workers in scrubs scurried among them.

The hospital was founded in 1887 with only eight beds. It had since grown to 72, but otherwise hadn't changed much, with aqua painted concrete blocks for walls. I remember as a kid tracing the grout lines with my finger anytime I had to wait with my parents. Dad often cut himself while working on the farm.

Peering through a few slightly open curtains as we passed, I could see one patient coughing, another moaning, another holding what appeared to be an injured hand. I found it hard to care—I really just wanted to get to Jax.

My legs were so weak they quivered under me. As we passed the nurses' station, some of them were on their computer monitors or talking to doctors, while others were talking about their weekend.

I overheard one say to a doctor, "When are you going to talk to the family?"

"When all of the family gets here," said the doctor.

Please don't let them be talking about Jax.

"Here he is. I'll leave you with him." The nurse gestured me toward trauma room 2, then turned and disappeared.

For a moment I stood where she'd left me, motionless. I had seen on one of those *Trauma: Life in the ER* reality shows that these trauma rooms are larger to give the medical team ample space to work on a patient in the case of a Code Blue.

Did they have to work on Jax? Did he Code Blue? I shook the idea from my head. *He'll be fine—it's Jax.*

I pushed the curtain aside and entered.

My eyes went first to the figure in the bed, the seemingly lifeless body of Jax. Amelia was sitting beside him, holding his hand. Her face was pale, and she'd been crying. Their mom was on the other side, pushing her son's hair off his forehead. She was talking to him. I detected a sense of sadness in her when he wasn't responding back. Their Uncle Arthur stood at Amelia's side with his hand on her shoulder. *Of course, that's where he'd be—he practically raised them.*

I saw a clear hose coming from Jax's mouth and realized he was on a breathing machine. *Not breathing on his own? How bad is this?* In the background, I could hear music, unsure where it was coming from. Don Henley. I recognized the lyrics from somewhere. *Where? When?*

Then it came to me: sixteen years ago, the spring of 1996, when I first saw Jax.

*

The window of the truck was down, and I took in a deep breath. The spring air smelled of hot pavement and cedar trees mixed with a floral scent I didn't recognize. The road ahead seemed to float in the mirage of heat. Don Henley played on the radio. The warm wind was blowing my hair off my face, though one strand insisted on making the corner of my eye its resting place. Peter

25

was turned and looking out his window. That wasn't unusual for Peter. He didn't talk much, and neither did I, making the silence awkward. His elbow rested on the window frame, and his fingers gripped the top. My mother's words, as we were leaving, were still ringing in my ears.

What are you doing with this man? Why can't you work things out with Michelle? She was such a nice Christian girl. I had hopes for you, Ben. And perhaps the most painful: *What are the children going to think?*

Turning up the radio to drown out her voice, I sang along, "*I saw a dead head sticker on a Cadillac.*" Tapping the steering wheel, I looked down at my gas gauge.

It was around noon when I pulled into the small Esso station at the corner of Mosley and the town line in Wasaga Beach, a small tourist town close to where I grew up. You can walk for miles on the longest fresh-water beach in the world. We locals refer to it as Wasaga, or simply, the Beach.

This drive always took me back to childhood days. I remember sinking my toes into the warm sand. My family would pack a cooler and head down for a day. We'd change behind towels on the open beach without a care in the world. The westerly sun would disappear behind the mountain, casting orange, yellow, pink, and purple rays that rippled out onto the water. They rolled and danced onto the sand, creating the most spectacular sunsets. The entire bay became a kaleidoscope of colour. I'd watch as the coloured waves melted my sandcastles away.

It has been said that Al Capone once owned a hotel right at the main end. The "main end" is what we call beach area 1, and it's where there are shops and bars as well as a cruising road adjacent to the sandy shore. You feel like you could be somewhere in Miami. Most locals stay clear of that part of the beach; it's too congested. We always end up somewhere around beach area five.

Pulling up to the gas pump, I leaned over to reach for my credit card, and when I turned back, there, standing at the open window, was the most gorgeous guy I'd ever seen. I sat staring at him, speechless. For a moment I completely forgot what I was even doing there, and that he was waiting for me to tell him how much gas I needed. He could have been a model or a film star, I thought.

I wondered if Peter, who was looking our way, had seen my involuntary reaction. Peter and I had met just a few weeks back, and we were going canoeing today. He had lovely brown medium length hair and sexy blue eyes, but he couldn't hold a candle to the gas attendant. I felt bad for thinking that this guy was hot, but I'm almost positive Peter was thinking it too. A confidence flowed from the attendant, drawing me to him even more. It was a confidence Peter lacked. In the two weeks we'd been hanging out, conversation had felt forced. Peter was reserved and quiet; words didn't come easily to him. He often bowed his head and stared at the ground, making it near impossible to engage him.

"Uh, oh, ah…could you fill it with diesel please?"

Heat rose to my cheeks. Mother would have quoted a scripture or told me to drive to another gas station. Again, I wondered if Peter saw my reaction. I thanked the Lord it was a hot day, so maybe this gas guy and Peter wouldn't notice my flush.

I watched him in the side mirror walk back to remove the gas cap. *Man, stay cool, Ben.* He pulled open the small door that hid the cap, unscrewed it, and inserted the diesel nozzle. As he stood there filling the tank, I couldn't stop looking. He was in his thirties, close to my age. It was hard to tell, but he appeared to be about my height. His face was a perfect oval shape with soft-looking, caramel-coloured skin. His hair was golden brown with lightened ends. The sun's reflection turned it into a halo. His large round eyes were hazel, I thought, but dark enough to appear brown.

He looked over then and caught me staring at him in the mirror. He smiled—I had never seen such a gorgeous smile— then looked at the ground. I had been wondering if he was interested in me, and the downward glance, for some reason, reassured me.

I quickly looked away and pretended to fiddle with something in my armrest, then noticed a bible. *Oh, for god's sake, Mom, even in my truck?* Since Michelle and I broke up, I'd been finding bibles all over the house. I glanced again at the guy in the mirror.

I think Peter might have said something to me, although I have no recollection of what. When I glanced back at this intriguing stranger, he was staring over at the other cars in the lot across the way. A click signaled the tank was full, and it startled me. *That was too fast.* I just wanted to sit there and watch him all day. I felt like a schoolboy. I wanted to ask him his name, but I didn't want to be rude to Peter. I decided in the end that I could maybe come back another day, without Peter. It was the appropriate thing to do.

"Hey, man, how much do I owe you?" With shaky hands, I handed this fine man my credit card. After paying, I drove off with Peter, trying to focus on our canoe adventure. But the truth is, I felt distracted all day.

In the days following, I did find myself going out of my way to get fuel even when I didn't need it—and without Peter. But the sexy attendant was never there, and I began to wonder if he'd moved on. How could my luck be so bad? I wasn't giving up, though. Was this just a part-time gig for him? Maybe he worked only one day a week? I wasn't sure, but I was determined to keep going back until I saw him.

Finally, a couple of weeks after that first encounter, my luck changed. I pulled up, and there he was. It was another gorgeous June day. My hands shook and a bead of sweat formed on my brow.

"Hey there, nice to see you again." He smiled. "What's your name?"

I was caught off guard. I said nothing, momentarily stunned. *He remembers me?*

It was a relief not to have Peter in the car. Maybe that was why this guy was speaking to me this time? *Don't worry, beautiful stranger, Peter is gone and won't be returning.*

I had explained to Peter a few days after our canoe trip that I felt we just didn't have enough in common. The forced conversation, the zero-eye contact. The relationship was going nowhere. "I think it's fair for you to move on," I'd said, but really, it was to let me move on. Each time I was with him, I could only think of this guy.

Finally, able to speak I said, "It's Ben—and you?"

"Jax. It's nice to meet you."

I smiled. "Jax, that's a cool name. Is it short for something?" Sweat was running down my back. I must have looked like I'd just done a workout, and I hoped he wouldn't notice.

"Jaxon. My mom named me after my great-grandfather. Do you live around here? I've seen you come in a few times."

He'd seen me? Why hadn't he said anything? Had he seen me from inside and was too busy to come out?

I put my hand out the window, and when he shook it, I didn't want to let go. His was so warm, and small but strong.

I reached into the armrest to grab my wallet and saw the bible I'd forgotten to take out. I pushed it under some papers.

This time I got out of the truck and stood beside him while he pumped the fuel. I wanted to be closer to him. He was wearing a soft musk aftershave. It smelled wonderful, and he wasn't wearing too much. Some guys drown themselves in it, especially gay guys. *Maybe he's not gay?*

"Yeah, I just live about ten minutes from here," I replied closing my door. "Hey, I was wondering if you might like to get together sometime, you know, for dinner or something. I'll bake a pie!" *A pie?* Shit, the words had flown out of my mouth before I could stop them. And now the saliva in my mouth had vanished, making it hard to swallow, let alone talk.

"Hang on, I just have to grab that other car—but I'd really like that." Jax looked back at me as he walked away. Then he flicked his hair out of his eyes and smiled.

That smile—it flaunted perfect teeth. It was definitely his best feature, although coming in a close second were his hazel eyes. I hoped he liked me, and I hoped that he was gay. I had met cute men before, but this one felt different. There was

31

something about him that seemed to speak to me. Like I knew him from another life or something. Now, I know that sounds weird, it sounded weird even to me, but I'd heard of that before—was it in church maybe? I wasn't sure; all I knew was that our connection, at least for me, seemed too strong to ignore.

My thoughts drifted as I watched him. I remembered being in school, I was never teased like other guys I knew. Some were beaten up on a weekly basis. A few gays in larger cities like Toronto were murdered for being different. Some killed themselves. I'm not sure if it was from the shame, the guilt, or something else. They couldn't live with their demons. I felt a little luckier than them, because I never had to deal with all of that on top of my family's disgust. I'm not sure I could have handled it. I guess in that sense I could understand why some took their lives; my family was more than enough to deal with. Then came AIDS, and that certainly didn't help the homophobes; it just gave more ammunition for them to be cruel, calling it the gay disease. Shouting things out like, "Well good, let that take them all out." Yep. This life can certainly test you. I wouldn't have chosen it, if in fact I had a choice.

I watched him with the other customer. He was friendly and had a great energy about him. He displayed a confidence that I'd always desired for myself. His smile seemed to make other people smile, and in their body language I could see that they felt good around him. His physique wasn't too shabby either. His jeans snuggly hugged his perfect butt.

I waited for him to finish the other car. Since no one else had pulled in, I thought I'd wait to set a date for the dinner. I didn't want to miss this opportunity. I couldn't.

He walked back toward the truck.

"So … how is this Thursday? Do you work that night?" My lips got stuck on my teeth.

"Nope, Thursday is my day off." He smiled again.

Man, he's sexy.

I never quite fit in with the "flaming guys" nor with straight guys. I fell somewhere in between. I felt different from everyone else, a sort of stranger to both worlds, it would seem. And Jax, well, he seemed more like… me. He carried himself like a straight man—no lisp, no floppy hand—yet he had softness, a kindness and confidence that were compelling. I wondered if he really did prefer men, or was he just being nice?

"Oh, that's great man! Okay, say, around 5? I can take you for a hayride around the farm before dinner, or we could go for a walk. Do you have a piece of paper? I'll give you directions. It's really easy—it's on the 6th."

I know what I'd like to do in that hay—Okay, stop that.

He brought his hand up and scratched his temple looking right at me. "6th Line? By the airport? There are many 6th's." His eyes peered right into my soul.

33

"Yes, that's the one. My great-grandfather built the place in the 1800s. It's old, but it's home."

"It's a small world." Jax leaned against the gas pump and crossed one ankle over the other. The warm breeze tousled his hair. "My grandfather built a farm and a farmhouse on the 4th Line, but it was in the early '50s. His dad, my great-grandfather Jax, built a small house before that on the same property in the late 1800s, when he and seven of his brothers moved over from Holland, but it came down when the new house went up. I practically grew up there, so I know exactly where the 6th Line is. He farmed pigs and had a couple of horses. We used to take the horses across the train tracks and ride them to the 6th." His voice rose and his expression had changed when he mentioned the farm; it obviously held fond memories.

"Then that must be the great-grandfather you are named after?" I asked, and Jax nodded. "Cool, man. By the train tracks … that's just about right across from me. I'm just past the bridge on the right when heading south, number 24111. You know the green 911 sign?"

"Yes. You must not be far from that dirt road not assumed by the town," he said. "I don't think I've ever known the name of it. We used to ride the horses on there too, and in the wintertime, we'd snowmobile up it. Anyway, we should

34

save some talk for the dinner. I'll see you at 5 on Thursday. Can I bring anything?"

He uncrossed his ankles, stood straight again and rubbed my shoulder down to my biceps. The heat continued to travel right into my groin, warming my whole body.

"No, man, not at all, just yourself is more than enough, and yes, I'm up not too far from that road." I noticed another car pulling in. "I'd better let you go. See you Thursday!"

Just get to the truck, just get to the truck. As I walked, my knees threatened to buckle under me. The inside of my stomach felt fizzy, like I'd guzzled a can of Coke. I wondered if Jax liked me. Did he find me as compelling as I found him? If he didn't, I'm sure he wouldn't have said yes. *Right?* I could hardly believe he said yes. The way he'd caressed my arm felt like he was letting me know. I could still feel his hand there.

4

❦

AMELIA

Around 10:30 a.m. a nurse guided Dad and me into Jax's room. The moment I saw him, sadness robbed me of my voice. Uncle Arthur and my cousin Tom were standing just inside the doorway, and Mom was by Jax's side. Both Dad and I approached gingerly. Strangely this was the same room Jax had been in the year before with his high blood pressure scare. There he was lying in the same bed, only this time he wasn't looking stressed. He wasn't glancing at the monitor every few minutes.

He wasn't moving at all.

I finally jumbled my way to his bedside across from Mom. Tom and Uncle Arthur followed. Tom rubbed my shoulders and Uncle Arthur wrapped his arms around me.

"I love you—you know that, right? You are my little girl and always will be. I'll be here as long as you need me to be and for whatever you need from me."

His arms around me gave me a small twinge of hope, but it was based on nothing more than the fact that I couldn't imagine losing my brother.

Uncle Arthur married Dad's sister in the '50s. Sadly she had passed away in '92 from cervical cancer. Uncle Arthur generously stood in for the absence of my dad while Jax and I grew up. I loved him with all my heart and was thankful he was here. Dad was grateful for him too thanking him for looking after us, each time Dad saw him.

Sitting in the chair next to Jax, I glanced tentatively across the bed at Mom. She looked over at me while leaving her hand on Jax. She must have seen the confusion on my face when she cleared her throat and blurted, "Amelia, the doctors believe Jax has had a stroke, like I told you on the phone,"

Her voice was clear and concise as if she were explaining a real estate closing to one of her clients. She had worked as a legal secretary for over thirty years.

"They've done CT scans, MRIs, and X-rays, bloodwork, and checked his vitals. He's stable but unresponsive. We are waiting for all test results to come back to confirm their suspicions. Once they do, the doctor will be in to see us and explain what happens next."

Despite her matter-of-fact voice, I saw the worry in the small wrinkles around her eyes. Mom and I were close; the three of us were, because outside of Uncle Arthur, we only really had each other. In my forty-four years, though, I'd seen Mom retreat inside herself in times of sadness or crisis. It wasn't as though she was unreachable, but she became quiet. Yet strong for those who needed her. If she ever caught me crying, or feeling sorry for myself, she'd tell me to give my head a shake and brush myself off. Not a very physically affectionate person, Mom showed her love in what she did for you, like cooking your favourite foods. For me, her peanut butter cookies, and for Jax, her tomato casserole.

Jax's eyelids were closed, his arms down by his sides. His face was the colour of ripe tomatoes. His cheeks seemed deflated until the ventilator filled them with air, and then he'd puff it out. He didn't look like my brother; he seemed a stranger to me in this setting. It was the quiet that surrounded him, so ill-suited to the man he'd been, vibrant and vivacious.

A large see-through tube coming from his mouth hooked into a large machine. I noticed condensation droplets on the inside. On his left arm was an IV line. Little sticky pads with wires coming from them stuck to his torso and legs, and a blood pressure cuff belted his arm. He was so still. Too still. Jax was never still. The ache deep in my stomach strengthened. I took a cavernous breath to try to make it go away.

Hearing the digital beeps of the heart monitor had me notice the unnatural puffs of the ventilator slowly pushing air in and out of his lungs. It seemed not in unison with his breath. I thought that must be positive, but I wasn't sure how these things worked.

I grabbed his hand, lifted it, and placed it back down. It was heavy. I squeezed it, but there was no squeeze back.

I wanted answers. Someone to explain what's happening in words that I'd understand. I wanted to know how no one had caught this, prevented it, whatever it is.

But really, I wanted someone to hold me and tell me that it was all a big mistake, that he'd wake up and all would be normal again. I feared because he'd not been air-lifted to Sunnybrook. I feared for him, for me and for my parents. I thought of all those who might never get the opportunity to know him—what a great loss that would be.

My mind stretched to wondering who will take care of me if Jax goes. Considered the strong one in the family, I didn't think I could be strong now, not without Jax. The someone I needed was motionless in front of me.

Out of nowhere, a childhood memory. I remembered being a kid and chasing those brown fluffy moths around our large front yard, trying to catch one and make it my pet. Jax and our neighbour Michael were playing lawn darts. The old-style ones, like weighted arrows. I wasn't paying any attention to them, nor were they paying any to me. One moment I was running free, then next, a sharp pain shot right up my leg. I looked down and saw a lawn dart sticking out of the top of my foot. Jax lost it on Michael, yelling and freaking out. I'd never seen him like that before. We typically didn't get along as kids. Sometimes I thought he hated me. But I remember that day how good it felt, him getting mad at Michael, even though it was an accident. It was one of the first times I remember knowing he loved me. That I had a big brother.

Watching Jax now, I silently begged him to wake up. I needed him to continue to protect me.

I checked my phone. There was a text from one girlfriend saying how sorry she was. The other friend hadn't responded yet. She shared a birthday with Jax, and they were close. I was worried about how she'd take the news.

Katie called. She and her husband Mark would arrive sometime after dinner. His parents were coming to watch the kids. I felt bad them having to travel so far but I knew there would be no keeping Katie away. My nausea eased at the thought of her coming. I told her that if there were any change I'd let her know.

I texted Ben again. No answer. Did he even know yet? I was sure that once he knew, he'd be right here—or would he? Could he handle this? Jax and Ben hadn't been together for twelve years, and although I knew how Jax felt about Ben, and had always felt about him, I wasn't sure exactly how Ben felt about Jax. I knew they still hung out when Jax was in Collingwood. Jax always included Ben at our family get-togethers. It was obvious Ben still cared for Jax, I just wasn't sure to what depth. And I was equally uncertain how he'd react to this news.

I called Stu. He said he'd stay and look after our dogs while waiting for Larissa to get home from school, then come straight to the hospital. She had a spare for last class and would be home around 1:30 p.m. I knew Larissa wouldn't be with him; she hated hospitals. Just a couple of years earlier, she had had a skiing accident. She was brought to the hospital by ambulance with a severe concussion. School trip gone bad. She's thankful to not remember the tree that jumped out in front of her, the ambulance ride or the six hours she remained in the room. She does remember Stu crying once he arrived, making her think she was dying. Stu was never good with these things. Crisis, death, injuries. Odd, being the son of a doctor.

l wondered though how Larissa would react to Jax's crisis. I wished I could be there to talk to her. Just this past July she'd lost her favourite little dog, Lila, to a heart attack. She cried for days. Could she take much more? I'd call her after school to check in.

I called Fredrik to see if he'd left yet. He'd finally found a ride and was on his way. Then I called our cousin in

41

Winnipeg. I called everyone I could remember to call. I knew Fredrik would notify all their friends in the city—*thank god*. I also posted the news on Facebook, so anyone I'd forgotten would see our situation. I hated to have to do that. I could hardly believe the words, even as I typed them: *my brother has had a stroke and is unconscious*. Then I texted Ben a couple more times.

Another hour passed, and still no answers. As I waited, I flipped through pages of a magazine, seeing and absorbing nothing.

Stu came to the hospital but, as expected, without Larissa. Nor could he bring himself to remain in the hospital room and see Jax in that state, finding it too upsetting.

Jax had been the best man at our wedding, and they'd had some great times together. Stu was closer to him than his own siblings. He loved getting Jax *ramped up*, as he called it. This crisis was a challenge for Stu—dealing with his own shock and at the same time trying to be there for me and Larissa. I could tell he was torn. He hadn't wanted to leave Larissa at home, but he'd wanted to check on me. Our neighbours had come to our house to look in on Larissa, and although she'd taken the news from Stu quite well, after Stu left, our neighbours called to say Larissa had broken down. She must have been trying to stay strong for us.

Trying to hide my roiling emotions, I said, "It's okay. I have a lot of people here to support me. Please go be with Larissa."

He hesitated but eventually left, after making me promise to call if I needed him. We'd met at a mutual friend's barbecue. Stu grew up in Toronto. A family not close. Having two older brothers and an older sister that he rarely spoke to made my relationship with Jax hard for him at first. An intimacy unknown to him. He adjusted and grew to appreciate our family but in these times his past reflected an awkwardness within him.

I called Larissa shortly after Stu left. She told me she didn't need to talk about it, that she was fine. I wasn't so sure. I understood, but it broke my heart all the same.

My uncle, cousin, and mom were talking outside the room, clearly stressed but just trying to make the time go by faster. Bart paced the halls of the hospital, shaking his head, still mumbling, "It doesn't look good." He was a man of few words who'd never been formally diagnosed, but I'd bet that he was part of the Autism spectrum. Once he got onto something it was hard to change his focus.

Dad stayed with me in the room pacing the floor around me, glancing occasionally at his son. No words were spoken. His naturally dark hair had remained for his seventy-four years, though it was now thinning and with a touch of grey around the ears. People had often commented on how much he looked like John Forsythe or Larry Hagman. He wore denim jeans with a red flannel shirt—fitting, I thought. Although a humble farm guy in appearance, he'd been successful in his career doing many different things, but mainly sales. He no longer worked a farm (our papa, Dad's father, made his living farming), but you couldn't take the farmer out of him. If you didn't know him, you wouldn't know he was well off financially. His attire was often rubber boots and a barn coat, typically waterproof, wind-resistant, and easily wipe-able materials that repelled smells—for obvious reasons. Style wasn't important, but Dad's coat was a lovely shade of red. He lived on his childhood farm in a modest farmhouse that my grandfather had built in the early '50s. Norma, his wife, or whatever she was, who had been his mistress when Jax and I were little, lived there also. She was snobbish, cold, and always sick. Everyone who met her said the same thing—*gold digger.* She hated Dad's rubber boots and farm jacket. It seemed as though she considered Dad's casual clothes affecting her self-inflated reputation. *Larry, what are you wearing? You aren't going into town in that, are you?* Sometimes I wondered if Dad wore them just to bother her. I looked around just in case she was here at the hospital with us. But this wasn't her family crisis, so it wouldn't be a priority for her. Anyway, she was probably feigning sick and laying down, which was fine with me.

When I was growing up, Dad worked a lot and wasn't around for much of Jax and my upbringing. It wasn't until my early twenties that we grew closer. Oddly, it had been an ex-boyfriend who made me see that having a relationship with my dad was worth every effort after all of these years. I'm grateful for that advice. It opened my mind and gave Dad, Jax and I a chance to learn more about each other.

Dad and Mom separated when I was just two weeks old, and Jax three and a half, after Mom had found out about Dad's affair with Norma. I hated Dad for many years, couldn't even look at him because of what he'd done to Mom, me and Jax.

I think as we age, though, we begin to see things differently, and thank god I did. We have our moments, of course, but overall, it's a strong, loving, father and daughter bond now. It still drives me crazy when he's absent for things because of some lame excuse but he has acknowledged his deceit and regrets it. I admire that. He and Mom should have been together—but doesn't every kid feel that way?

I put the magazine down and began pacing with Dad, thinking that might numb the dread I felt each time I looked at my unconscious brother.

Another hour passed. The anxiety melted into exhaustion, leaving me a wrung-out shell. Every once in a while, I would reach for Jax's hand, hoping for a response.

None came.

Wake up, Jax, dammit, just wake up.

At one point the nurse came in and recorded numbers in his chart, the numbers that changed on the monitor with every fake breath and every squeeze of his cuff.

"We have to draw more blood now," she said. "Would you like to stay or leave for this?"

Even though she was a stranger to us, her voice was caring. I silently hoped they were doing more bloodwork to prepare him for Sunnybrook and possible surgery.

I forced myself to say, "No, I'll stay, thanks."

She pushed the needle in, and I watched as his heart pulsed the blood into the tiny plastic tube she'd snapped onto the end of the needle. It appeared dark red and filled the tube quickly, which surprised me. I'm not sure why. Seeing that life flow somewhat calmed me. His heart was still beating; he was still alive.

As I hovered there holding his hand, I wondered if he was feeling anything. This morning when it happened, was he frightened? Had he wished I'd been there? At least he had been at Mom's house. Should I have stayed last night like he'd wanted me to? The thoughts were like physical blows, and I silently vowed to stay with him now. I would do anything to help him, whatever that meant.

Leaning my head on his chest, I willed the life in my body to enter his. I felt his chest rise and fall with every fake breath, and I convinced myself that that was a good thing. He was still here and with me.

Unaware that anyone else was in the room I felt a hand touch my shoulder. The nurse. I wasn't even sure when Dad had left.

"I need to empty the catheter bag," she said.

I looked down and saw yellow liquid bulging the edges of the bag. Instead of leaving the room, I wandered to the other side of the bed. I was going to be right by his side the moment he woke up. *Why isn't he waking up?* It had been hours now. That familiar ache returned to my stomach. Where were his test results? When were we going to get some answers?

I drifted into thinking about my mom. I thought of my daughter's birth and how the hospital hosts both the best and the absolute worst moments in our lives.

I heard someone behind me say, "Here he is, I'll leave you with him."

I turned to see Ben standing in the doorway. His face was white.

5

❦

BEN

"Oh, Ben. Oh my god, Ben." Amelia spotted me, ran over, and pulled me from my thoughts.

Her voice was soft. She looked so much like Jax, only with longer brown hair. Same smile, same eyes, although maybe hers were slightly darker. She placed her hand on my shoulder in the same way Jax had so many years ago.

Like on that first day I met Jax, and seeing him on the hospital bed now, my legs threatened to buckle—but for a much different reason.

I stepped forward toward her and into the room. I couldn't believe that was Jax lying there. I thought I might throw up.

Barely able to talk, I mustered, "I'm so sorry that I didn't get here sooner. I did get your messages, but I…couldn't bring myself to come."

"It's okay. You're here now. Jax showed me your message from yesterday, and he felt so bad that he couldn't reply. He'd started to but couldn't see the screen for what he called jiggly images. I knew he'd want me to call you and have you come."

"Oh, *that's* why he didn't text me back?"

"Yes." She wrapped her arms around my neck and sobbed, dampening my shoulder.

Her arms felt heavy, like she might collapse. I didn't mind. What she didn't realize was that we were holding each other up like the foundation of a house of cards. The sound of her anguish felt like my own.

How did I let him go? We had so many plans together— what the hell happened?

I didn't know what to say to Amelia. I didn't know what to say to anyone. I looked over at their mom, their poor mom. The lines in her forehead were clearly visible…more so than normal. *What will this do to her if she loses him? What will it do to me?*

We stopped hugging. I braced myself placing my hands against the back of the chair she'd been sitting in.

Gazing at Jax, I took myself back to that first day. It was easier to live there right now.

*

I couldn't get Jax's smile out of my mind. I could still feel his hand on my shoulder; his touch lingering the rest of the way home. I was so happy he'd said yes to dinner. I had to pinch myself over and over again to make sure this was real.

The rough part was that it was only Monday, but I had my train club tonight. I had to work tomorrow night, and I needed an evening to prepare. Ours would have to be Thursday.

Last night, Michelle had picked up the kids. Our three beautiful kids: Sophia seven, Josh, five, and Caroline, three. The best days of my life were the days they were born. They all have their own unique personalities. Soph was outgoing, and I could see her running a farm one day. I was told Josh was a mini-me both in looks and personality. Caroline was a combination of the two of them with a heart for animals. At three, she already loved cats, dogs, sheep, whatever animal she could cozy up to.

Michelle was to have the three of them all this week. We alternated weeks, because we each craved time with them, and to split the cost. But she'd come to the door an hour early.

Sitting at the kitchen table I spotted her out the window. She walked up the front steps and stopped on the porch.

As I opened the door, she looked past me. "Are they ready?"

"They … aren't here?" My tone made it sound like more of a question than an answer.

"Where are they, Ben?" She shoved me aside and stormed into the house. I closed the door. My nose had an angry twitch from her strong floral-scented perfume.

I wasn't sure what she thought I'd done with them.

"Well, why are you here at 7? The kids don't get back until 8."

I could tell, as per usual, that she didn't even hear me.

She snapped, "What the heck? Where are they? You knew I was coming!" She flounced into the living room, searching, then the kitchen, and finally ran upstairs to the bedrooms.

She must have thought I was hiding them like I used to hide my *Playgirl* magazines. I don't know.

I yelled up the stairs, "If you'd just calm down, you'd remember that they're in Bible School from 7 to 8 p.m. Remember? You used to drop them off and pick them up yourself."

Maybe she should start doing that again.

She appeared at the top of the stairs. "I thought it was 6 to 7. Wasn't it always 6 to 7?"

Her tousled red hair looked like she'd been in a windstorm. Her face was flushed, hiding her freckles. I swore that from where I stood at the bottom of the stairs I could hear her heart beating. She kept looking over her shoulder as if she was expecting them to appear, like she still didn't quite believe me.

"Nope, never 6 to 7, always 7 to 8. Wanna come back in an hour?" I didn't want to spend a minute with her, let alone a whole hour.

"I'll wait thanks. I'm not driving back into town just to turn around and come back."

"Well, it's hardly fifteen minutes into town and fifteen back," I said, still trying to convince her to leave. "You could go sit with the kids. I'm sure they would love that."

"If I didn't know any better, I'd swear you were trying to get rid of me." She finally came down the stairs, crossed her arms and plunked herself right on my sofa. "You have company coming or something?"

"No, why?" I followed her and stood at the side of the sofa.

"You seem desperate to get rid of me."

"We aren't exactly friends. I just got the letter from your lawyer yesterday. You're clearly are out of your mind, man. I don't have *that* kind of money. Besides we are going with joint custody and agreed to split all costs."

I really didn't want to get into it with her. I just wanted her to leave.

"We shall see. You still have to pay for the three kids you spermed." She crossed one leg over the other and flicked her hair over her shoulder.

So smug, I thought.

I took a deep breath. "That's not fair. You knew I was gay, and you still wanted to marry me. I was honest with you right from the start. You knew what you were getting into. Besides, I love Sophie, Josh and Caroline."

We'd discussed my urges while we were dating. I'd never hidden that from her, nor denied it. For me, our relationship was an attempt to appease my family. I'm not really sure what she was doing. Did she marry me because she thought she could change me? I didn't care. I suppose. I just knew my getting married would stop all of the questions and condescending stares...for a while anyway.

"But you never loved me, right?"

"That's not true either. I did love you. I just couldn't live with you questioning and ridiculing my every move. Nothing I did was ever good enough for you. I'm always the bad guy. And you weren't happy either. Anyway, I'm a bit uncomfortable talking about this now. I think you should go before it gets heated." I was generally the rational and calm one, but with Michelle, things could turn really bad really fast...as the past had proven.

"I'm thinking of going after full custody. I'm sure no judge will grant a *gay* man joint custody. No judge wants children to be influenced by that." She looked at her nails, bit a piece off, then wiped her hand on her shoulder.

"What? Since when did you decide *this*?" My worst fear, and she knew it.

"Last week when I was with my lawyer. She feels that I deserve full custody. With the amount that she said I could get, I really wouldn't have to work anymore. Oh, and I get them on every holiday too." She sat on my couch looking like she owned the place.

I wanted to grab her by her arm and throw her out. I'm not a violent guy, never have been. I kept my cool in situations where I've seen other people lose theirs. I pride myself on that, but in that moment, it felt harder than normal. I let out my breath, unaware I'd been holding it.

"Bring it on, man. You left here, remember? You walked out on us. I will be responding through my lawyer from now on. I think it's best if you leave now. Moving forward, why don't I have Mom drop the kids off to you, so you never have to come here again. Or you can pick them up right from Bible school."

She let out a loud humph, stood up, and stormed out the door. Leaving nothing but the scent of her perfume behind.

I experienced a moment of relief immediately followed by dread. *What if she succeeded in taking the kids?* This woman had the ability to destroy my life as I knew it. At least I'd known enough to watch what I said. Knowing Michelle, she could have hidden a recorder somewhere.

The clock on the wall seemed unusually loud. The ticking was a constant reminder of how the next few days, waiting to see Jax, would feel like an eternity.

My thoughts drifted to Peter. I felt bad about ending it with him, although in truth, he'd only been there to meet a physical need. We'd really struggled to talk. I think we were both introverts. The canoe ride, a few weeks back had been enjoyable, but I couldn't stop thinking about Jax. I kept wishing he were sitting across from me instead of Peter.

I spent most of the canoe ride with Peter wondering what the conversation would have been like if it were Jax. What his favourite colour was. His favourite foods. What his childhood was like—was it good or bad? I wasn't even sure he was gay. If he was, did his family accept him? Would he accept my bad habits? I leave the water running while I brush my teeth, and squeeze the toothpaste from the top. Or would he mind that I have to have all of the same glasses together in the cupboard, neatly stacked and containers labelled? Does he like the toilet seat down after someone uses it? Or does he even notice those things? Did he have any bad habits? Would I be able to live with them? *Slow down, Ben, you're getting way ahead of yourself.*

That day with Peter changed drastically after I'd seen Jax. I'd planned to take Peter to my favourite spot along the river but instead detoured and went a different way. That place was too special for Peter. And now, it was hard for me to believe that in just a few days, Jax, the sexy gas attendant, would be sitting at my table.

The week dragged, but Thursday finally arrived.

I was baking an apple pie. The aroma filled the kitchen. From as early as I could remember, I had always loved being in the kitchen. The smell whisked me back to the times when Mom prepared our meals and was about to start baking the pies.

"Can I help? I want to learn how to bake one of those."

"Hop on up here, and I can teach you." She tapped the counter.

I wondered if she had any inclination that I might be gay. What ten-year-old boy asks to learn how to make pies? Shouldn't I have been wanting to play baseball or something?

She showed me how to mix the flour, water, and lard for the crust. Then she had me cut the apples into wedges and place them on the bottom and sprinkle over the cinnamon, flour and sugar mixture. I helped put the top on and made the little indents around the rim. While it baked, I remember not taking my eyes off it to make sure it didn't burn. It was one of the few heartwarming memories of my mother that I could recall.

The warm breeze that came through the window blew the curtains. I glanced around the kitchen, the same one in which my mother had helped me bake that pie. Little had changed. The stove was newer, and by newer, I mean 1950s. It was white with silver knobs and had two ovens without windowed doors. It stood where it had stood since it arrived, in the corner. The cabinets and cream linoleum floor hadn't changed for as long as I could remember. My grandfather's ash table needed varnish but otherwise didn't show its age. I loved this place, and now I would have a chance to share it with Jax.

The cuckoo clock chirped once. It was 4:30 p.m. and the fizzy feeling had returned to my stomach. He'd be here in half an hour.

I ran upstairs to hop in the shower. The warm water felt soothing as it streamed over me. Droplets made their way down my chest to my groin and over my legs, finally swirling into the drain. I loved being naked. Showers always seemed erotic to me. The heat, the massage of the water, touching, caressing, slippery soap cleansing sweaty skin, awakening all my senses.

I thought of high school and how I was so reluctant to shower after gym class. There was no hiding an erection in there. It was next to impossible to not get one around all those naked guys standing next to me. It was such a confusing time.

All that I'd learned or that had been ingrained in me through the Church had left me believing my inclinations were wrong. I'd have to go relieve myself in the bathroom stall afterwards.

After drying off, I rubbed the condensation away from the mirror with the towel, revealing my naked body. I stood looking at myself, light-coloured body hair running down the middle of my torso leading to a semi-erect penis and testicles hanging low from the warm shower. *Not too shabby, Ben, not too shabby.* A quick shave, hair gel, deodorant, teeth brushed, jeans, favourite white shirt, and I would be ready.

I heard the back door open. *Shit, not now.* I knew it wasn't Jax; he'd be coming to the front. I wrapped the towel around my waist and walked to the top of the stairs in time to see my mom, who lived in the back of the house, standing at the bottom. She sniffed in a critical way.

"Pie? You are baking an apple pie? What for?"

"I… Yes. I..."

"Do you have company coming again? Michelle has the kids, and you think it's free time for you to do whatever you choose? How do you ever expect to reconcile carrying on the way that you do?" She glanced at the piano, where I'd tossed the bible. "Is this the bible out of your car? I put it there for you to keep beside you, not to bring back into the house. You need to be reminded of God's words. You need to stop the nonsense and get back with Michelle."

I'd forgotten that I'd put it there. How on earth did she recognize it as the one from my car? Did she mark them or something?

Mom's arms crossed tightly against her breasts and her lips pressed together. She moved one hand to her forehead and the other to her stomach, like she had a fever and was about to be sick.

I didn't budge from where I was standing. When she finally stopped talking, I tried again.

"I'm having a friend for dinner," I said, keeping my voice even. "I'm allowed to entertain friends, aren't I? I moved the bible because it was taking up the entire armrest space, and besides, I have a dozen all over the house. I have explained about Michelle and me several times. I can't help who I love." I tightened the towel around my waist.

She huffed, turned, and walked out, slamming the door behind her.

Sighing, I walked back into the bathroom and finished getting ready. I wished she would just understand me. I was thankful, at least, that her surprise visit had happened before Jax got there.

Back down in the kitchen after getting ready, I had about five minutes before Jax would be here. I'd marinated the chicken earlier. I took it out of the fridge and slid it in the oven. I took the potatoes out of the fridge and cubed them, then put them into a covered bowl. I turned the pot of water on the stove to medium to warm it for faster boiling.

I hope he likes chicken, I never asked, I should have asked. What if he doesn't like chicken? Breathe, Ben, breathe.

6

≈ ≈ ≈

BEN

I somehow managed to hoist my weight from the chair and stagger closer to the side of Jax's hospital bed. I placed both my hands on the bedrail, thinking there was no risk of his falling out; he wasn't even moving.

The machines were beeping, and the blood pressure cuff was expanding around Jax's arm. I watched it until it stopped. I looked at the monitor: his blood pressure was almost normal. I bent down and kissed his forehead.

"I'll leave you with him for a while," Amelia said to me, grabbing my hand and squeezing it tight. It's as if she could read my mind, like she knew I needed to be alone with him and my thoughts.

I was still not sure what was going on. I wondered why they hadn't air-lifted him to Sunnybrook. I wondered why there hadn't been more signs that something was wrong. I hadn't even really known Jax was having problems. He'd kept it from me. I knew that a year ago he'd been taken into the Emerg for not feeling right. I knew that his blood pressure was 266/144, but I thought the doctor had got it back to normal. I glanced at the breathing tube inserted in his mouth. This was the most still I'd ever seen him.

Amelia put her hands around my shoulders, and I felt a big tear hit my shirt.

She whispered, "He loved you, Ben. He always did and never stopped." Then she left the room to join her mom.

How did she know those were the words I needed to hear? And yet somehow, they also made me feel worse.

I sat back down in the same chair touching Jax. I rubbed his arm. I was happy to be all alone with him. There was so much I needed to tell him.

*

When I heard a vehicle pull up into the circular drive, I ran to the front door and peeked out the tiny window. I almost missed Jax's green truck camouflaged among the evergreen trees that lined the driveway. To the left of our driveway was a huge pond, and on the edge of it sat my mom's five geese honking at each other. Sometimes the male would chase incoming guests, but he seemed uninterested in Jax. I was thankful, although it might have been amusing to watch.

The original historical fire engine red and black brick covered the entire house. The white window frames popped in contrast against the brick. On either side of the front steps stood

62

large white pillars that held up the small curved balcony above. To the right of the house was a large field that was home to a few goats and a small horse. Around the corner of the house, we had a red barn with white trim. It reminded me of a *Fisher-Price* barn I played with as a kid.

I stood still peeking out and tried not to let Jax see me. He stood in the driveway for a few minutes looking at the front of the house, the geese, and the field beyond. I wondered what he was thinking. He was wearing a blue shirt with *Mexico* in white lettering across his chest, and I could see something hanging from the *M*. It was hard to make out from where I stood—a lizard? An iguana? He had on blue and white shorts, the blue matching that of the T-shirt, and white running shoes. He looked so good standing there. He walked around the half-circle, and I saw him peer behind the house. His expression softened. Gentle breezes brushed his hair from his face, his T-shirt blowing with it. It looked like he was taking a deep breath.

Cicadas sounded in the distance as I opened the door and stepped out onto the front porch. Birds chirped in a nearby tree. The hay was growing, the air sweetly scented with it. I couldn't help feeling aroused.

Shrugging that off I called out, "Hey, man, are you just going to stand in the driveway all night or what?"

"You're funny. I was just taking it all in. This place is beautiful, Ben, wow. You weren't kidding when you said it was old. It so reminds me of my Papa's farm."

The field went on for miles behind the house. Huge hundred-year-old maples gave us the best maple syrup every March. We'd finished this year's and still had a few bottles left over for winter. The rest would be sold.

"Why don't we go for a walk? Dinner won't be ready until about six, so we have time."

I stepped down off the porch and met Jax where he stood. We walked around the side to the back of the house and headed for the field. My mind was racing, the anticipation of what was to come was almost too hard to take. Was he gay? Was he feeling the same way?

"You look really nice. I should have worn my jeans," Jax said.

"You look great in that outfit."

"Thanks, although I think you're just being nice. Your white shirt and jeans look so good." He rubbed my quad and felt the denim. My early questions of whether he was gay or not started to diminish.

"Thanks." I'd pulled out my nicest white shirt and tightest fitting jeans. I was happy that he'd noticed.

We walked for about an hour, the field turning sepia as the sun started to set. We talked about horses, and I took him to see mine in the barn. I have two large Belgian pulling horses, Jake and Budd. I prefer their look to Clydesdales. They aren't ridable; they're working horses. Jax walked right up to them and placed his hands on each of their noses. He spoke in a soft, calm voice while stroking them. He wasn't intimidated by their size at all. After a few minutes, we wandered past the old sleighs and wagons that I hitch them to. I mentioned the Rhode Island red and Plymouth Rock chickens in the barn. On the way back to the house I pointed out the rear renovated portion. I'd done most of the work myself, with some help from my dad. The house was too big for just my kids and me, so we'd decided to section some of it off as an in-law suite for my parents.

"My great-grandpa bought the farm in 1856. He married my great-grandma in 1857. They built the current house in 1874. They came from Germany, poor and looking for a better life."

"It looks like they found it."

"It was a tough go, but yes, I think they found it, and I'm happy they did. I love it here."

"You're so lucky. The horses remind me of my papa's farm, only his were riding ones. The wagon and sleigh in the barn… Do you hook them up to those?"

"Yeah, I take guests on sleigh rides in the winter and wagon rides in the fall. I built a cabin near the sugar shack. I make ginger snaps and hot chocolate and have it ready when we get there." I hoped that Jax would still be around to come with me this year.

"Beautiful." He stopped and turned around for a moment, standing very still and gazing back at the barn and the field.

What was he seeing?

Then we headed inside.

I turned the burners on to cook and shut the oven off, leaving the chicken inside to rest. In the living room, Jax went straight over to the family pictures on the wall.

"You have kids?" His neutral tone made it hard to decipher whether it bothered him.

I stood next to him, shifting from one leg to the other and clenching my fingers. Being gay and finding someone to love is hard enough, but for many, kids can be a deal-breaker. "Yeah, they're the best gifts I ever got."

"So, you were married or...?" He didn't appear to be phased.

I nodded. "Let's save that for another conversation. I don't want to spoil the night."

But he was clearly curious. "What are their names and how old are they?" His gaze bounced from one photo to the next.

"This is Sophie, she's seven," I said, pointing. "That's Josh. He's five. And this is my little baby Caroline. She's three."

"Josh sure looks like you."

"Thanks, that's what everyone says, although I really don't see it. He's quiet like me. Sophie is like a mother hen to the other two. If there is an animal of any sort Caroline is crawling toward them as fast as she can; she's got quite the heart already."

"They're adorable. Where are they now?"

I found myself relaxing. "With their crazy mom. We alternate weeks, as we agreed on joint custody. But…let's not get into all of that. I'll gladly tell you all about my kids, but Michelle…I'd rather save that for another time if that's okay. It's…messy and stressful. My kids are my life. I'd do absolutely anything for them." Truthfully, I didn't want to tell him much about my situation with Michelle for fear he'd run. I came with a lot of baggage.

I continued to talk about my kids, probably too much, but Jax didn't seem to mind. He asked a ton of questions and seemed genuinely interested. I felt relieved.

I'd forgotten about the potatoes until I heard them boiling over. Hurrying to the kitchen, I lifted the lid. I asked Jax if he wanted anything, and he said just a glass of water. When I came in to give it to him, he was sitting on the couch flipping through a photo album he'd found of the kids. He asked me casually what I did for a living. I told him I sold farm insurance. I knew what he did, although he'd mentioned that he had applied to a local car dealership to sell cars and was hoping to find out soon if he'd gotten the job.

Returning to the kitchen, I poked the potatoes with a fork and cut into the chicken. Everything was done. I drained some of the water into a pan to use for the gravy. If I'd had it my way, I would have let the potatoes burn and taken Jax into the backfield…but I had to be patient. Besides that, I was too shy to act on my thoughts, at least this early in the game. I knew already that I wanted this one to be more than a one-night thing—

Yet the idea of it scared me. I'd never allowed myself to think like that. I was raised in the Mennonite Church, which forbade homosexuality, a deed seen as devil driven. Long term relationships were meant to be with women yet my urges for men only got stronger with age. Unable to deny those urges, I'd convinced myself that if it was only for a night it was okay. This was the first time I allowed myself to think beyond that. I was still unsure whether Jax had the same feelings as me, but with each passing moment and the connection we seemed to be building, I was growing more confident.

The thought of explaining any of this to my family felt overwhelming, and I pushed that aside. Too early for that anyway. The younger of my two sisters, Sasha's words, at a Thanksgiving get-together not that long ago, were forever engraved in my mind. I remembered us all gathered around her wooden harvest table, about to give thanks for our food.

"I'm so tired of Wilson only preaching about God's love and acceptance of everyone." Sasha turned her gaze toward me. "He needs to preach more about fire and brimstone. Especially to those whispering and giggling teenagers in the back seat this morning. They need a sermon to scare the hell right out of them. That's the way we were brought up, and all this lovey-dovey preaching is just wrong." Her chunky face reddened, and she smirked. "Did you see Charlene obviously showing this morning? When is her due date anyway? Doesn't her husband have a really bad back? I wonder how she got pregnant in the first place? Maybe she likes to ride on top." A boisterous laugh came out of her, although no one else was joining in. "And when Lilian stood up and said how thankful she was for her family—pfft, with all of their problems? Please!"

My other sister Bev looked as uncomfortable as I felt.

"John! Get in here and give the blessing!" Poor John, her husband of five years, looked brow-beaten most of the time.

Everyone shuffled toward the table like herded sheep. My tiny cousins giggled as they jostled each other claiming their seats. One of them reached for a pickle, and my sister slapped their hand. "Not before the blessing," she barked.

Once everyone found their seats and the blessing was over, she started in again.

"And what did you think when the preacher said that bit about same-sex marriage and them being allowed to adopt children! My word. Poor little buggers having to grow up with that. It makes me sick just thinking about it." She wiped her hands on her napkin and shook her head as she shot another look my way.

I remember swallowing more than normal. It wasn't as though any of this was a surprise. Each time we gathered, the conversation always ended up here. The last tirade was about the atrocity of Walmart dealing with gay-owned and-operated suppliers.

I just sat there quietly. My everyday stress was enough for me to handle. I was exhausted. And anyway, it wouldn't matter what I said, she'd carry on. My situation was never discussed in a compassionate or empathetic way, only judgement, disgust and denial. No one even wanted to try to understand—it was wrong, and that was that. Being here had me feeling like a wounded deer as the wolves circled about. I wouldn't come if it weren't for my kids. I felt it important for them to be around family.

Now my cousin Luke was fired up: "Yeah, my dad says they should put all the fags and Taliban together on an island, give them tons of guns and let them shoot at each other."

Sasha exaggerated her laugh and muttered, "What is this world coming to?"

I would never take Jax there. I wouldn't do that to him.

Needing to shake off that memory, I stood for a moment before walking into the front room, where Jax sat. I told him that dinner would soon be ready.

He took a deep sniff. "The house smells wonderful. I can't decide if I like the smell of the chicken or the pie more. My papa's favourite pie was apple, and he'd eat it with a huge chunk of the oldest cheddar cheese you could buy. This place is so much like his." He got up and followed me into the kitchen from the front room. "Is there anything I can help you with?"

"No, I'm good, thanks."

I looked at his Mexico shirt.

"Hey, man, have you been there?" I asked, pointing to it.

"Yes, I go to Puerto Vallarta every year—it's the best place ever! You been?" His eyes brightened, just like they had when I mentioned the farm the other day.

"No. Is it nice? I haven't been out of Ontario except for Pennsylvania. I have cousins there." I felt embarrassed. He seemed so worldly.

"Oh my god, you so have to go. I can't believe you've never been. The beach is long and wide, the waves huge, and the town is so safe that you can walk everywhere! They have this martini bar, Apaches, downtown—it's legendary. A couple of lesbians from Toronto own it. There's a donkey out front of a bar called Undules just down from the Apaches that you can sit on and get your picture taken—like, a real donkey. You should come this year! The Mexican guy that owns the donkey makes a living by charging for sitting and taking pictures with it. Well, I might not call it a living—it's more supporting his drinking habit. The guy is tanked most of the time. And the place is full of gay men."

I listened in wonder as Jax spoke. Unlike Peter, Jax talked...a lot. I felt relief in that; he made our being together easy. I already felt like I'd known him my entire life.

He grabbed a stool that was tucked under the small kitchen island. I stirred the gravy. He said he was thirty-two—five years younger than me—but I thought he looked twenty-two. He had such a youthful appearance and personality. It was nice to see him light up when talking about Mexico. I'd heard about Puerto Vallarta being a popular gay area.

"I sat on the donkey once; it's a pretty patient one. You can take a ride on it too. There are a lot of drunk people falling into it, stumbling all over it, and it just sits there. I suppose if you think of it, it's pretty used to that. I just kept buying its owner drinks. He loved me!"

I watched him during this tale. His hands moved with his speech—no, it was more like his elbows flapped while his hands stayed by his armpits. I wondered if he did this often when he found something funny or amusing. It looked like a move straight out of the chicken dance.

"We will see. I have a lot of expenses—let's call it a Champagne taste on a beer budget." The thought of going did intrigue me. I somehow knew that it would be a lot of fun with Jax.

I stirred the gravy once more and poured it into the gravy boat, grabbed the potatoes from the oven along with the chicken and headed toward the larger table.

"Dinner is ready. I'll bring it over."

"Can I grab something for you?"

"No, it's okay—thanks though. Just make yourself comfortable."

I watched him walk toward the table. His blue shorts snugged his ass like a glove. I brought the food over. He grabbed the wine I'd set out and poured us each a glass.

"Dammit, do you have some paper towels? I spilled some." There was a puddle of wine around each glass.

I shook my head in mock disbelief the way I do when one of my kids has done something silly. I grabbed some paper towels. "I noticed you pouring with your left hand. Are you left-handed like me?"

"No, I'm right-handed, but for some reason I always pour stuff with my left. Mom and Amelia tell me all the time to pour with my right—believe it or not, it's actually worse. I'm not the most coordinated individual. I should've left the pouring to you, I'm so sorry."

"It's just a little wine." I handed the paper to him, and he wiped up the spills.

"If you can believe it, I was actually a bartender while I went to the University of Guelph, to help pay for school, but everyone spilled there, so no one really noticed." He smiled at me.

I noted for future reference that his smile would definitely break me should we ever be involved in an argument. Something told me that I shouldn't let him know that—but who was I kidding? He was probably very aware of the power of that smile.

After dinner I noticed that he hadn't eaten many potatoes.

"Do you not like potatoes?"

"They aren't my favourite. Sorry. I didn't want to say anything. You worked so hard on everything."

"What kind of a Dutchman doesn't like potatoes?"

"This Dutchman. Again, sorry about that."

"Don't be silly, it's fine. Anything else I should know about?"

"Cilantro and coconut. I don't know why anyone would eat either of those things. Cucumber too."

I smiled. "So…no cucumber and coconut salad with a cilantro garnish and potato salad side?" He scrunched his nose and made a gagging noise.

That night we talked for hours about his papa's farm, the pigs, and harvesting the hay. He mentioned his mom and papa's vegetable gardens, his sister Amelia, and how they had hated each other as kids but now had to talk every day. He talked about all his trips. I was right that he was well travelled. He'd been to so many places with his aunt and uncle. I spoke more about my three kids and touched on Michelle briefly—I again didn't want to ruin the positive atmosphere in the room. We laughed a lot, and before we knew it, it was 2 a.m. He'd had a few drinks, and I wasn't comfortable letting him drive.

"I have a spare room, so please don't feel that you have to rush out or drive tipsy."

He put his hand on my leg really close to my groin. I felt his finger graze the side of my penis; it rose to the occasion.

"I thought you'd never ask." He leaned over and placed his lips on mine. His other hand brushed the side of my face as he ran his fingers down my neck to my chest. He was so gentle.

Unsure of what tasted so good, the wine, the pie, or just his lips, I kissed him a second time, it was definitely his lips. Standing up, I took his hand and guided him upstairs.

"I want to show you the balcony. I sleep up there sometimes to stare at the stars and think. Don't be alarmed by the mattress."

"Alarmed? If I didn't know any better, I'd think you're hitting on me."

"Maybe." I shrugged and flashed him a mock sinister grin, then led him upstairs. The balcony was only accessible from my bedroom, which I hoped might be convenient for the near future.

The full moon cast silver highlights on the treetops and silver ripples that bounced on the pond. The stars were so bright they looked like fireflies skimming the water.

The mattress was soft under our bums. We sat side by side, nestled up against each other. The warmth of his skin felt good. June is a weird month around here. There was a chill in the air. In the corner, sleeping bags rested against the brick. I grabbed them and covered our legs.

"Listen to the crickets, and the frogs in the pond. That and the smell of the air takes me right back to my papa's farm. I know I keep mentioning it, but those were some of my best memories as a kid." The moonlight silhouetted Jax's face. His skin was like porcelain. There was a definite twinkle in his eye.

"The stars are so bright," he said, gazing up. He pulled out a cigarette.

"You smoke?

"Bad habit, I know. I think it's my mom's fault; she's smoked like a chimney for years. I'll quit…someday."

He took a drag and blew the smoke away from me. I'd never smoked myself, but somehow Jax lighting up just added to his intoxicating presence. Here I was, the good Christian farm boy, with Jax, the rebel—mysterious, tantalizing.

He hadn't made a move toward me other than the kiss in the kitchen. It made me nervous. Usually by this time in a date, gay men had made their desires pretty clear.

Maybe he'd changed his mind?

My hand shifted under the sleeping bag and found Jax's by accident. He responded with a gentle caress. Our conversation stopped. I felt my pulse speeding up.

Slowly we began to explore each other's bodies. His forefinger ran down my chest following the fine line on my sternum. I wrapped my arm around his back feeling every inch with my hand. In the darkness, the sense of touch ruled. A soft tingling urge to be with this man overtook me. I'd never really been with a man before in the true sense. I was a sort of virgin. Oh, I'd sucked cock many times, given countless hand jobs, but never allowed penetration. The fear of AIDS was always in the back of my mind. It's an awkward topic, especially in a romantic situation, but it's something I think all gay men fear. Many people had died, and no one was sure even what AIDS was. Celebrities couldn't escape it. It was over ten years since the disease took Rock Hudson and five since Freddy Mercury had been gone.

"Are you okay?" Jax asked, brushing a strand of hair from my forehead.

I guess he could see my concern on my face.

I stiffened. "Well, I hate to ruin the moment, but before we go any further, I think we should bring up the elephant in the room." His eyelids lifted, like he was confused. "Are you clean? Like, HIV negative?"

He thought for a moment. "Oh…that elephant. Well, I'd better be. I've never been with a man…like I've never…you know. Nor have I had it done to me. I've only sucked dick, wacked guys off, you know that sort of thing. Too afraid to go there with experienced guys—don't know where they've been, and I don't want to die. I've been experimenting more lately, but I could still only count on one hand how many men I've been with." His expression was so genuine.

"Really? But you are so damn sexy. I can't believe that." Not sure why I was shocked, at the beginning I wasn't even convinced that he was gay, but he was so hot. Now, knowing that he liked men, I couldn't believe he was like me and had never been with anyone.

"So, we are both virgins?"

"Yes, I guess so." He smiled.

I felt in that moment that somehow, I'd waited for him.

My breath became heavy. "You are so beautiful."

"So are you." He gently kissed my forehead.

I felt his hand go down the front of my pants, his touch almost making me explode. He then undid my pants and slid them down around my ankles. His finger caressed the waistband of my underwear. I was so hard. He then lifted to his knees and looked down at me. The expression in his eyes deprived my body of its strength, and I laid back. The feel of his tongue around my shaft sent vibrations through my body. Like it was my first time. In a way, I suppose it was. I moaned like an injured animal and prayed my mom couldn't hear. And then suddenly I didn't care who could hear me. I felt too good to care.

After about an hour we went back into the house to my bedroom, where we lay down on my bed, and I held Jax all night. We reenacted the balcony scene several times before drifting off to sleep. He dozed off first, but before I allowed my eyes to close, I sat for a while, staring at him feeling like I was in a dream. I had been with men before, but it had seemed only to satisfy my physical, not my emotional, needs. This was a whole other dimension. One I was eager to explore.

7

❧

BEN

If you took the ventilator away, Jax appeared much as he had when sleeping. He wasn't a complicated man, but he was a hyper one, at least while awake. I remember thinking back then, when we were together, how nice it was to see him just lie quietly.

Now I longed for some of his hyperactivity. And watching him, I felt scared. I leaned in to place my mouth near his ear.

"Jax, Jax can you hear me? Do you know that I'm here?" I straightened out his hospital gown, then traced my finger around his nipple as I always had. It would usually wake him up—but not this time. I heard a beep and looked up at the monitor. I saw his blood pressure stats down the left side from previous readings. The cuff had just finished a blood pressure cycle. It read higher than the previous one. His heart rate had gone from 80 beats per minute to 94. I felt a twinge in my stomach. *Does he know I'm here?*

His blood pressure was returning to normal, his heart rate decreasing. I felt destitute. *He isn't waking up.* I looked at his arms, and a chill consumed me at the thought that they might never hold me again.

Positioning my head on his chest as best as I could without getting out of my chair, I grabbed his arm. I tried to wrap it around me, longing to feel his squeeze. It slid off me and back down to where it had been resting. I lifted it again and again, each time with the same result. I felt an overwhelming sorrow. For so many years I had taken those arms for granted.

*

"Wake up."

I felt the warmth of his whisper. Was I dreaming? Did last night actually happen? I took a deep breath, stretched my arms up over my head, and rolled over placing my arms around Jax's waist. He smiled, and I felt such intense pleasure.

"What a great way to be woken up," I said.

I brought my lips to meet his. Our kisses felt as soft as cotton, our lips moulding together as if designed to do so. Pulling back, I propped myself on my elbow far enough away to look into his eyes, and drew little circles with my finger around his nipple.

"Wow, man, last night." I grabbed his hand and held it against my chest. "Do you feel that? Do you feel my heart pounding? What have you done to me?"

"Feel this." He brought my hand to his dick. "How's that feel?"

I grinned, and we kissed again.

Before I knew it, we were replaying last night. Sucking toes, fingers, and dicks. I just couldn't get enough of him, his touch, his kiss, and his body against mine. It was like the feeling you get just before you jump off a cliff into water, a surge of endorphins—your breath stops and your senses heighten, until you take that leap and plunge right in. I never wanted to quit this. Reaching up, I rested my hand on his chest sure I could feel it pounding too.

I thought of the balcony and how I had wanted to stay there the entire night. But Mom usually got up early, and I didn't want her seeing us up there.

My bed was king size and comfy. Tons of room to snuggle in. The morning light slanted in through the sheers creating soft shadows throughout the room. It was decorated with light mocha walls and white trim. I choose mocha thinking that it made me look masculine. Not that I wasn't what with my woodworking skills and no lisp, but if anything, it made me feel better. The crown moulding met the coffered ceiling seamlessly. I suppose I got my talent of woodworking from my great grandfather, he's the reason the coffered ceiling is there. He built all of the mouldings too. The walls were covered in the original plaster. The bedroom smelled of a mix of musk, fabric softener, and sex.

"Do you have today off?" I asked.

"Yes, I booked it off in hopes that what happened with us would." Jax winked.

"Good, get dressed. There's somewhere I want to take you." I jumped out of bed and grabbed my jeans and the white shirt I'd worn the night before. "Come on—we have to make some breakfast, then sandwiches for the adventure."

Shoving the covers back I saw his naked body. His muscles moved like harp strings. He was flawlessly built. The outline of his quad muscles travelled right down into his calves. He had a small six-pack, and his nipples were proportionate to his chest. His pecs seamlessly led into his toned biceps. His chest had no hair except for a thin tiny patch around each nipple. I was happy about that. Although I'd always wished I'd had a bit more. I thought he would make a great model for one of those nude drawing classes I'd taken a while back.

"Oh, I'm always up for an adventure!" he said.

I left Jax in the bed and ran downstairs to the kitchen. There was a pain in my jaw. At first, I wondered if it was from last night and this morning, but then it dawned on me that it was from the smile I couldn't seem to wipe off my face.

Growing up as a gay kid in a Mennonite family, I was deprived of these special moments. Unable to share it with anyone. I couldn't bring home dates like I could if I were straight. I had to hide everything, my boyfriends, my insecurities, my moments of happiness. The excitement from family for that first date was never there. It hurt. I remember my mom telling me that if I couldn't control myself, perhaps I should go to my doctor and get some pills. That stung—still does.

For breakfast I whipped up some eggs and put bread in the toaster while the bacon cooked in the microwave. After getting out the cooler bag, I grabbed more bread and some salami, mustard and mayo. I made sandwiches and threw them in the bag, along with a couple of apples and bottles of water, and some leftover slices of the apple pie from the night before. As I cleaned up the counter, I called for Jax.

After we ate, Jax went back upstairs to use the washroom, and I went out to the barn and loaded the canoe atop my 89 Ford truck. I could see my mom glaring out her back-door window at me. *Did she hear us last night?* Her face was just above the arm of the metal cross my dad had welded into the screen door. The room, where she stood, used to be the old living room before we did the renovations; it's more of a mudroom now that leads into a smaller den area.

Her eyes pierced through me like lasers, as if she knew what had happened between Jax and me. For a moment, I felt guilty, ashamed and pretended to not see her. I didn't want her to spoil what I was feeling.

I suppose she'd been what people refer to as a helicopter parent —always hovering. *Sit up straight, don't touch that, don't look at that boy that way*. Apparently, she still was. I knew it came from a place of love, although it wouldn't appear that way to others.

My dad must have been in the barn that morning, because as I was loading the canoe, he came over.

"Going somewhere, son?" His voice was concerned, like Mom had kept him up all night talking about what a failure I was and how come I couldn't just be with Michelle.

"Yeah, I'm taking a friend canoeing." I couldn't look at him, or he'd know Jax was more than a friend. I heaved the canoe up, still avoiding eye contact.

"Ah well…" He walked away mumbling something to himself, his hands in the pockets of his overalls and his head down.

He clearly didn't want to hear anymore, and I was okay with that. I knew he was disappointed in me. I knew I was sinning and going against everything my parents had tried to teach me. Didn't they understand what a struggle this was for me too? I had always known the rules. I had always known what my mom and dad believed. They stressed responsibility. They believed in consequences for your actions, and the Church came first. I knew that wasn't always a bad thing. I had adopted some of the Church's doctrine with my own kids and knew they were better for it.

The difference was that my mom always seemed so confident about everything, so content in who she was and the choices she'd made. Like dancing to the beat of a song, it just came natural to her. I wondered if she had any regrets at all. I wondered if my dad had.

Returning to better thoughts, I couldn't wait for Jax to see this place. I went back in the front door and watched him slowly coming down the stairs. What I didn't see was my mom following me.

"My knees are weak. What did you do to … Oh, hello, you must be Ben's mom? It's nice to meet you. I'm Jax."

At the bottom of the stairs now, he reached past me to shake my mom's hand. Of course, she left hers right on her hips. She wouldn't even look at Jax. She ignored his introduction and asked me where I was going.

"Mom, please don't be rude. This is my friend Jax, and we're going canoeing."

She turned away, slamming the door as she left.

"What the hell was that about? Did I do something wrong?" Jax asked.

He went to the door to peer through the window and watch her go. Then he turned back to look at me. My embarrassment and sadness were evident, I'm sure. He seemed such a caring guy, and I could see this broke his spirit. Liking guys comes with a certain judgement and ridicule that you never quite get used to.

"No, you didn't. I did." I went to him.

"Is she unusually grumpy this morning or always like that?" he asked.

"Well, that's a tough question. I'm going to say both."

"I feel so bad for you. I haven't told my parents or family that I prefer men, but even if I did, I'm sure they wouldn't act like that—at least I hope not."

I remember the shame I felt as a kid whenever I disappointed my parents. I suppose all kids feel that to a certain degree. I could always make up for it by doing a chore or getting good grades in school.

But this part of me—this evil, as my mother always puts it—I couldn't make up for, I couldn't change, and that was the most difficult thing to deal with. I had worked hard at trying to change. I bought *Playboy* magazines, but looking through the pages evoked nothing. I'd look down at my penis and wonder why it wouldn't move. I'd poke it to try to get it to wake up; it was supposed to grow when I saw a naked woman, I thought. It sure rose to the *Playgirl* magazines. I spoke to other guys about girls. I dated girls, befriended girls, hung out with many different girls to see if I could generate any kind of spark, but nothing. I'd exhausted all avenues and tried for years to ignore the impulses. I even spoke to the church counsellor in private sessions. He told the bishop, who told the congregation and asked me to leave the church. It wasn't long before I'd found another church who accepted me. The pastor of that one even had a lesbian sister. It felt good to be understood after the humiliation experienced at the Mennonite church. Aren't you supposed to feel safe there? I'd become quite good friends with this pastor. He asked tons of questions about being gay. I think it helped him to understand his sister. My family, to my surprise, were disappointed in our church and left with me. I believe it was more about their own embarrassment than support for me.

They claimed they had a cure for my gay disease, like I had cancer or something. Of course, none of the conversion therapy camps or the preaching worked. The years passed, and what was inside me only got stronger. I tried marriage, giving it my best shot. It's a good thing I like sex, straight or not, but picturing men while sleeping with my wife didn't hurt.

I do know some guys who have never been with a woman, and they never could. They said it made them physically ill. I guess in one way, when I think about it, I'm lucky. I'm not a flaming type, so I can hide it when I need to. Not many people know I'm gay, and many would be surprised to find that out.

But standing here in front of me was a man who seemed to understand me, who was like me, and it felt like a miracle.

"I hope your arms are good," I said, changing the subject. "We're going canoeing! Come on."

We got into the truck and headed to the boat launch in Edenvale.

"When was your first gay experience?"

His question didn't surprise me, as gay men ask this all the time, especially after they've had sex. Besides, it would make the forty-minute drive to the boat launch interesting.

"Are you ready for this?"

He nodded. "I wouldn't have asked if I weren't."

"Okay, here it goes. When I was nine, we had a farmhand come for the summer to help, and he was thirteen. The first day he came, I remember feeling a tingling in my groin, and it confused me at first."

"That's called being horny," he offered.

I laughed, "At nine? I guess so. Anyway, every summer I'd look forward to him coming. For four years I admired him from afar, until one day he approached me. After that we'd suck each other's cock and jerk off together under the bridge on Batteaux Creek or in the hay mow. To this day the smell of fresh hay excites me." I didn't bother sugar coating it. "That continued until I was fourteen and he was eighteen. My summers were the best…"

89

He was quiet for a second, and I wondered if he was upset.

"Huh." He rubbed the tiny scruff that was showing on his chin. "Yours was a farmhand too?"

Good. He wasn't offended or bothered by the news. But wait, what?

"What do you mean? Don't tell me yours was too?"

"Yep. Sure was. My papa hired this guy who was eighteen when I was fifteen. I remember doing the chores and staring at him. He'd look over at me and catch me staring, but he'd smile instead of looking away. I had that same tingling as a matter of fact." He rolled down the window, for which I was thankful—it was getting warm. "My Nana would make us sleep in the same room, because it had twin beds. He'd make me suck his dick every night, sometimes returning the favour."

"He made you?"

"He was older, and I was always taught to respect my elders." He turned toward me and smiled. "Don't worry. I enjoyed doing it as much as he enjoyed receiving it. That's when I realized I was into guys."

"That's why you are so good at it—you had lots of practice with him."

He couldn't suppress his smile. "I suppose so." He paused. "You know the funny part is that he was my sister Amelia's first crush too. She was eleven and completely smitten

90

with him. I never told her that he was my first male experience. Who knew we'd have the same taste in men."

I found it both fascinating and unbelievable that our experiences had been so similar.

I pulled the truck into the boat dock at Edenvale and parked. Jax helped me lift the canoe off and into the water. I was excited to be bringing him to this place. My secret haunt. A place I'd always gone to when life didn't accept me, where no one could find me. A place where judgement didn't exist, and I could be myself, alone with my secrets. Where I had dreamed of someday taking someone like Jax. And now, here we were.

At the Nottawasaga River, where we stood, the ground was a mix of spicy pine needles, leathery soil, sand, and old leaves. Those leaves have a mild sweet smell, especially after the winter melt or a rain. There are houses all along the river until you get to a small patch of nature with an abundance of trees and birds. There is an energy here that can't be explained, only felt.

I couldn't wait for Jax to feel it, smell it, and experience it. As soon as he had talked about his papa's farm, his face aglow, I knew he appreciated nature. I craved to see that same glow on his face in this place. I somehow knew that he would appreciate it the way I did.

When we got into the canoe, Jax in front, me in back, it rocked from side to side, and Jax almost fell out. He giggled

91

and looked back at me. He got up off the small bench and squatted, putting his hands on either side of the canoe rocking it again, purposely.

"What are you doing?" I asked, even though I knew.

"Nothing really. Just trying to get my sea legs."

"Are you trying to dump me?"

"Nooo."

Rapidly, I was discovering that Jax had a mischievous side. It was obvious in some of the stories he had already told me about his childhood. He'd mentioned that he and his sister would ride his papa's horses. Dock, the pony, was smaller, so Amelia would ride him. Mony was tall, so Jax, being older, would ride her. He'd purposely get Dock to follow Mony under the clothesline knowing Dock, when spooked, would buck Amelia off.

When he was two, his mom and nana took him to the local fair. Against his mom's advice, his nana bought him a fuzzy bear on a stick. He took his little fuzzy bear on a stick and ran with it. He was short enough to fit under the tables—tables at which sat many mini skirted women. My mom heard screeches coming from various tables, saw women jumping up out of their seats. Jax would pop his head up over each table and shout, "Here I am, Mommy," and before she could stop him, he'd move on to the next.

"That little bear on the stick saw more that day than most men see in a lifetime," Jax said, making that excited chicken motion with his arms.

Now he rocked the boat harder, stopping only when he noticed it wasn't fazing me. He sat back down on the small wooden bench in the canoe and started paddling. The wind blew his hair back. It also made his blue T-shirt —the one I'd taken off him the night before—puff out in the back. His gaze bounced from side to side as we passed the beautiful riverbanks. I wondered what he was thinking. He wasn't saying anything. I couldn't always see his expression, what with him sitting in front of me, but his profile showed a partial grin. There was a calmness that surrounded him in this setting. I was happy that he seemed to be enjoying it.

High in an oak tree an oriole sang his wooing song, but at the sight of our approaching canoe, he chattered his disapproval. His bright orange chest stood out against the green of the leaves. It was a flawless almost summer day. Puffy white clouds glided in the sky. Renewed shades of green tinted the trees along the riverbank. Willows bent and swayed dangling their knobby limbs in the flowing water as we passed. The poplar leaves bopped in the light breeze. The river had not yet fallen to its summer level, so it moved vigorously. Nature seemed to be showing off its finest features.

Our paddles dipped into the water, making tiny swirls. Little splashes leapt up onto my arms.

"This is stunning—it smells so earthy," said Jax. "It reminds me of when I used to go camping as a kid. We would sleep in tents on the ground, and it would smell like this." He inhaled. "Almost musty, but in a good way."

I felt as though I'd finally met someone like me. I'd doubted they existed for years.

Sitting on the edge of the canoe on Jax's right side was a dragonfly, perched there as if it were our pet. I had recently bought a book called *Animal Speak* by a Native American, Ted Andrews. I'd bought it at another place I knew Jax would love.

Andrews wrote about nature and all things in it. How we all used to live together in harmony and speak to one another. Man has forgotten this, but animals and insects have not and thus still come into our path to give us messages. Coincidentally, I had just read the meaning of the dragonfly the other day. One had landed right on my nose while I was working in the barn. Andrews wrote that the dragonfly is the symbol of change and light, and it appears to remind you to bring more lightness and joy into your life. I was comforted at the thought that Jax was my dragonfly.

After a couple of hours of paddling downstream, we crossed Jack's Lake and were on the final segment of our voyage. Sometimes we chitchatted as we floated along, while other times the incredible beauty called for a veneration beyond words.

I watched Jax as he paddled. I was so drawn to him. His extrovert nature was gravitational. I'd always seen myself as a cat, cautious yet curious. Around him, it was hard to keep guard. The fortress of protection I'd built around myself from previous fallen relationships and family ridicule was slowly crumbling.

The river snaked and twisted. Up ahead, coming into view, was a wide bend. On the far side of that bend, a sandbank rose tall from the water's edge. Carved by years of floodwaters, it formed a vertical wall, a perfect place for bank swallows to dart in and out of their burrows, busy with their lives, paying no never mind to the two of us.

On the opposite side of the river was a cobbled shore and fresh green, grassy flats. The river became shallow here. It gushed around the rocks, sloshing and splattering as it went. We were coming up to the place that I wanted to share with Jax. Montgomery Rapids.

"We're going to lift the canoe around this next bend. The water rushes pretty fast, so you have to be ready, okay?"

Jax looked back and nodded. Small rapids pushed us farther into the swirls, and we paddled hard, really hard. I saw sweat drip down the back of Jax's neck. The next thing I knew, water gushed into the side of the canoe, tipping it and plunged us straight into the water. Jax had a hold of the canoe and was floating on top when I came to the surface. *Good thing I tied everything down.* I quickly scoped the area and saw nothing making its way to the surface. I was confident that everything had stayed inside the canoe.

Out of breath, Jax yelled, "That was mind-blowing!" He looked back at me, shaking his wet hair from his forehead. "Over there, is that where we're going?" He pointed to a small flat piece of land about half a mile down, and by small, I mean about the size of an average bedroom.

"Yes, that's the place. I'll swim over to you. Hang on." I spotted the paddles and grabbed them on my way. The current was strong but manageable.

"Okay," he said. "I'll flip the canoe."

A strong swimmer, Jax was able to flip it upright in one motion. I arrived soaked and tired moments later. Again, I did a visual sweep, but everything appeared to be as it was before the flip. The cooler bag was still intact under Jax's seat. We both laughed at how silly we were and managed, not gracefully I might add, to get back into the canoe. After my breath returned from the coldness of the water, I concluded that the unexpected dunking had actually been quite refreshing.

"That sure got the blood pumping," I said.

There was an indescribable smell from the poplar trees. Strong but pleasant. White cotton-like seeds danced through the air. The sun's rays caught them, making them sparkle yellow and pink. I looked around at them and at Jax. Despite my doubts about who I was, in that moment nothing seemed clearer. Every sense was awakened. I felt comfortable in the body that God had given me. For the first time in my life I didn't feel ashamed, I didn't feel guilt, and I was proud to be me. Maybe all the previous ridicule and self-hate was worth it, if it had brought me to this point. I wondered how I ever could have fought it. I wondered how something this exciting, this exhilarating could be against God's wishes. Why could He create something so beautiful, yet tell us it's wrong?

Jax held his hands up to catch the fluff. "What is this stuff?"

I paddled the canoe to the edge of the small bank. "It's from the poplar trees. They seed at this time of year."

"It couldn't have come down at a better time. As if this moment weren't magical enough. It's like the universe is throwing confetti down on us." He took one and put it into his water-logged shorts pocket.

Magical—yes. I wondered if it were a sign from God. Maybe He was giving us His blessing. Maybe it was Him throwing the confetti.

8

❦

AMELIA

I peeked in the doorway of Jax's room watching Ben with my brother. I knew I shouldn't, but I couldn't help myself. I wanted to see how he'd react with no one around. I knew he needed some time to absorb all this. We all did.

Jax hadn't wanted Ben to know he'd been struggling and kept it from him. I'm not sure why. If this was a shock for my family despite knowing of his health issues for the past year, it must be an even bigger shock to Ben.

I saw Ben trying to wrap Jax's arms around him, with no success. It was heartbreaking. I knew I should turn and walk away, but something inside told me to stay. I made sure Ben couldn't see me, and luckily no one else was around.

What was he whispering to Jax? Was he wishing they'd had more time together? Was he saying goodbye? Maybe both. I remembered the love they'd had, and how different my brother acted when they'd been together. He'd been calmer, more at peace, and happy—happier than I'd ever seen him. Ben was good for Jax, keeping him grounded, like taming him without trying to change him.

When Larissa was a year old, Jax had quit smoking because of Ben. I couldn't believe it. He'd always been one of those "light one cigarette off another" types. I suspected he always thought Ben didn't like it, and so one day he quit. Ben had never made any negative comments about it, not that I'd heard. I think because Ben didn't smoke, Jax assumed that he didn't like it.

Ben also beat Jax at his own game, either by not reacting to Jax's pranks, or by returning a prank of his own. At one of our summer parties Ben told me about the time they'd gone on a Caribbean cruise together. Nicely dressed, they went to their assigned table for dinner. Around the white table cloth and royal blue napkins, they introduced themselves to what Ben called, "pretty stuffy" tablemates. After a couple of glasses of expensive wine that Jax had ordered, Ben started to feel tipsy. He rose from his chair to go to the washroom. Before leaving the table, without thinking, he leaned in and planted a full kiss on Jax's lips, saying he would be right back. He left Jax to deal with the stares and open mouths of their new acquaintances. Ben hadn't done it on purpose, but in the bathroom, it sank in. He chuckled to himself. *It serves you right, you bugger, for all the things you've done to me.* He laughed when he told me the story.

The remembrance sparked another memory of a different cruise they took, where on the formal soirée known as Captain's Night Ben suggested attending it in their bathrobes instead of the suits they'd brought. Of course, Jax agreed. Ben confessed later that he'd never done or even thought of doing anything like that until he'd met Jax. He also reassured me that they'd worn shorts underneath—thank god.

Jax just had a way of making you want to be wild and crazy. He had brought that out in Ben. Yet as crazy as he could be at times, he was also the sweetest, kindest man you'd ever meet. I remembered him running dinner out to Ben at the sugar shack during maple syrup time, knowing that he'd be stuck in there all day. Even after they broke up, Jax continued to do that. Jax would sometimes bake cookies for Ben to give out on his sleigh and hay rides often going with him to help out. That was Jax.

I worried for Ben. Would he ever be the same? They hadn't been a couple for twelve years, but if Jax didn't recover... It dawned on me that Ben had never dated anyone since Jax. He might have gone on dates here and there, but he hadn't had a serious relationship. Was he waiting for Jax? Even after they'd broken up, they'd met at least once a week. Jax often invited Ben to our family events. They'd remained close. My husband, Stu had referred to it jokingly as their *booty calls*, but I felt it was more than that. Why else would they have gone to Europe together twice?

I often wondered how Fredrik felt about the lingering friendship between them. Did he even know? He'd never mentioned it to me, and he seemed cordial to Ben. I worried about Fredrik too. For the last few years his relationship with Jax appeared strained. Jax said little about it, except the time he told me that Fredrik had cheated on him with an HIV positive guy, and Fredrik was now HIV positive himself. They lived together, but because of Jax's fear of HIV, their sex life had changed since the indiscretion. Jax appeared less upset about the indiscretion than about the cold fact that Fredrik had slept with a guy he knew was HIV positive. I had tried to reassure Jax that I really didn't think Fredrik would sleep with a guy he knew was positive. *Who would do that?* But it hurt him just the same.

9

❦❧❨

BEN

Off to one side of the bank stood a tree casting a soft shadow over the small patch of young grass. This is where I came when I needed to reflect. I sat here often thinking about my life and finding someone with whom I could share it. I couldn't believe that that someone was Jax and that he was finally here.

After we got out of the canoe, Jax grabbed the small cooler bag containing our lunch and placed it under the shade of the tree. I lifted the canoe out of the water. I watched him as he squatted over the bag, reaching in to pull out what we'd brought. He carefully arranged the plates and food on a small blue plaid plastic tablecloth that he'd unfolded from the bag, its creases still visible. He was so focused on what he was doing that he didn't notice me watching. He placed the white plastic plates across from each other with the utensils on either side. Under the fork he placed a small napkin. He then unwrapped the sandwiches and put them on the plates. He pulled two water bottles from the bag and set them in front of both plates. He looked inside the bag, then shoved his arm right down to the bottom and pulled out two apples, and the leftover slices of apple pie which he placed beside the water bottles. He stood and with pride on his face, admired the little picnic arrangement he'd created.

I realized, while watching him amidst all the white poplar seedlings falling around us and the sunbeams dusting the air, that I was already falling in love with this man. For the first time in my life, I saw my future. A part of me felt relieved that I'd found someone who saw the real me. But another part was an insecure little boy, back in the conversion camp, being told that these feelings weren't real. That a boy was supposed to like girls. It was God's way.

Feeling overwhelmed, I focused on hauling the canoe far enough up the bank to secure it from floating away. I then walked toward the river's edge. I stood there, unable to speak or look at Jax. A rush of familiar shame filled my head. I'd tried so many times to make sense of me, of who I was born to be, of who I was meant to become.

My mom's voice echoed in my ears as if she were standing beside me. *These feelings aren't normal! It's the devil trying to take your soul!*

But here we were, and God had just sprinkled his blessing down on us, hadn't He?

Why me? Why couldn't I just be like everyone else?

"Damn, why does that always happen?" said Jax, looking down at his chest. "I really don't know why my entire life I've slopped shit on my shirt. Almost every shirt I own has a stain right here."

Looking back at Jax, I saw him point to a glob of mayonnaise he tried to flick away. His sandwich half eaten.

"Hey, Ben, you okay?" Jax asked, licking the mayo off his finger.

"Yeah, man, just taking it all in," I lied and turned back toward the water.

"It is beautiful, isn't it?"

I nodded.

"Please tell me what's wrong. Did I do something? You seem...distracted."

I felt bad for going so quiet on him. "Nothing you could ever do would change this day for me, man. It's been absolutely perfect."

"Then what's wrong? Something's weighing on you, I can see it."

I thought for a few moments before answering. "You don't know much about me yet. I can't wait to tell you everything. Just know that nothing you've done has affected me in a bad way; it's the opposite actually, and that scares the heck out of me."

I turned to look back at Jax. Lines rippled his forehead. He looked down, still wiping his shirt.

"Where do I begin? There is so much to tell you. This place knows all my secrets. I wish it could talk."

Jax finished with his shirt, got up, and joined me by the edge of the water. His body stiffened as he approached.

"Secrets... Oh, so you've brought other people here? Is that what you mean? Did you bring that guy here? I completely forgot to ask about him. I'm so sorry. I mean, if you did bring him and he is your boyfriend, I'm totally okay with that, don't worry. I really don't mind. I know you had a life before ..."

"What guy?" I was confused.

He smoothed a strand of his hair back with his palm, his eyes staying steady with mine. "That one in your truck the first time I met you at the gas station. Seriously, if you guys are a couple, I totally get that, and I'll back off, as disappointed as I'd be by that, because I think we've connected really well. Is that what's wrong? You're trying to find a way to tell me?"

He stepped back. My cheeks warmed. I moved closer to him. He put his hand over mine, intertwining our fingers.

It dawned on me. "Oh, you mean Peter. No, no, we didn't go canoeing here that day. This place was too special to me. He and I never really connected. Nothing like you and me. It was only a few dates. After I saw you that day, I told him that I didn't think it was going to work out between us. Truth was, I couldn't get you off my mind, and it wasn't fair to him. I didn't tell him that of course. Didn't want to hurt his feelings. I just said that we didn't connect. You made quite the impact on me. And I've dreamed of this moment ever since."

I squeezed his hand. He let me talk.

"You see, all my life I've never felt that I fit in. I always knew that I was more attracted to guys than girls. I never felt comfortable with straight guys or gay ones, you know, the real princess types. I guess I just never knew where my place was. Almost like I wasn't straight and I wasn't gay. Know what I mean?"

Jax looked at our interlocked hands and rubbed the top of them with his free hand. He closed his eyes and sighed.

"I do." He opened his eyes again. "In one way I feel totally relieved. I thought you were going to tell me that this was over before it began. On the other hand, I feel your pain. I can relate to what you're saying. It's sort of like being at a party around lots of people that you don't know, so you just casually find a corner. No one is familiar, and you feel alone. You look through the crowd comparing yourself to all of them, never quite matching up to what you feel is normal or what you've been told is normal. I fake it most of the time and become the life of the party; that way no one really knows what's going on in my head." He tapped my hand after he let go of our intertwined fingers and looked at me. "I tease a lot and point out traits that make people uncomfortable. I sometimes wonder why I do that. I've done it my whole life; maybe it's to get them to realize their own insecurities or to avoid my own. I'm not a hundred percent sure—Listen to me, I'm babbling, jeez."

"You're not babbling. I know what you mean." I wrapped my arm around his waist and rested my head on his shoulder. "I met you, and brought you here to this place, this special place that I come to try and find myself. Where I don't feel like a freak. I didn't even have to tell you what it stood for, and you were already setting up the food and making us a romantic lunch. You know?" I removed my head from his shoulder and looked into his eyes. "You didn't look at me like I was just a dumb farm kid or wonder what the big deal was with this place. You got it…you get it."

I could see goosebumps on Jax's arm.

"You are saying exactly what I was thinking. Finally, someone who understands me too. I feel like you. A lot of people don't even know that I'm gay, nor would they suspect it, and I suppose that's what attracted me to you—that and a few more things." He smiled and shot me a wink. "I liked that I wasn't sure you were gay at first. I mean, I had my suspicions, and I sure hoped that you were, but it wasn't obvious."

Feeling a bit relieved I said, "I thought the same thing. That's funny."

"I've also always had such a pull toward nature and animals. You saw that in me somehow. And I'm so glad that you have it too. I suppose growing up on the farm with my papa influenced that for me; he taught me compassion and appreciation for all things living. I always admired that about him. He ran a pig farm, and we all know their fate, but he cared for them with tenderness and kindness. Some farmers feel they are just money and mistreat them—nope, not my papa. He knew they had feelings and deserved a level of respect. He taught me to have that same level of respect for nature."

He looked around where we stood. "Like this place. Look how lush it is, so undisturbed. That's what's so beautiful about it." His lips curved into a gentle smile. "I suppose I get my whimsical nature from Papa too. He used to get us to ride the pigs. He'd really get Nana going with that. She hated risky adventures, especially when it included her grandkids. He also made me take a bucket of testicles to her after he'd castrated the boars. He told me to tell her to fry them up for dinner. It wasn't difficult to get me to participate. Boy, she'd get mad at him. He'd just chuckle and carry on with the farming chores. I'd also chase my cousin Tom and my sister around with the pig prod, jolted them straight!" He slapped his leg while he laughed.

I think he was trying to lighten my mood with such crazy stories, and it was helping, but I still felt I had to explain why I was a little distant. I really didn't want him to feel it was him.

"Man, it sounds like you had some crazy times on the farm. Your papa sounds wonderful." I paused, cleared my throat. "I also want to tell you everything so you understand who I am, and I never want you to blame yourself."

I sat down on the edge of the river, and Jax followed. I crossed my legs. "I start to feel so free here and let myself go. The poplar trees released their seeds when we rounded the river bend to this little piece of heaven. It is almost too good to be true, and it scares me."

He placed his hand on my thigh and rubbed. The water was dark, and the sand—if you could call it sand—was paper-bag brown.

I lifted my knees and placed my feet in the water, tapping my toes, making little waves while I talked on.

"See, I grew up in the Mennonite Church, with a family that feels homosexuality is wrong. The Church says it's wrong, my mom and dad say it's wrong, and I struggle with myself daily. That's why my mom was so rude to you. She knows when I bring a guy over to the house, he isn't just there for chatting." I looked down at the water. "But then I get caught up in you and this, and I feel like I'm going against all I believe in. I hear my mom's voice shaming me. I also have to think of the kids. How do I explain this to them?"

"They're young. It will become the only way they know. Besides, kids are resilient; they will be fine. I had no idea you were religious, though. That makes sense then—about your mom, I mean."

"It's hard sometimes." I continued to splash the water with my toes.

"I can see the battle going on inside of you. It makes me sad. If it helps, I've struggled too." He kept rubbing my thigh. "My family doesn't know that I prefer men, nor do I want to tell them. I'm not ready yet. I don't think they have any idea, as I've slept with several women, probably trying to convince myself more than them. I'm not religious, though my nana is, and I get the struggle. When you're young and start to hear your friends talking about that pretty girl in class, but you are staring at Rick sitting beside her. Yeah, I get it. All the while you try to understand it. I mean, we are born this way, but don't always understand why. I see the beauty in women, but I just prefer men."

He moved his hand from my thigh to my back. His fingertips felt good as they circled my shoulder blades. It relaxed me.

"Yeah, I remember thinking that too. And the boys' locker room? Oh, man." I leaned into his hand just a little more. "And I know kids are resilient, but I still worry for them. I mean, what if they hate me? Then there's my ex-wife who will

110

use any ammunition she can to keep them from me. She also wants sole custody. I worry about that too—what will they think, and what will a judge think? They may not admit it, but I bet they won't like a gay man raising children. Or maybe they'll think I have AIDS, and if I did ever get AIDS, where would that leave them?" I turned my head to look at Jax. "With their crazy mom, that's where."

I tried instead to picture us—Jax and me—happy and in love, being accepted and living on the farm, his or my family's farm—it really didn't matter. Getting to know him, sharing my three kids and maybe him helping to raise them—I could see it all. We had talked extensively about them the night before, and I couldn't wait for him to meet them. I just hoped that my fears wouldn't get in the way.

"Listen, I believe a judge will see you for the dad that I can only imagine you to be. Just never lie to them, ever. My dad lied to me and Amelia more than he told the truth, and you know what? We always knew. Like I said, kids are resilient and smart. They can handle more than we give them credit for. I'm sure they love you just as you are, and a judge won't want to take them away. I mean, it's not like because you're gay, you're abusing them somehow. Just seeing how much this is bothering you shows me how much you care about them. There are so many dead-beat dads. You will be a welcome change to any judge, gay or not!" Jax reached for my hands. "You know what?

Angie Vancise

Let's not talk about it now, in this place. Let's just enjoy nature and each other. We'll pretend the world accepts us like we accept ourselves, pretend the mess with your ex-wife is already solved. I mean... look at it here—he swept his arm theatrically—no churches, no family members, and certainly no ex-wives."

He pulled me toward him.

10

BEN

My nausea hadn't subsided, and I wasn't sure that it ever would. I sat back up and reached out to grab Jax's hand again. It was warm, which caught me off guard. I wasn't really sure why I'd expected it to be cold. I stared at the tubes coming from his mouth and the IV lines trailing from his hand.

Now the steady beat of the heart monitor made it even harder to believe that he might never wake up. It sounded strong and uniform, with a regular rhythm, no more rising beats. But it wasn't his heart that was failing him. It was as strong as ever, and I wished that he could hear that. I knew that it would settle him. He had worried in the past year that he had clogged arteries or that he was going to have a heart attack. I did know that much. Maybe he could hear it. I studied him for any signs that he might, but all that was moving was his chest in unison with the ventilator.

*

Jax grabbed my hands and pulled me down on top of him. The grass was damp. It didn't matter. My shy smile was met by his unforgettable grin. *Yep, that smile is definitely my weakness.* His eyes shone back at me. His lips pressed up against mine. His hand was on my groin. He undid my zipper.

Unaware of the human connection happening far below him, another oriole hopped from branch to branch. He too sounded his disapproving squawk once he spotted the intruders below. He bounced farther away and focused on reciting his splendid musical chorus, almost as if he were hired to serenade us.

"Are you okay with this? No one is around; it's pretty secluded here," Jax said, looking around. "I also don't want to seem insensitive to your feelings."

"What do you mean? We're in the middle of nature; this is beautiful and couldn't be more perfect. Oh sure, I am okay with this. You do have a way of helping me to forget my troubles. Besides is there anything that could make you not want to get your dick sucked?"

We laughed. I put my hands on his cheeks and pulled him in close to me.

He went down on me and gave me the most intense blowjob I'd ever had. I forgot about my shame. I forgot about the stern Church and my critical family.

Out of the corner of my eye, I noticed a fisherman wading in the water about fifty feet away. He reeled in his cast so fast that I thought he might break the rod.

"Jax, look! We aren't alone," I said, yanking up my fly.

Jax sat up. "Oh no, do you think he was there that whole time?"

"Not sure, but if he was…poor guy. What he saw will stay with him like smoke on clothes."

"Look how fast he's reeling in his line. I think we freaked him out." He grinned, looking like he enjoyed having caused this man distress. "Do you think he liked what he saw? Maybe he liked it *too* much. Now he's been caught watching, so he's disappearing, trying to pretend he never liked it."

"Man, you are so bad. That poor guy will be scarred for life. Every time he closes his eyes, we'll be tattooed on the inside of his eyelids."

"Well, I didn't know he was there—but don't you find it just a bit funny?" He shot me a look of accomplishment. "I have an idea: how about from now on we try to shock someone at least once a week."

"You are crazy—do that once a week? I might go to hell." I hesitated, then grinned. "But… I guess that means we're going to see each other again?" I said it like a question, although I trusted that this day marked the beginning of our life together.

He gave a slight nod. "I guess it does. I mean, I'd like to see you again if you'll have me. I feel I should warn you, though."

"Warn me?"

"I call myself *Wolfie*, like my dogs."

"Wolfie? What does that mean?"

"Wolves mate for life, so you'll be stuck with me."

"I like the sound of that."

Jax moved closer and kissed my cheek. "And by shocking I didn't necessarily mean a blowjob in front of someone each week, although that sounds pretty good too." He smirked. "I'm thinking more along the lines of holding hands in your church, or cuddle-sitting on a bench down on Main Street. Small towns like Collingwood have people who'd faint at the sight of that, right?" Jax withheld nothing. His free spirit drew me in even more. "Or we could plant a kiss on each other in the bank line?"

The thought intrigued me—I'm not going to lie. Jax made me want to live, to try new things. He lived out what was only in my head. What the hell, why not? The kid is always inside us, but rarely present. It's like Jax's inner child had never left. The good farm boy image I tried to keep up just didn't appeal to me when Jax was around. I wanted to try things I'd never thought I would. I wanted to skydive, jump off cliffs, smoke a joint, go to my church in drag—it really didn't matter, as long as I was with him.

Giving a defeating small eye roll I finally said, "Okay. You have a deal. From now on we will try to shock at least one person every week. And … I'll definitely have you." There was no way I was letting him get away. The thought of seeing him regularly made the future look exciting despite my idiosyncrasies.

When my stomach growled, I realized I hadn't yet had a sandwich. I got up and picked one from Jax's nice plate arrangement, then returned to the side of the riverbank with Jax. After I ate, we lay back and watched the clouds pass overhead. The sky was a baby blue, making the white of the clouds stand out.

"Look, there's a lamb's head," I said, pointing.

Jax looked in the direction of my point. "I see an elephant."

"Over there to your left, that cloud looks like a hand petting a dog's head."

"Again, an elephant … Look!" Jax pointed up.

"Let me guess…an elephant?"

"Yeah, you got it!" He winked. "I'm the math guy. Amelia's the creative one." He looked so youthful. His laugh lines were only visible when he smiled.

Nearby, I heard a tree branch crackling and leaves brushing together. A few leaves and small twigs fell to the ground. Tilting my head back, I sat straight up.

"What? What is it?" Jax jerked to a seated position.

I pushed myself right around, almost not believing what I was seeing.

"Oh, man. Look, up there, in the tree," I whispered and pointed.

Jax looked around. "Where?"

"Shh, try to be quiet. Right above our heads. It's an osprey."

"A what?"

"An osprey, or otherwise known as a sea hawk. It's rare to see them away from wide-open water. They eat fish and are usually only around the bay."

"What's it doing here?"

"It's nesting. That's the only reason for coming inland. Wow, this is really rare, Jax. I usually only see them on Flowerpot Island."

"Its face is completely white."

"Yes, that is how I know it's an osprey. They live up to twenty years and mate for life. They have two cries?"

"Cries?"

"Yeah, crows caw, budgies chirp, owls hoot. Ospreys cry. Anyway, they have two, one for communication and one for warning."

"Are you one of those crazy bird-watcher people?"

"Nooo. Well, maybe—"

Just then the osprey flapped its enormous wingspan and flew out of the nest, her unique cry bouncing off the riverbank.

A warning or communication?

I wondered if there were eggs in the nest, or babies, or if it was just building the nest in anticipation of the new lives to come.

"That's a beautiful bird. It's huge." Jax stared in the direction of its flight.

"I'm surprised you didn't see an elephant."

"Ha ha. Funny guy."

The darkening sky cast a long shadow over Jax's face. I glanced at my watch.

"We'd better get cleaned up here and make our way back before it gets too dark." What I really wanted to say was that I didn't want the day to end and for him to undo my jeans again.

We gathered up the picnic and loaded it into the canoe, securing it in case we capsized again. Together we paddled upriver. The headwind picked up making paddling slower than when we'd arrived. I didn't mind. The more time I spent with Jax, the better.

We reached the truck a couple of hours later. The sky was turning a darker shade of blue as twilight fell. The breeze was now gone. The trees' branches were still and quiet, allowing the crickets' and frogs' song to echo for miles. We loaded the canoe back up onto the truck, and I drove the forty-five-minute drive back to my house to pick up his truck.

Once there, we got out of my truck and stood next to his.

"I had an amazing time. I sure hope we can do this again soon," Jax said. He took a couple of steps toward me.

But just then I saw my mom emerge from around the corner of the house, and I backed away. Jax turned to look.

"Hi, Mom, can I help you?" I said, trying not to sound rude even though I wasn't thrilled with the interruption.

She glared at Jax.

"Never mind." She turned abruptly walking away, disappearing behind the house.

"Are you okay?" Despite having been snubbed, Jax seemed more concerned with my feelings than his own.

"Yeah, I'm okay. I'm sure she'll be waiting in the living room for me. You'd think that at my age she'd just leave me alone." I leaned toward Jax and rubbed his arm. "I really enjoyed spending time with you too, and I'd absolutely love to do this again. Let's plan something soon. Hey man, let's do something that you want next time."

Jax nodded. "Sure! I'd like that. I'll think of something that we can do, although I don't think I would care what it was as long as I was with you." He put both hands on my cheeks and kissed my forehead. "Bye, Ben."

I watched as his truck drove off, getting smaller and smaller. Even then, I stood in the driveway for what seemed a long time before going in, possibly to face my mom. Her world was so very different from mine. She was who she was without question. She had never shared much about her upbringing, and I wondered if her family had been anything but loving. I knew my grandparents, but only from a distance. All I knew for sure was that confiding in my mom at this moment would only lead to more trouble than I was prepared to deal with.

But when I walked into the house, I was pleasantly surprised she wasn't there.

Later that evening, my head full of the events of the last forty-eight hours, I wandered restlessly around the house. I walked into the living room and stopped by the couch. I stood there staring aimlessly down at the cushions caught up in the day's actions. When my focus finally returned to the cushion, I recalled a moment about a month before I'd met Jax. I had come into the living room and knelt where I now stood. And I had prayed to God to fix me. I'd cried, leaving wet marks on the fabric of the couch. I reached down now and touched where the ghost of them remained. Even the warmth of the sun through the window on my back that day didn't comfort me. My chest rose and fell, and my breathing was loud. I was broken. I hated who I was.

Why, God, why did you even create me? Why didn't you just let the barn ceiling fall on me when I was a teenager? Are you just keeping me here to torture me?

I can't change, God. I've tried, you know I've tried, and it still won't go away. What am I supposed to do? It's wrong. I've been taught that. The Bible says it's wrong, but I can't change it. Why won't you do this for me?

I sobbed under the tremendous load of grief. I had succumbed to His mercy. That's when I heard the words *I love you, Ben.* I remember looking around the room, stunned for a moment. And then I knew: He had spoken to me. He loved me despite who I was.

Did He send me Jax? Was this God's way of saying it was time for me now?

The phone rang. I opened my eyes to darkness. I must have dozed off on the couch. It took me a moment to get my bearings, then I ran to answer.

"Hello?"

"Hey, whatcha up to?"

I was so excited to hear his voice. I felt like a teenager again. I'd just seen him a few hours before, but it felt too long.

Still lost in the memory of speaking with God, I decided that I would tell him someday, but now wasn't the time.

"I was just lying on the couch. You?"

"Doing the same. Mom is knitting or something, and I'm bored."

In the background, all I could hear were barking dogs. Jax mentioned living with his mom after falling on hard times.

"I can barely hear you. Where are you?"

"I'm at my mom's… BE QUIET! … Sorry about that."

"How many dogs are there?"

"Well, there are my two, Nikko and Girdy, but then we have Gracie, Amos, and Andy, and my mom's dog, Mia. They're all German Shepherds accept for Girdy. I rescued her, she's a Lab cross."

"Holy, man. What on earth are you doing with all those dogs?" I asked.

"I used to have a kennel before I moved to Mom's. I bred shepherds. I sold most of them to these two guys I know who are starting a kennel. They have to build a few more kennels before these dogs go there, so they stay in my mom's garage for now. I guess I forgot to mention how much I love animals?"

I could hear his mom in the background trying to stop them from barking.

"Yes, yes you did. Which ones will you keep?" I asked, surprising myself by questioning how many might come to live with me one day.

"I'll just keep Nikko and Girdy. Mom will keep Mia, and that will be it."

I was relieved to hear that. I like dogs, but it sounded like mayhem there. I was raised by a farmer who believed animals were for making money, and if you had a farm dog it was to protect the livestock. It didn't live in the house, never lived in the house.

We talked for about three hours. Conversation came easily. I could be myself and didn't have to watch what I said. There was never any judgement, just understanding and acceptance. He'd told me that he'd landed the job at the car dealership and would start on Monday. I was excited for him. We'd also made plans to go to Flowerpot in July. Flowerpot Island is about two hours west of Collingwood just off the tip of the Bruce Peninsula. Michigan is directly across the lake from there. A ferry travels back and forth all day between Tobermory, on the mainland, and the island.

I had planned to go to Flowerpot already. I volunteered on the lighthouse committee, and each volunteer had to run the shop at least once every summer. Jax was excited, and so was I.

Four days of just us—hiking, climbing. And he could bring his dogs. Well, not all of them.

The next morning the largest bouquet of flowers I'd ever seen arrived with a card.

Dear Ben:

Thank you for such an amazing night and day. I'm so happy that we met. I can't wait to see what our future holds but as long as you are in it I know it will be great.

Love Jax.

11

BEN

I laid my head on his shoulder. I wanted to crawl into the bed next to him. I wanted to hold him and tell him how much I still loved him. I wanted to right all of the wrongs. I wanted the past twelve years back. I wanted our life back. I wanted to stand up to my mother the way Jax had always wished me to, and I wanted to show him that I could.

I'd thought we'd have time.

I always felt that we'd be a couple again. Our story didn't feel over; it never had. I'd always believed we'd have our second chance and felt angry that it hadn't happened. Would I now not have that opportunity? I needed to tell him how stupid it was that I had wasted all this time—and for what? Jax never held back who he was or what he wanted to say. What I'd admired most about Jax was that he'd mastered the art of being who he was, unapologetically. He didn't fear the judgement of others. In fact, if I was being truthful, it was what I had always desired for myself. Watching him now only made me realize that being around him, even with no movement, no speech, no shenanigans, somehow made that easier for me. It also scared me. How could I do that now without him? Jax was my future—he had made me, me. Suddenly everything seemed bleak. Like deep black water. I wanted him to sit up and tell me it was all a joke, that I was on the receiving end of the shock this week.

The only words I seemed to be able to muster were "I'm sorry, I'm so very sorry."

The doctor hadn't been in since I'd arrived. Why was Jax still lying here? All I got from Amelia was that they thought he'd had a stroke and they intended to airlift him to Sunnybrook in Toronto for surgery. *How is it possible he'd had a stroke? He's only forty-eight.* I looked up at the clock. That was six hours ago. If they did get it right and it was a stroke, wasn't this an emergency? I got a horrible feeling in the pit of my stomach. Caressing his warm hand, I saw Larry and Elizabeth, Jax's parents, walk back in the room, Amelia right behind them.

"See, I told all of you it was something more than anxiety. I knew something else was wrong," Larry said.

I saw anguish on his face, and a tear trickled down his cheek. He was about to start pacing, which Jax told me Larry often did when emotion became too much. He kept clearing his throat and then placing his hand across his neck to find his pulse.

"Now, Larry, it is definitely not the time to be placing blame. I know you are scared, we all are but that's not helping." Elizabeth was a very strong woman. Her parents were Scottish and Irish, and when it came to her family, she loved deeply and wore her heart on her sleeve. I admired her so much.

For the first time, I saw Jax in both of them. He had his dad's eyes but his mom's cheekbones. He walked like his dad but was clumsy like his mom. I saw her trip over air several times, just the way Jax sometimes seemed to, something I'd kidded him about. Elizabeth always said she was thankful that neither Jax nor Amelia got her nose, which she felt was too big. One thing I knew for sure was that they had created a man who was one of a kind.

"Mom, remember when we all went to Mexico. How we saved for two years in our 'trip- jar' to go?" Standing behind her mom, Amelia placed her hands on Elizabeth's shoulders.

Elizabeth just kept gazing at Jax. "Yes, I remember, the locals called me the hen with her chicks." Her face reddened, and her eyes filled with unshed tears. "That was such a fun trip." She rubbed Jax's arm. "I'm so glad we did that, Amelia. I knew it would be a long time before we'd get the chance to do it again, what with it being Jax's last year in high school and your first."

"And you were right. It was a long time before we did it again, but we've been to Mexico twice since then, and Costa

Rica was so much fun this past year. Even if you called it Cost-a-lotta."

Amelia forced a smile as she walked over to where I was standing on the other side of the bed. She flopped in the chair next to me and let out a big sigh. She always tried to lighten any situation, not because she didn't see the depth of it, but because she hated seeing anyone sad.

Both Amelia and her mom seemed lost in their memories. Staring at his son, Larry shook his head, again clearing his throat. Jax and I had discussed his upbringing many times. His dad wasn't around much. I wondered if the memory of their many adventures left a sadness deep within him. He wasn't there. Not there for any of the trips, the sporting events, the graduations, and although he'd been there more in the later years, I suspected that looking down at the shell of what had been a vibrant and vivacious man caused him a degree of guilt that I would never know.

My own guilt was making it hard to breathe, for I didn't love him the way that my heart had said I should. I closed my eyes and sent a silent message to Jax. *Please come back to me. I love you so much.* I pictured his unforgettable smile and how he could get away with anything. The way he would look at me, the soft delicate way he'd run his fingers through my hair. I remembered every moment we'd spent together, and couldn't help but see every moment stolen. Jax had never known how much I missed and loved him and this, I felt looking at Larry, was something that the two of us shared.

I felt Amelia's hand on my shoulder. She was now standing beside me.

"We're waiting for Fredrik. He had to find a ride. I think the doctors want everyone here before they speak to us. He shouldn't be much longer. I texted him about ten minutes ago, and he was just coming into Barrie. My stomach is in knots."

"I should probably go," I said. I wasn't comfortable being here with Fredrik coming. "I don't want to overstep my boundaries."

"What? Why? You have every right to be here, and besides, I know Jax would want you here. Fredrik too."

"I don't really have a place here anymore, Amelia," I said, "like I'm not sure where I belong. I'm not his partner, and I don't have a say in anything. The nurse was in and asked what relationship I had to Jax, and I didn't even know how to answer her."

"You have a very important role in Jax's life," she said. She looked me in the eyes. "You were the love of his life."

Her words soothed me. I hadn't realized she knew what Jax and I meant to each other.

"The whole family sees that you and Jax should be together. I'd never seen my brother so at peace as he was when he was with you. You tamed his wild side."

"Really? I never knew you felt that way."

"We all did. He seemed to bring out the wild in you. You guys complemented each other perfectly. I wish I'd said something sooner. I can see your pain at the possibility of facing life without him. Had I said something sooner, perhaps it would have pushed you guys together. I just wasn't sure how you felt—I didn't think you wanted to be with Jax in that way, or I would have spoken up. Jax wanted nothing more than to be with you; he never got over you. He's happy with Fredrik, they love each other very much—but the two of them would be better as friends. I...I don't even know what I'm saying. I'm so sorry, Ben. None of this is helping."

She turned and leaned over Jax, putting her arm around him. She was staring at his face, and I knew that like me, she was praying he'd wake up.

"I don't have a good feeling about this, Ben. I don't want the doctor to come in, but I do... You know?"

"It's like driving alongside a crash. You don't want to look, but you can't help it, right?"

"Exactly."

I moved closer and placed my hand on her back. Not having had strong relationships with my sisters, I had always admired the love these two shared. When I was with Jax, he had spent a great deal of time telling me about Amelia. Even in the past twelve years when we would get together, that hadn't changed. They talked every day.

The entire family was close. It sometimes made me uncomfortable, because I'd never known this sort of intimacy. I just wasn't sure how to handle it. They were supportive of me right from the start, and because I truly didn't love myself, I wondered how these people could love me too.

Amelia sat quietly for a few moments, then asked, "Remember my fortieth birthday?"

"Yes. Hey, didn't Jax arrange the entire thing?" Four years ago already, I realized.

She nodded. "He and Stu planned it as a surprise. I had no idea. Stu said it was Jax's idea. He and Fredrik even got into a fight the Friday night. Did you know that?"

"A fight? How come?"

"I was feeling really sad that no one had arranged a party for me, because I certainly wasn't going to arrange my own fortieth, you know?"

"For sure," I said.

"Jax said he and Fredrik would come up on the Friday night to spend it with me but that they had to leave early Saturday to go see a friend of Fredrik's who was visiting from far away somewhere." She shifted, looking at her brother, and brushed the back of her finger down his cheek. "On the Friday night Jax said abruptly that he couldn't believe Fredrik was making him leave his sister's birthday for some lesbian he hardly knew." She looked back at me. "Fredrik lost it on Jax, telling him that she's not just 'some lesbian' and that he hadn't seen her in years. They went back and forth for quite some time, and it ended with Jax saying that Fredrik was heartless and that he couldn't believe he was making him do that. It was a full-on fight."

"Really? They did that?" I laughed.

"Yeah, and it was totally believable too. They even packed everything up in the car the next morning and left." There was a slight excitement in her voice. "Stu suggested we head to the mountain and wander around. That's when they came back and decorated the entire house and greeted everyone that Jax had invited."

"Jax would have played that fight up for sure. Anything to make the surprise that much more special." I smiled even though the memory made me sad. It reminded me of what we all would be missing if…if Jax didn't wake up.

"Speaking of special, I've also been thinking about Christmas," said Amelia. "I'm not sure why, maybe because it was Jax's and my favourite holiday. No…no, I think it's because he would always get the best gifts. Ah—maybe both, I don't know. How will I get through this Christmas if—" Her voice cracked, and she stopped talking.

I studied her features closely. Her face looked sad. My heart ached for her. I tried to find the right words.

"Yes, he sure did. Don't think about this Christmas, Amelia. It's early yet, and we have no idea what will happen. We have to hope for the best."

But she seemed lost in her memories.

"He always knew what people wanted before they even knew," she said. "The first Christmas after my papa, Mom's dad, passed away in '91 my nana held an auction of all his belongings, because she didn't want anyone fighting over stuff. 'If you want something, you can bid on it at the auction,' she said. Papa was so musical; he could pick up any instrument and play it. My favourite was his banjo. That's all I wanted was his banjo. The day of the auction, I had to work, so I asked Jax to get the banjo for me. I told him the most I could spend was two hundred bucks." She reached over and grabbed a Kleenex off the small shelf beside her. She wiped her nose, then squished the tissue into a ball and closed her hand tightly around it.

I moved closer to Jax and held onto his hand.

"When I got home from work, Jax told me that he'd been outbid on it, that it went for over two hundred. He looked so sad. I told him that it was okay and thanked him for trying, even though I was disappointed." She was quiet for a moment.

"That Christmas following the auction, we were at Mom's, and I'd opened all of my gifts, or so I thought. Then Jax stood up and said that he'd forgotten one, and he'd be right back ..."

"The banjo?"

"Yep, Papa's banjo. He kept it a secret until December to surprise me. Of course, first he gave me some awful, ugly jacket." She managed a small smile.

"That's so something Jax would do. He's the only guy I know who can drive you mad one minute but melt your heart the next."

Amelia walked around the bed and crawled up beside her brother. She lay there, holding him tight, and her next words were for him.

"Please don't leave me, please ... Just wake up."

12

❧❧

AMELIA

W hat will I do without him, if he doesn't pull through?"

Ben's question caught me off guard, even though I'd been harbouring the same fear.

"I'm sorry—that isn't a very nice thing to say to you. I just don't quite know what to say."

I shifted on the bed. "We don't know that we will be without him yet. Just like you said a minute ago, let's just wait and see what happens. And it's okay. I think we've all been wondering the same thing. We are all very scared of what is to come, but let's try not to get to ahead of ourselves and wait to see what the doctor has to say. Where the hell is he?"

I looked behind me toward the nurse's station. Fredrik had said in his last text that if the doctor came to us with the results, we weren't to wait for him.

Katie still hadn't arrived.

Mom and Dad came back into the room. They looked as though they'd aged ten years.

"Do you mind if I ask what happened? Was Jax okay last night?" Ben asked Mom.

I could see in his posture that asking this made him uncomfortable, but I knew he needed answers. Jax made us all promise to not let Ben know anything was wrong with him. At the time, I remember thinking why? Why wouldn't he want him to know? I think he didn't want Ben to treat him any differently just because he was struggling. He knew of the high blood pressure scare, but not of the recent events.

Mom explained how Jax hadn't been able to see and how he had felt pressure at the base of his neck and that he'd been to the RVH Emerg.

Even today, on the day her son had to be rushed into the hospital, Mom looked incredible. She was such a pretty lady with the most stunning green eyes. I'd always wished mine were her colour but Dad's brown eyes dominated. She kept herself looking great all the time. Her mix of grey and highlighted blonde hair sat perfectly placed, and her makeup was always done.

"Had he been having issues? When I texted him, he never texted back."

"He complained of this jiggly stuff in his eyes, and some blacked-out areas in his peripheral. We thought it was an ocular migraine but…" Mom turned toward Dad and bowed her head. "I guess it was more serious."

"Why didn't he tell me? I had no idea." Ben looked at Jax, his lips quivered into a frown. "I would have tried to help too."

I heard his longing. For years they'd continued getting together once a week, but lately Jax couldn't focus on anything other than his health.

"Like I said, I tried to tell you all it was more. Why didn't anyone listen?" Dad said.

"Larry, please." Mom tapped his arm. "Like I said before, now is not the time for blame or rehashing. Our son is lying here, and doesn't need I-told-you-so's. He needs us to be strong for him."

Dad nodded grudgingly.

"Let's go see if we can find the doctor," Mom said, and he quietly followed her out of the room.

Norma was still nowhere in sight. *Good.* Mom and Dad needed this time together. This was their son, and only they could understand.

Watching Jax, my throat tightened as I fought back tears.

I leaned into him and whispered, "Jax, please wake up. We've been through so much together. How would I face this world without you? All of the times you've gotten me through. Like the time I found that letter. Remember the letter?"

The house had smelled of Mom's, melt in your mouth peanut butter cookies. Friends would come over just for those cookies. She'd been in the kitchen all day Saturday. It was her favourite pastime, baking.

It was raining, so Jax and I had stayed in. I was eight and Jax twelve. We were playing hide and seek, and I always found the perfect spot in Mom's closet. It was long and skinny and jammed with clothes to hide behind. When I pushed the line of hanging clothes forward as hard as I could to make more room at the far end for myself, something fell from the shelf above.

A letter. It was addressed to my dad.

I knew I shouldn't look, but curiosity got the better of me. I opened the door to the closet to let in more light and started reading. The letter was from my Uncle Theodore, a minister and the husband of my great-aunt on my dad's side.

I didn't understand it all, but I understood enough to be upset.

Just as I was finishing it, Jax barged into the room yelling, "Found you. You're it!" When he saw the look on my face, he stopped.

"Hey, whatcha got there?"

I couldn't speak. With shaking hands, I handed him the letter. He read it.

When he finished, he stood there looking at me in silence. Then, together, we went to find Mom in the kitchen.

"What have you guys got?" She was washing a large bowl.

Our uncle's letter had said that the door would be open only for a short period, and when it closed, it would close forever. That Dad should consider his beautiful wife and two beautiful kids. Not to act on a whim. Marriage and kids are difficult, but don't let that push him into another's arms.

"Why didn't you tell us Dad had a girlfriend?" Jax was never one to mince words. He held up the letter.

She stopped washing and spun around to look. "What? Were you guys snooping in my closet?" Her tone was angry.

"No. I pushed clothes out of the way to hide in there, and this fell out."

"Would it matter, Mom? Why didn't you tell us?"

Jax's surprised tone wasn't all that convincing. I wondered even then if he had known but kept it quiet for my sake.

"Sit down, you two," said Mom. "We need to have a talk." She had calmed down.

We all sat down at the round pedestal table.

She explained to us that Dad had been having an affair since I was two weeks old, but she didn't want to tell us for fear of poisoning us against him. When we asked how and why she was still with him, her response was that she knew that if she left, it would kill our great-grandmother. Gram loved my mom. She was my dad's grandmother and a wonderful lady. It wasn't until years later, the day after Gram's funeral, that Mom filed for divorce. My mom made sacrifices for a lot of people in her life. Including me and Jax.

The monitor beeped, diffusing the memory.

"You were always there for me, always. Please, Jax, I still need you."

The cuff started to squeeze his arm again. It was programmed to do so every few minutes. His body went stiff like he was stretching, but only for a second, and he quivered like he had a chill, then lay flat and lifeless again. I overheard my dad mumble "That's not good," as he walked out the door. He was starting to repeat himself, like Bart. *Where was Bart?* I looked behind me and spotted him out in the hallway, pacing.

Jax's heart rate read 92 beats per minute, and his blood pressure was a little higher than the previous reading.

"Did you see that?" I said. "Jax's blood pressure—did you see that it went up when I grabbed his hand?"

Ben moved closer to the bed to look. "Yeah, I didn't want to say anything earlier, but a similar thing happened to me. When I approached him and told him I was here while I rubbed his chest, the monitors started beeping. His blood pressure went well above normal. I thought, *Does he know I'm here?*— but then I figured I was crazy. What do you think it means?"

I saw the same hope on Ben's face that I was feeling. I was starting to believe that Ben cared even more for him than I had thought. "I'm not sure, but that can't be a coincidence, can it?"

I turned to see that my mom had come back into the room and stopped the conversation with Ben; the last thing my mom needed was false hope. I couldn't imagine the pain and fear she must be feeling, although I figured it had to be worse than mine. I got up and motioned for her to sit. I had to pee anyway. She said she couldn't find the doctor.

The mirror in the bathroom was old with permanent streaks and black specks that wouldn't wipe off. A few hairline cracks ran across the centre. The face reflecting back at me was barely recognizable. I was pale with dark circles under my eyes. My hair, although I didn't remember touching it, was dishevelled. I turned on the tap, splashed cold water on my face, and ran my damp fingers through my hair, taming it into place.

I left the bathroom and instead of turning right to head back to the room, I turned left, aimlessly wandering the halls. I rounded a corner and came to the end of a hallway. Hanging on the walls were old pictures of nurses long gone. Pictures from the mid-1800s and up. Graduating classes from when the hospital was built until present. In a couple of photos, I caught a glimpse of a familiar face. There, grinning that same grin as my brother, was my Nana Vanbeermen. She'd been a nurse here for many years. I found comfort in that, as if she were somehow watching over all of us.

"Amelia!" my mom called down the hall. "What are you doing? The doctor has Jax's results, come quick." She hustled back toward Jax's room. "Katie and Mark just arrived too."

As I followed her, a wave of panic weakened my legs.

Standing in the room were Dad, Ben, Tom, Uncle Arthur, Bart, Katie, Mark and Norma. Norma stood at the end of the bed, looking concerned, of course. I wondered how she had reappeared so quickly—and where the hell had she been? Crocodile tears on her cheeks. Once I let that thought sink in, I felt bad. It was unkind, especially at a time like this, but it's hard to feel compassion for someone who lacks it.

I was paralyzed as the doctor walked into the room. I searched his face for answers, but his expression gave nothing away. Feeling the strength leave my body, I grabbed for the chair behind me. I looked over at my brother, as I always did, seeking comfort. But there was none.

"Hi, I'm Dr. McIntyre, I've been on Jax's care since 7 p.m. when Dr. Jones left."

I looked at my watch. It was already 8:30 p.m.

"We have not only reviewed all of Jax's test results, but also sent them to Sunnybrook for a specialist to confirm what we found. That's what has taken so long, but we had to be sure." He flipped a page on his chart. There was something defeated in his posture.

A bright white haze clouded the corners of my eyes.

"We all agree that the damage done from the stroke is irreparable. There is no point doing surgery, as it won't help, which is why we haven't sent him to Sunnybrook. I am so sorry to say that after reviewing all tests, Jax is not going to recover."

I heard my uncle say "What? What does that mean?" He squeezed my shoulders.

"The damage from the stroke has rendered Jax unresponsive, and he probably won't ever wake up. I'm afraid to say that he is basically brain dead and I feel that the conversation should now switch to organ donation. I'm so sorry—I wish I was delivering better news."

I blinked hard, so hard that I felt my eyelashes touch my cheek. He continued to speak, only I could no longer decipher the words. His voice was echoing, and I felt the walls closing in. The white haze now covered my eyes.

I knew it would take more than this one conversation for me to fully understand what he'd just said, but my legs could no longer hold me up. I slammed down onto the chair, almost missing it. My cousin, who was standing on the other side of me, caught me and shifted me to the centre of the chair. My uncle grabbed my hand. The doctor stopped for a moment to look at me. His curly black locks had dustings of grey. Although he was probably younger than me, I think that these conversations had him with premature silver.

"No! What? ... No." It was all I could muster. I felt the scream start in that familiar ache from earlier in the day. There was nothing I could do—it came hurtling out like the cry of an animal being attacked. The next thing I knew, a nurse was dragging me, like a ragdoll, down the corridor and out through the wooden doors, past the waiting room and into a small room, saying nothing as we moved. Me still screaming. All I remembered was the horror on the faces of the people in the waiting room as we passed. Following the nurse only paces behind was my cousin Tom. She left us in the room and closed the door behind her as she left. I can't remember if she spoke then or not, and if she did, I'm not sure I would have heard it over my screams.

I'm also not sure how I ended up on the floor, but I couldn't get up. The walls were covered in a textured beige wallpaper that was fraying at the seams, and the carpet smelled of bleach. In the corner stood a reclining chair, and along the one wall was a loveseat with a velvet flower pattern. Both had *donated by* plaques above them. I didn't read the names.

I couldn't breathe. I just kept hearing those words: *He's never going to wake up.* My body shook uncontrollably. How could I lose my best friend? How could I go through the rest of my life without him? It seemed such a long time—*the rest of my life.* How could I never hear his voice again? Grief was so paralyzing that it even stopped my tears. How could someone I loved so suddenly be unreachable? Somehow, I knew already that his absence would feel like a missing limb.

"I don't understand, Tom." I heard my voice quivering. "How could this happen? He's too young. Forty-eight isn't near enough time for him."

I knew that this was a blow to Tom too, but I wasn't strong enough to be strong for him.

Tom joined me on the floor. He had no words. He just placed his hand on top of mine to stop it from shaking. Or perhaps to stop his from shaking.

13

༺༻

BEN

I barely remembered the drive home. It was dark. I think it was raining. I hoped Amelia was okay. I was glad Tom had followed her and the nurse. I just couldn't stay.

Jax is never going to wake up. The words nearly broke my heart, and something perished inside me. Once inside, I collapsed on my couch, the room around me distorted through my tears. I couldn't breathe. The truth was mostly a terrible thing, and this truth was no different. I wished I was someone else, was somewhere else.

The room was cold. The wood stove had gone out, and I wondered how I'd ever get the energy to start it again. It was quiet, too quiet.

Brain dead.

I repeated the words out loud, trying to make myself believe them. How could that be? How could someone so vivacious be...gone? How did no one catch it sooner? If they had, would they have been able to save him? So many questions that I just didn't have answers to, and I wasn't sure I ever would. The past twelve years yawned with emptiness—an emptiness I'm not sure I knew until now.

Too exhausted to start the stove, I climbed the stairs to my room.

Entering, I stared at the top drawer of my dresser as I had many times. Something stirred in me and I paused. I crept toward the dresser and placed my hand on the handle opening it. Closing my eyes, I inhaled. My hand found it immediately as it instinctively knew where it sat. It had been in this spot for sixteen years. I pulled it out and opened my eyes. The pictures edges curling from all the times I'd handled it. Us...in our happiest time.

*

The warm July morning sun smiled down and made pink sparkles dance on the clear lake. It was just over a month since we'd met. There was a light breeze and the smell of fresh fish— noticeable but not offensive. A seagull cried out as it floated effortlessly on an updraft. It had been a fun weekend, but now the warm sun, fresh breeze, and gentle listing of the ship was making me drowsy.

Jax and I had driven his green Dodge truck around the "circle route" of Georgian Bay and were now on the 364-foot *Chi-Cheemaun* ferry crossing from Manitoulin Island back to Tobermory. We would spend the night in Tobermory before heading out tomorrow morning on the ferry to Flowerpot for four days.

The *Chi-Cheemaun* was launched in 1974 after being built in Collingwood at the Shipyards. Its name in Ojibway means "Big Canoe." It allows dogs, and friendly Nikko was more than happy to seek the attention of most of the 638 passengers.

We had both booked the week off work. We'd decided to head to Manitoulin first for the weekend, then make our way to Tobermory. The *Chi-Cheemaun* travelled back and forth between the two, making it easy to visit both. The residents of Manitoulin are First Nations people, and the island transportation is horse and buggy. It always reminded me of when I hitch Jake and Bud up to wagons, old-time buggies and sleighs in the winter. Jax mentioned the other day how he preferred Bud over Jake. Jake is a trouble-maker, where Bud is much more reserved. I remembered that we were trying to hitch them to the wagon a couple of weeks back when Jake reared up and knocked Jax back. His face had turned red. He was annoyed with Jake. I found it amusing. Now that I think about it, I suppose those two horses aren't very different from Jax and me.

The back of the truck had been our accommodation for our last night in Manitoulin. Neither of us had much money, and we tried to save where we could. Jax was doing well at selling cars, but the summer time was always slower.

149

Angie Vancise

"What about here?" Jax had asked, gesturing toward the tourist information centre, where we'd left the truck after getting off the ferry.

"Seriously?"

"Why not? It's cheap." He shrugged.

"All right…sure, why not."

We pulled up and found a quiet spot to rest our heads. There was a line of cedars at the base of the parking lot. We backed the truck in, so when we lay in the bed of the truck we had a better view than just the road. Yes, it was a line of boring cedars, but at least it made us feel like we were out in the wilderness.

It was a cool northern night. We hadn't expected the coldness of the steel truck bed to seep up through the air mattress but boy, it sure did. We'd brought blankets to cover us up but had only a sheet for the bottom. We'd thought the mattress would be thick enough, but we were wrong.

"Here, come closer. I'm always warm, and I can feel you shivering." His voice was soft.

When Jax placed his hand on mine, I was surprised at how natural it felt and how well our hands fit together. He pulled me near. It felt good to cuddle with him. Once I got warm, I rolled onto my back. Jax did so too and placed his head on my chest. I wrapped my arm around his waist and held him tight.

150

"I love to listen to your heartbeat and feel you breathe when you sleep," he said.

Jax wasn't a great sleeper. According to his mom, he never had been. I wasn't sure Jax could turn his brain off for more than five minutes at a time. Although once he finally did fall asleep, he'd be dead to the world.

I had just started to doze off, when a stray cat found the underneath of the truck a perfect place to bless us with the call of its people. After an hour of us trying to shout it away, I finally got out of the truck to see if I could scare it. Nikko thought he'd try to help. I had Jax hold onto him while I tended to the cat. All we needed was for Nikko to run off in the dark. I crawled back into the truck bed. I was thankful that it had a cap to shelter us.

"Did you bring the kitty into the truck?" Jax asked with a wide grin.

"Oh, yes, definitely, it wants to cuddle. Are you ready?"

"So, you did? Where is it?" He sat up and moved the covers around. These are the times when he drives me crazy.

"Okay, well, clearly I didn't—let's try to get some sleep." A moment later, "Man—!"

Nikko was attempting to crawl up between us, all 110 pounds of him. I wasn't sure if Jax had encouraged it, but I begged him to put the dog in the cab. We left the little window open between the cab and the back of the truck, so he could see we were still there. I think he actually had the better sleeping quarters.

Jax fell asleep fast, and as the moon silhouetted the darkened sky, it cast small shadows across his face making him appear mysterious to me—and I liked that. I dozed off, waking a couple of times, once in the middle of the night while it was still dark and once just before morning when the hint of light beamed through the window. Both times when I looked over at Jax I saw a stillness, a calmness. Watching him, the rhythm of his chest rising and falling, his breathing even—in moments like these I realized we were good for each other.

Now, while on this huge ferry with the wind blowing in my face and the warmth of the sun penetrating my skin, I felt the previous night's lack of sleep catching up with me.

"I'm going to lie down for a bit. I'm so tired," I said.

"Okay. Sure." He tapped his legs. "Why don't you lay your head on my lap."

We were out on the deck, and no one was around. I nestled the back of my head up against his stomach, letting my cheek melt into his thigh. I felt his arm across my chest. Nikko looked up at me from where he lay at our feet. He too needed a nap. The engines of the ship droned. The gentle breeze cooled my face. I looked up into Jax's eyes, and there again was that brilliant smile. There was silence, a peaceful silence, and time stood still. Jax placed his hand on the side of my face, tucking a small piece of hair behind my ear.

"You are so beautiful. I love you," he whispered. "I really, really love you."

I wasn't sure how to respond. I didn't want him to think I would say it back just because he'd said it first. It was the first time the *L* word had come up. But I did love this man. I loved him like I'd never loved before.

"I love you too," I whispered back, feeling myself drifting toward sleep. I'd never felt so safe—

"Oh my god! It was so funny. You won't believe it."

My eyes were barely open, but Jax was just itching for me to wake up.

"What?" I asked, rubbing my eyes, yawning and pushing myself up to a seated position. "How long was I asleep for? What time is it?"

"I don't know, but it doesn't matter. I didn't want to wake you—well, I did, but…I could hardly stand it. I almost poked you to wake up. You were missing the best parts." His eyes were so wide that his eyebrows almost touched his hairline. "You fell asleep, sound asleep when this deck was empty. Moments after you fell asleep, people started roaming around." He paused and snickered.

When he laughed I couldn't wait to hear what had gone on. "Well...what happened, man? Come on...tell me. The suspense is killing me."

"I'd stroke your hair or rub your shoulder. Some people looked and didn't care, but most of them went from this reaction of 'awe, look, how cute, two lovers on the deck' to disgust once they figured out we were two guys."

In the couple of months I'd known Jax, I'd come to realize that he loved this sort of thing. What people thought never mattered to him, or if it did, he didn't show it. He succeeded in drawing reactions out of people by barely trying. Not in a mean way but in a sort of playful way. He was entertained at their expense. Sometimes it drove me crazy, but somehow it also made me love him more. Making me aware of how trivial others' opinions really were. He'd lived up to once-a-week-shock promise without even trying. He was such a kid at heart. So many things excited him. He was a "now" kind of guy. Everything had to be done now, lived now, planned now. He made me live, made me want to live, to experience everything at least once. His energy was so large that when he'd walk into a room, everyone would notice. Nothing big seemed to frighten him, though strangely, he would worry about the most trivial things, especially concerning his health, like if a pimple were red without a white head on it, he'd think it was cancer or something.

"You seem to have enjoyed yourself while I was asleep. You and your scandalous ways," I teased.

"I couldn't have planned it any better myself!" Jax looked smug. "Wait! I got so entertained by the reactions and telling you about them, I almost forgot to tell you something else." He lightly touched my shoulder, then placed his hand back on his leg. A gentle nudge to make sure I was listening.

"Do I really want to know?"

"No, it's not a bad thing. I pretty much told you all the trouble we caused."

"WE?"

He chuckled. "You remember the big bird we saw at Montgomery Rapids?"

"The osprey? The one that was nesting right above our heads?"

"Yeah, that's the one. Well ... while you were sleeping and entertaining the guests"—he paused to get a reaction, and I chose to ignore that one— "one flew right above us. Oh, and it had a fish in its talons, a big fish." He stood up excitedly to finish the story. He was looking into the air as if he were seeing it again.

14

☙❧

BEN

I rubbed my fingers across the photo of us both standing there in the happiest time of my life. I felt sad that I was unaware of it then. I mean I felt happy of course, but we had the world in the palm of our hands. For a moment I'd wished I'd never met him, at least then I wouldn't feel this pain. On the other hand, though, I wouldn't have found that love either. I felt angry at him for leaving me. It wasn't supposed to happen this way. We would grow old together. I was supposed to die first.

That sparked a memory of the time he'd asked me to see *Brokeback Mountain*. He'd seen it and said that it reminded him of the two of us. We'd been apart for five years, but always found time to meet up. That awkwardness after a breakup had vanished, and we'd found a comfortable place with each other. We both protected our hearts, but that didn't stop us from enjoying one another. We'd been good for each other both then and now. He'd always joke about buying me muscles to get me horny. I surely didn't need that, horny wasn't the problem,

Fredrik was, I really tried to respect their relationship. Tried and failed, I'm afraid. Jax was my weakness, as I said, we were good together. When I would ask him about Fredrik and what he might think, his response was always that Fredrik wouldn't care. I felt bad about that and wondered what kind of a relationship it was that they had or was Jax just saying it because he'd wanted me and he knew I'd feel guilty. I'd now never know.

He'd said during the movie, "It's you and me. See? Ennis is you and Jack is me. He almost has the same name too." *Brokeback Mountain* wasn't a gay cowboy movie, as I'd originally thought, but a story of two human beings falling in love and wrestling with the complications.

In one scene Jack says, *"I wish I knew how to quit you. Tell you what...the truth is...sometimes I miss you so much I can hardly stand it."* Jax had leaned over and whispered, "That's exactly how I feel."

*

After another night in the back of the truck, and breakfast, this time in Tobermory, Jax, Nikko, and I finally got to the dock at Flowerpot. It was almost 9:30 a.m. We all stepped off the boat onto the long wooden dock. Jax stood staring out at the water.

"This place...wow."

The island was called Flowerpot because as the glaciers melted, the rock wore away over time, leaving tall structures that resembled flowerpots. We were tiny compared to them. There were three along the north shoreline of the island. The island was surrounded by icy blue water so cold it took your breath away—not to mention shrinking various body parts. The shallow portion was so clear it looked like glass exposing the shale underneath. It only extended out about 12 feet. Beyond that, it just dropped off into black darkness, 300 feet of darkness. That was part of the reason why the water was so cold, it's too deep for the sun to penetrate it and counteract the winter temperatures.

There was that fish smell again, probably from the coating of algae that grew on the shallow shelves of shale making them slippery.

Jax's bag was over his shoulder. His hair was windblown from the twenty-minute boat ride, it didn't appear to bother him. He raised one hand into the air and fist-pumped. "Yeahhhh."

My aunt and uncle had been the lighthouse keepers on Flowerpot Island for almost thirty years. As a kid, I spent countless hours there exploring the caves, swimming in the bay, and laughing with my aunt and uncle hearing stories of times gone past. I was never judged. I felt free. It's a place where I found peace, and where I could truly be myself. It was similar to Montgomery Rapids for me in its sense of peacefulness, but

Flowerpot was so much more. My childhood belonged to this island. Being gay didn't matter here.

Once I met Jax, I knew instantly that I would bring him here. Laying everything on the line for him to see. That surprised me because I had never trusted anyone to see this side of me. I had never wanted to be that vulnerable, but with Jax it was easy. That thought both scared and rejuvenated me, but at this point in the relationship, it was time.

The day was brilliant, the sky a warm blue, not a cloud to be seen. From a distance, the shale looked like sand. Tourists often comment on how Georgian Bay resembles the Caribbean with so many striking shades of blue. The island was always three or four degrees cooler than home. The shale covered the vast space from one end to the other, spreading out so far that it seemed designed by man. The inner part of the island is dense forest consisting mainly of evergreen and cedar trees with quite a few caves to explore.

Jax inhaled deeply. "I can smell the cedar from the trees. Doesn't it smell good? I think it's my favourite smell." He stood on the dock for a few more moments, as if in a trance, reminding me of when he stood at the farm staring back into the field on our first date. He had that same look. After one more breath he turned toward me and grabbed the handle of the cooler. "Where do we go from here?"

"Just follow the dock to the end, and you will see a path. Here, let me grab the other end. It's about a twenty-minute walk through the forest to reach the lighthouse keeper's house."

I was surprised we'd been the only ones on the ferry—usually there are more on the first boat. It gave us time to get everything ready. "Come on, Nikko."

Jax had decided to leave Girdy, the Lab, at home. She was older, and he felt the trip might be too much for her. Nikko was such a friendly dog, and he was happy no matter where he was, as long as he was with Jax. I couldn't blame him.

I looked up at the trees; they were just so green and full in early August. Jax was appreciating our surroundings too.

"Listen to the birds—they sound so happy. But who wouldn't be being here? What kind of bird is that?" He paused and listened. "It feels like I'm in the middle of a jungle." He tripped on a small rock sticking out of the path.

I chuckled. "Better watch where you're walking, man. And that bird's just a chickadee."

"Really? Well, don't I feel dumb. It sure sounds different here, more exotic."

"Did you know that the chickadee, in the First Nations totem, means higher mind and higher perceptions? Chickadees are social birds; they usually travel in groups, and this is reflected in their totem people. They love being with people and are usually cheerful and fearless."

I waited for a reaction. He looked over at me. His hazel eyes widened. I hadn't told him about the book yet. I had wanted to but feared he might think I was insane if I started talking about animals communicating with us.

Jax lifted and eyebrow. "Animal totems?" he said. "What's that?"

"This is in your heritage, Jax. Didn't you mention that your grandmother had Indigenous blood?"

During one of our many long conversations while spending the weekend on Manitoulin Island, Jax had mentioned that they always believed they were descended, on his dad's side, from someone aboriginal. His grandmother would never admit it. She came from an era when it was shameful to associate with an "Indian," and therefore one wouldn't even talk about the possibility of Native blood running through one's veins—even though Jax's dad called his grandmother Maha.

"Yes, but she never spoke of it"—he stumbled again— "and she never mentioned animal totems."

Unable to control the snicker again at his klutziness, I looked at him shaking my head. I did eventually compose myself. "It's believed in the Aboriginal culture that animals come into our lives to give us messages. At one time, we all lived together. We have evolved and lost touch with that, but the animals haven't."

Ignoring my snicker, he looked down at the ground, probably for more tripping traps, and said, "That's pretty cool and actually makes sense. How do you know this stuff?" He switched his grip on the cooler handle.

I wiped the sweat off my brow with my free hand. Boy, it was hot. Humid too. My shirt was soaked.

"One day in Tobermory, while waiting for the ferry, I was talking to a guy. He was a Native man who lived on Christian Island. He had a book called *Animal Speak* sticking out of his knapsack, so I asked him about it. I've been reading up on the subject ever since."

"So, this book, it tells you what each animal means?" Jax seemed intrigued.

"Yep, and insects and birds. It's really interesting stuff. I bought it once I got home. I'll loan it to you one day if you like." I felt a sense of relief that I could share this with him and that he didn't think I was crazy.

Jax nodded. "Sure, I'd like that."

We were making our way along the trail, which wound up over the rocks and tree roots of the forest. Jax stumbled three more times even when keeping an eye on the path in front of him. The roots from the evergreen trees protruded but were the same colour as the earth, making them hard to see. The shale blended in too. The tree roots proved to be helpful, though— only apparently not for Jax—as they formed natural steps. I'd walked this trail many times in the years. I never tired of it. My insecurities and hatred for who I was faded with each step.

The last few feet of the trail rounded into a small S bend. Then it opened to a vast clearing where stood two houses. The lighthouse couldn't be seen from there, because it was to the right and up a small hill. Once I stepped out onto the short cobblestone path that my uncle built with rocks found on the island, I was swept into memories. I saw him standing there with open arms, waiting for me to jump up into them. I was so excited for my summer to begin. My Aunt Ruby was never far behind, welcoming me with a plate of my favourite freshly baked chocolate chip cookies for my little hands to grab.

We put the cooler down on the walkway but kept the knapsacks on our backs.

"This is where my aunt and uncle lived from 1960 to 1987, when the park finally shut down the lighthouse. I would come up here every summer, but at that time, we stayed in the older house over there." I pointed over Jax's shoulder. He turned to look. "This smaller house was built in 1957, for a helper of the lighthouse keeper to stay in, but we always preferred the other house."

There were three buildings on the island: the lighthouse, the lighthouse keeper's house, and another smaller house where the keeper's helper would live. The lighthouse was a tall white structure with red trim around the top and a red cap.

163

It was no longer in use and had been shut down and locked several years before, because people had been stealing bits and pieces from it. The older house, which had been built in the summer of 1900, was a two-storey that looked like something out of a storybook. The red trim popped against the white of the walls. The old wooden screen door creaked when you opened it and then slammed shut with a thud. The paint was about three inches thick on the wooden siding, having been redone so many times. Across the longest wall of the house where the porch wrapped around were painted varieties of butterflies and bugs that inhabited the island. Underneath each was a detailed description. On the porch sat four rocking chairs and two benches, all painted the same red as the trim.

Jax admired the house. "Are we sleeping in there?" A grin crossed his face, the one that said he was about to get up to no good. His mom had warned me about that cheeky grin.

"No, we're sleeping in this one. It's for the volunteers." That house, which we'd always referred to as "the smaller house," was built to look like the larger older house, only it was more modern. It had white wooden siding and was one storey, with a small crawl space. "We could sleep in the older house, but people have said it's haunted now. I've seen one of the three rockers rock when there's no wind, and when the others aren't moving. And one volunteer said the radio came on one night without any power to it." I shivered.

"Oh, then all the more reason to stay there! That could be fun. Don't you want to sleep with the ghosts?" Jax rubbed his palms together eagerly.

I ignored his comment about ghosts. "It's a museum of sorts now, so, as much as I can see the pleasure it would give you to sleep there, we will be sleeping *here*. This is our home for the next four days. Come on, man, let's get our stuff inside before the visitors start coming. The next boat has probably arrived by now."

Nikko stayed outside, exploring every invisible footprint with his nose. Jax and I placed the cooler inside the smaller house and moved the food into the solar fridge. We put our knapsacks in a corner of the kitchen.

"There used to be power to the island. All the wires were placed into submarine tubing and run under the water to the island, but the government shut it off years ago. There are solar panels now that power it, but only the small house. You can use the toilet, but you have to shower out there." I pointed to the bay.

As a volunteer with the lighthouse historical committee, I was there to run the small store located inside the older house that helps fund the organization. I was really looking forward to it, as I did every year, only this year I had someone extraordinary to enjoy it with. Of course, my mother had had words for me before I left and had slipped a bible into my bag when she thought I wasn't looking.

You shouldn't be taking HIM with you to the island, Ben. God will punish you for your sins. He knows what you will be doing there with that man. You can't hide from Him, for He is always watching.

I shook off the memory of her words as I grabbed the key to the old house in one hand and Jax's hand with the other. "If I didn't volunteer, we'd be on the other side of the island at the campsite. Hey, man, that could be fun if we want to come back again this summer. We could camp!" Our time here had just begun, and already I was planning the next.

Jax pulled on my arm and brought me up against his body. He felt so warm. The world froze in that moment. We looked into each other's eyes. Then I heard voices and pulled away.

"Let's go out there holding hands and really freak them out." He laughed.

In my mind, I could still see the image of the poor fisherman that day on the river. I pictured the *Chi-cheemaun* travellers returning home with lasting nightmares. I wondered if I really should have agreed to this. But I couldn't resist the pull of Jax's enthusiasm.

Side by side, holding hands, we walked out of the kitchen, went down the three concrete steps and headed toward

166

the old house. Nikko received a lot of attention from the incoming guests. His tongue hung out one side of his mouth while a small boy caressed his head.

I unlocked the door of the old house, and we stepped inside. It smelled of mould. The décor remained unchanged from when I used to visit as a kid. The same blue flowered wallpaper lined the walls in the entrance and kitchen, the corners turning down where the glue had given in to gravity and old age. Set out on a rickety chair for guests to flip through were two photo albums containing pictures of all of us from years gone by.

"Aunt Ruby sure made use of this kitchen. I remember her being in here most of the day baking and cooking. Her chocolate chip cookies were still the best I'd ever had. One of my favourite dinners was her chicken pot pie. It always warmed the belly. Look, it still has the same old cast-iron stove. It would help heat the house when Aunt Ruby cooked." I took Jax over to show him.

"This is still the original one? Does it work?" He placed his hand on the burner. "It feels like sandpaper."

"I'm not sure, I haven't tried. Oh, just a sec, there are visitors coming." I turned back toward the door. The volunteers' dates were booked way back in February. Only one volunteer at a time was allowed to visit and run the shop, although I could bring my kids. The shop in the older house couldn't hold more than one or two people at a time, and there were only three bedrooms in the smaller house.

After the actual lighthouse building was closed down, they no longer needed a keeper to stay in either of the houses. The historical committee took over in order to save all three. They converted the original tiny back entrance of the older house into a gift shop. It was clever, really, because visitors had to pass through it twice, once on the way in and again on the way out, as they explored the place that felt like a second home to me. Their purchases helped to fund the upkeep of the lighthouse and the houses as tourist attractions. To the left was a small counter with chocolate bars inside a small rectangular plastic holder. Straight ahead, in the old kitchen, stood a solar-powered chest fridge containing assorted beverages. Pinned to the walls in the entrance were souvenirs like postcards, magnets, colouring books for kids, and hand-knitted quilts.

Jax pointed to one of the handmade items. "What's that?" He reached up and grabbed a knitted monster. It had a purple and green body with large eyes. Horns stuck out from its head. He chuckled. "It looks like they may have knitted it with their eyes closed."

I laughed. "Oh, let me tell you about that." A younger couple that had entered the shop stopped to listen. "In 1948, a liner out of Michigan, holding several people, apparently spotted a sixty-foot green and purple scaled monster, with a huge horned head. No one has seen it since, but everyone on the ship saw it, or so the story goes. They called it the Tobermory Sea Monster. Some of the volunteer ladies knit these to sell to visitors."

I took the knitted monster from Jax and went to hang it back up, but the woman stopped me and bought it for their daughter. She said she'd liked the story. I placed the $15 in the cash box and thanked her.

After the couple left, I winked at Jax, "We hardly ever sell those. You should come here more often asking questions." We both laughed. "Hey, after I close the shop, I want to take you to the cliffs." I placed my hand on top of Jax's and felt a surge of desire. "Ah ... maybe you should go and check on Nikko. I'll mind the shop."

I looked down at my watch. It was finally 6 p.m. The day had dragged, even though there were plenty of people through the shop. I loved this time of day because it meant that other than a few campers on the other side of the island—if there were any—we'd be completely alone. I wished we were just camping that way I could have spent the entire day with Jax. We'd have the evening to ourselves and that appeased me. I always closed the shop around six. The last boat off the island was 6:30, and guests needed twenty minutes to get back to the dock so that meant there wouldn't be any more coming. The first day is always somewhat daunting trying to get your bearings and remembering how to do everything. Jax popped in and out throughout day, which was nice because I was missing him. He said he'd explored the Island with Nikko, while I kept the shop running.

I stood on the path just outside the doorway and looked around for Jax. He and Nikko must have gone for a walk, I decided. As I locked the door I looked left toward the small garden that some of the volunteers had planted and noticed a large bird sitting in a tree above the sunflowers. I focused my eyes by squinting and realized it was an osprey. First seeing it at Montgomery Rapids, Jax seeing one on the ferry and now, I couldn't help but wonder if it meant something. Shaking that thought off I remembered that inside the smaller house was a book in which volunteers documented and recorded all birds spotted on the island. We are to do the same. I figured I'd record it and balance the books at the same time while waiting for Jax and Nikko to return.

I turned and headed down the thirty-foot long patio-stone path toward the smaller house. Approaching the door, I spotted Jax sitting on the rocks to the right. I stopped and watched. He sat with his arms crossed resting on his knees. His eyes were fixed on Nikko, who was standing at the edge of the shale ledge staring into the water. Jax stood up, bent over and picked up a piece of shale. He tossed it skipping it three times out into the water. Nikko jumped in to chase it. Jax sat back down and watched him as he swam back toward where he'd been after unsuccessfully finding the piece he'd thrown.

Jax's hair glistened in the sun. I liked how the top was slightly longer than the bottom. He wore a white T-shirt and brown plaid swimming trunks. I wondered what he was thinking.

Mom would be angry if she could hear my thoughts. It made me angry and uncomfortable knowing that I had to hide these feelings from my family and pretend that we were just friends.

Just then, I heard a familiar cry and saw the osprey soar overhead past Jax. It hovered above the water, wings outstretched, wind blowing in its face. How lucky it was to have such freedom. It could go anywhere without worry, condemnation or ridicule, embarrassment. I was envious. My life had always felt like I was trying to fly without feathers.

I slipped into the house to grab my camera.

Coming back out I realized the osprey had left. I turned the corner to head down to where Jax and Nikko were. Nikko spotted me and came galloping up. He was bouncing and shaking water everywhere like a furry sprinkler. He jumped up on me, soaking my shorts and legs. Jax turned with a huge smile. Then he got up and headed toward me, his arms swinging as he navigated the rocks.

"Hey, is the shop all closed?" He watched as I wiped my hands over my legs to get rid of the water Nikko had sprayed at me. "Yeah, sorry about that."

"I grabbed my camera to take a picture of the osprey that literally just glided above your head but when I came back out it had flown off. Don't you wish you could just disappear like that sometimes...?"

"I didn't even see it. I was watching Nikko. But yeah, I guess I do, sometimes."

"Ah, never mind that. Now that I have the camera let's get a picture of the three of us down where you were sitting instead. My camera has a timer, let's get it set up and snap the picture." We made our way back down to the water. I squatted setting it up on one of the rocks, pushed the button and ran to join Nikko and Jax where they had been sitting earlier. Nikko sat so still. He was such a good dog. I couldn't wait to get that one developed.

After a few minutes we headed back to the small house. I told Jax there was a place I wanted to show him. We packed egg salad sandwiches and a couple of waters into the knapsack, fed Nikko and headed out the door. We left Nikko behind, I was worried that he could get hurt on some of the terrain. We walked on the main path about a quarter of the way back to the dock, and then we veered to the left.

We entered a part of overgrown forest that had no signs of previous occupants. No one knew about this place. I had explored every inch of the island as a kid.

"Are you sure you know where you are going? Did you bring a bush whacker or machete?" He said in disbelief.

"Yes, I know where I am going. I've been to this spot many times, it's just not well known." When I said that I saw Jax's shoulders bounce, knowing he'd got a rise.

He then pushed a tree branch out of the way. "Are you sure Jason isn't going to jump out of somewhere with his hockey mask and axe?"

"Don't worry, it will be worth all of this where we're going. It's a bit of a walk with a few steep hills to climb before we get there."

Minutes later we came to a wall of earth and trees that stood around twelve feet tall. It was one of the more challenging parts of the trail, because we had to climb a small earthen cliff, followed by sixty-degree-angled algae-covered flat rock.

"Hope you are up for some climbing." I looked back at Jax, whose face was red from the heat. I grinned at him. He must have thought I'd lost my mind.

"Absolutely!"

Going first, to show Jax the way, I stepped on a couple of those roots that formed natural stairs. Then I found some earth that provided a flat spot to place my foot onto. I grabbed onto a tree and circled around it until my one suspended foot landed on another flat patch behind the tree. Getting into a sort of downward dog position I side walked over to the steep rock. I looked down at Jax, who was already attempting to follow me up. *Awesome.* No one I knew, other than my kids of course, would want to try this. A moment later, Jax's foot slipped. He fell back onto the ground, landing on his butt. He got up, brushed off his pants and started again. I backtracked to make sure he was okay. Standing on the solid ledge again, I grabbed Jax's hand and pulled him up.

"You okay? Want some help getting to the top from here?"

Jax brushed off more dirt. "No, I'm fine. My ego is a little bruised, but otherwise I'm fine." Laughing he said, "I'm not sure I can do it."

We finally did make it to the top but not before Jax slid down the slanted rock twice. He never gave up. I started to turn right and then backtracked to the left. It had been a year since I'd been up here, and the foliage had grown in a lot. I certainly didn't want Jax knowing that I might be lost. I saw a break in the trees to the left and remembered something.

"Come this way." I bounced with each step.

The ground went from packed dirt to flat rock. I led Jax under a ten-foot-tall overhang that spanned twenty feet. It was supported by a surprisingly small column of rock that looked worn from years of snow, ice, wind and rain. I could never quite figure out how it held up such a large wide mass. While standing beneath it, I saw Jax pick up a dead branch and place it into the tight small cave above his head. Something flew out from underneath, just missing my head. A bat!

"Hey, man, did you seriously just poke that to make it fly out at me?" I instantly regretted telling Jax, on the boat ride over, that bats are one of the few things that I don't enjoy about the island. I had a nagging suspicion that this bat wouldn't be the only one over the next four days.

Jax stood with the stick in his hand, looking for more. His voice full of excitement and mischief. "I would never do that." He flashed that smile again, as he looked up under another ridge, searching for more bats. Oddly it had no friends, but you didn't hear me complaining.

Relieved to lead Jax out from under the overhang, we headed up the slope through trees and small bushes. He tossed the stick into the crevasse beside the overhang.

As we rerouted back onto the original path I almost sprinted to get to the large oak tree, I had to keep my cool and walk at a regular pace.

Jax mentioned a couple of his heterosexual relationships as we walked. They were almost as awful as my marriage. I understood all too well how hard heterosexual relationships were for us.

I wondered why some women thought they could make the gay go away. My mom and my Church were of that same belief. Gays were sick, and with some medicine, we were sure to recover.

"You have brought your kids here, right?" Jax said, breaking into my thoughts.

"Yep. I've brought Soph and Josh, but Caroline is young yet. They love it here." Suddenly I wished they were here, but I knew that day would come. For now, I was happy to just be with Jax. "Being a dad is the most rewarding thing I've ever done. I'd really like you to meet them soon. I think they'd really like you."

I hadn't yet introduced him to the children because I wasn't sure where our relationship was going—that, and I'm not sure what they would think. They might just be young enough yet that they wouldn't care.

"I'd like that very much. Small little pieces of you."

My heart surged. I somehow knew that he, unlike the people of my church and my family, accepted me and wouldn't use this personal confidence against me.

He walked behind me, following every footstep I made.

"Family means everything to me. Take Amelia, for instance. We never got along as kids, but I now can't imagine my life without her. We talk every day. She saved my life, you know."

"How? What happened?"

He explained to me about how Amelia had arranged an intervention after he'd visited her place. He entered really drunk, puked and then opened another beer. He'd said she'd been concerned previous to that as he was bouncing cheques and not cleaning up after himself, but that just pushed her over the edge.

"What happened? Did the intervention ever happen then?"

"No, I guess they cancel it when the receiver is told about it. Dad never could keep a secret. Turns out I didn't need it—the threat of it was enough to snap me to attention. I've realized since then that Amelia was right: I was drinking way too much. I'd screwed up a lot. I took a long hard look at myself. The inner demons came out and like it or not, I had to live my truth."

"Your truth?" I tugged at my shirt. I thought I was the only one that seemed to struggled with that.

"Yeah, it was the first time I truly admitted to myself that I was gay. That's why I was drinking so much—it made it easier to deny." He rubbed his chin with hand. "I suppose when you think about it, it's because of Amelia that I'm even here, with you. If she hadn't planned that intervention, I'd never have admitted to myself that this was the kind of relationship I needed, nor would I have been working at that gas station when

I met you." He twisted a vine he'd picked off a nearby bush an appreciative expression on his face.

I was thankful to Amelia too, even though I hadn't yet met her.

We walked for another few minutes, making our way through overgrown grass, until I saw the opening just under the large oak tree. I angled left, and Jax followed. *Thank goodness it stays light until 10.* Pushing through the thick branches and brush, we stepped out onto a bulky dark grey rock that stuck out about eight feet from the edge of a cliff. Jax walked toward the edge, his mouth dropping open. He stopped and took in the view in one direction and then the other. I would come here as a kid, as a teenager, and as an adult, spending hours alone sitting and gazing at this view.

The horizon melted into the water with a slight haze. The sky was clear and a beautiful light blue. Hints of pink yellow and orange were visible as the sun began to set. The moon's white glow was slightly detectible as it started to rise, signalling nightfall was approaching. Seagulls squawked as they flew past looking for food. The breeze was warm and sported a soft fragrant smell. You could see Bear Island clearly across from us. The solar powered lighthouse light peeked out from above the trees to our left. It was still too light out to see it flash. Where we stood was marginally higher than the lighthouse. Directly below us about fifty feet, were trees and more rock.

You could appreciate, especially from here, how the glacier had left its mark in the rock.

"Do you see that rock formation? The one straight ahead looks like a Native person, and the one over there, that one looks like a monkey." I pointed to the left of us. "Oh, who am I kidding? You'll just see an elephant."

"You really are a funny guy... As a matter of fact, I do see the face of the Native person...but the monkey? I'm just seeing a clump of rocks for that one."

The sides of the cliffs were sharp in places and smooth in others, making the view interesting. The water lapped against the lower rocks, creating a delightful soothing sound.

I sat down with my legs dangling off the edge. The rock felt warm from the day's sun. I grabbed the sandwiches and water from the bag, and then I tapped the ground, motioning for Jax to join me. We sat close, our thighs touching. I handed him a sandwich, he unwrapped it placing the cellophane back into the bag. As he brought the sandwich up to his mouth and bit down, a blob of egg salad squished out the other side and landed on his shirt. He really hadn't been lying when he said that always happened.

He looked at me and shook his head. We both laughed. I watched as he used his finger to wipe the blob off his shirt. He licked his finger, opened his water, and dipped the end of a napkin into it dabbing the leftover stain.

Angie Vancise

We talked for what seemed like hours. Small talk mostly about some of the adventures on the island and his on the farm. It was so natural with Jax and just got easier and easier. Eventually we sat in silence and listened to the trees rustling in the forest, and the waves crashing against the rocks.

The sky had turned into a brilliant red and pink spilling out onto the water. The moon was now glowing a soft yellow but still hovered low. The haunting calls of the loons were nature's romantic music for us. Looking into the sunset, I spotted the osprey soaring in the distance and pointed it out to Jax. It seemed to be hanging around. Its message unclear.

Jax leaned against me and placed his arm around my waist.

I pulled away. Those damn thoughts creep in at the worst of times.

"You okay?"

"It's just more of the same. All of it, Michelle, my family, my inability to love who I am." I lifted my legs from dangling, bent my knees and placed my feet on the edge of the rock. I then rested my elbows on my knees, with my chin in my hands. I stared out at the water. I clenched my jaw to hold back the tears.

"It is who you were born to be. I had trouble accepting it too, hence that intervention scare, but now that I have, I finally met you. What is wrong with what we are doing? Does it

180

feel wrong to you? I mean really feel wrong? Are you happy?"
He paused for a moment. Unable to find any words, I kept
staring toward the water, listening. He continued, "We've both
been through so much. I'd like to think that's what led us here,
here to this beautiful place and into each other's arms." Jax
placed his hand under my chin and turned my face to look at
him. I resisted at first, but only for a moment. "How could
something that feels this good be wrong? Why aren't we
allowed to feel love in the same way as straight people?
Because your family, some hypocrites, and some book written
thousands of years ago says 'this' is wrong, we should be
denied these feelings? How is that right? How is that fair?"

Jax inched closer and placed his other hand on my
cheek. He traced, with his finger, up my cheek to the top of my
head resting his hand there. His touch was so soft and gentle.
He pulled my face in close to his; pausing for a moment to
make sure it was okay. I thought of the timing of when God
spoke to me, how it was a month before Jax. It brought some
comfort. Did he send Jax to help me be the person that he wants
me to be? We closed our eyes, leaned into each other and our
lips met. The sensual touch of his tongue against mine put my
mind and my heart into a battle. My head was hearing my mom
and my Church, while my heart was beating for this forbidden
love. I felt a tear roll down my cheek to our lips, melting into

our saliva. I pulled Jax in so close that I thought for sure we had become one. I gave in. We made love until the sun went down.

*

Setting the photo on the bed next to me, I reached for a tissue. My body felt weary. Wiping my eyes and blowing my nose, I felt I'd snapped that picture just yesterday, and at the same time, a lifetime ago. I got up and walked to the bathroom, splashed my face with water, and returned to the bed. Resting back on my pillow, I pressed the photo against my chest, then lifted it staring into it. In the background you could see the cliff. Flowerpot held some of the best memories of me and Jax. Every year after that, that we were together, we'd gone there, both camping and volunteering, always managing to make it to the cliff. It was our spot, our secret hideaway.

I tried to imagine an alternative version of the past lonely twelve years and what it would have been like to wake up to his warmth every day. To hold him as tightly as I had that day on the cliff. To live a life without lies, like an osprey.

I got up and went back to the dresser. In the opposite corner of the drawer were cards Jax had given me over the years. Remembering one he'd sent right after we'd been to Flowerpot, I reached in and grabbed it.

I want you to know what a huge part of my life you have become over the past month. It's probably the best it has ever been. Sometimes we don't always take the time to say thanks for

all of the little things we do. I want you to know how much I do appreciate the sacrifices you've made. I will always love you,
Love, Jax

My upper lip quivering, I placed the card back in its place along with the photo.

God, I prayed, *if you let Jax come back to me, I promise to live the life that you set out for me. I promise to honour you and myself. I promise never to let him go again. But please, please let him come back to me.*

My phone rang. It was Amelia.

15

⁓⁓

AMELIA

"Jax has brain activity!" I blurted, barely giving Ben time to say hello.

"What? How do you know?" He sounded sad, tired and confused.

"I just got off the phone with the doctor from RVH in Barrie. He called after examining Jax. He said he has brain activity, so they couldn't do the donation. Sorry, I didn't wake you, did I? I know it's late. And I just sprung that on you."

"No, I was up," he said quietly. "What…what does that mean?" His voice sounding stronger and louder into the phone as the news sank in.

"I have no idea, but we have to be at RVH for 11 a.m. to meet with the neurologist. He may have more answers." I couldn't help myself. "I hope…I hope this means Jax's coming back to us."

I had phoned Ben right after the call from the doctor. I was so tired my eyes hurt. My body felt like an empty shell. I had just gotten back from the hospital shortly before, and was lying in bed when the phone rang around 11 p.m. The doctor had called after Jax arrived for the organ donation.

The discussion had been painful, but it had been decided that we would donate Jax's organs. That meant sending him by ambulance, forty-five minutes away to Barrie, since they don't handle that service in Collingwood. None of us were convinced this was something Jax would have wanted, as he was petrified of doctors and operations. But we felt it would help to give his death some meaning, and give us a sense of purpose amid all that was happening. There was comfort, too, in knowing we'd be saving another family from the devastation that had become our lives.

I'd said my goodbyes and left the hospital trying to accept that he was going to Barrie to be cut apart, that his organs would live on in other people. And now this call from the doctor two hours later saying they couldn't proceed. To be officially considered clinically dead, a person must have either no heartbeat or no brain activity—and apparently Jax had both. Was this some kind of sick joke Jax was playing on us? It was just his style. *Psych! Just kidding, I got ya, I'm not really dead.* What the hell?

"Did you ask what that meant?" I heard the renewed enthusiasm in Ben's voice, and I recognized it—it felt just like mine.

I'd never been quite sure how Ben felt about Jax. Hell, I wasn't aware they were a couple until a few years after they broke up. We all thought they were just great friends hanging out. And that's what they kept telling us. What did I know? I wasn't aware then that my brother was gay. Growing up he was always just Jax. I didn't have much to compare him to. Collingwood is a small town. He'd dress in Mom's clothing and put silly curlers and funny things in his hair but that was always just Jax's ordinary. Anything to get a reaction. He was also what you'd call a male slut sleeping with many women. I would have never guessed him to be gay.

Over the past twelve years—since their breakup and since realizing Jax was gay—I felt bad thinking that as close as we were that that was something he felt he had to keep from me. I had also come to realize just how much my brother loved Ben, always wanting him near, secretly wishing they could get back what they'd once had.

"I'll never be a priority in his life, Amelia," he'd said less than a month ago, at the fall fair, after seeing Ben with another guy. "I think it's time I move on and give up on anything ever happening."

I guess they were supposed to get together that weekend, and according to Jax, Ben blew him off—again. His defeated posture had made me feel so bad for him. He wasn't feeling well, either, so it seemed a double whammy.

To me Ben had always appeared guarded and cautious. But my thoughts on that were changing as I watched him react to this heartbreaking situation. I wondered if deep down he really did love my brother the way Jax loved him, and if that were true, the tragedy of Jax's stroke was compounded. Jax lying on that bed not able to see the way Ben looked at him, just how broken Ben was, how lost and alone he seemed. Perhaps Ben himself hadn't realized the depth of his feelings till now. I wasn't sure, but then again, I wasn't sure about anything anymore.

"He said that it doesn't really change anything, that Jax is still unconscious and needs the ventilator. He's still unresponsive, but the doctor has seen people come out of comas with as little chance as Jax seems to have. Then he just advised me to wait and see what the neurologist will say after he examines him. He sounded a little angry about us being told that Jax was brain dead when he clearly wasn't."

"Oh, man, do you think I'll get my second chance after all?" Ben blurted out.

I hesitated. I wasn't sure what to say. So, Ben *had* wanted to reconcile with Jax? That made me happy but also very sad. Sad for Ben *and* for Jax, because they'd truly loved each other but were either too afraid—or too dumb—to dive back in.

187

I wished I'd known back then that they were a couple. I would have supported Jax. If only he'd known that. All I'd seen was the peace that Ben brought to my brother. Jax was always the party guy and appeared happy, but it felt like something was missing for him. When he was with Ben, he was calmer and much happier. Like he was truly content with his life for the first time. *How did I not know that he was in love back then?* His energy was lighter somehow. I felt a tinge of guilt that I hadn't tried to push them together just a bit harder. Why hadn't I said something? Many reasons. *It wasn't my place ... awkward topic ... none of my business* to name a few—but the main reason? Fredrik. He was part of our family and had become like a brother to me. I loved him, too, and I'd never want to hurt him, even though I believed he and Jax maybe would have been better as friends.

"You wanted that?" I said it gently, afraid of making him regret confiding in me. The unfairness of this tore at my heart. The one thing Jax had always wanted was for Ben to come back to him.

"Man, I never stopped loving him. If I don't get my second chance—"

I swallowed hard and cut in. "Don't think about that now, Ben." It was all I could think of to say to comfort him. "Let's just focus on this call being the hope that we all so desperately need."

"Would you mind if I brought my pastor to be with Jax early tomorrow morning before anyone arrives?" His voice was shaky.

Ben knew our family weren't church-going people, but I figured some God and prayer wouldn't hurt right now.

"No, of course not. Please do, and please wait for us to come, okay? Like, don't leave when your pastor does—I need you there with me."

"Okay, I will. See you tomorrow. We should both try to get a little sleep. Thanks for calling."

I hung up the phone with a twinge in my heart. Maybe, just maybe, we were going to wake up from this nightmare. Maybe Jax would turn the corner, and tomorrow would bring better news. Maybe this was all happening to force both Jax and Ben to live their truths. Ben would help him through physical rehabilitation from the stroke, and they'd be closer than they'd ever been. Miracles happened, right? With that thought, I was able to close my eyes and rest.

Morning came early, and I felt weird. Physically and emotionally weird. I felt alone for the first time in my life. I thought of the neurologist's report, and the determination we were waiting for. Though, I knew in my heart it was dangerous to hope.

I had to call Fredrik and let him know as soon as I could, so he could again arrange a ride to Barrie from the city, but I didn't want to make that call. I didn't want to be going through any of this. At least Fredrik would let everyone else know, which was comforting. I grabbed the phone from the side of the bed and dialled his number. After that I called Mom. She sounded scared but remained calm, still not sharing how she was truly feeling.

I checked my phone for messages. I had a couple from my friends telling me they were sorry, but they made no mention of meeting me at the hospital. Why were they being evasive? Maybe they just didn't know what to say to me. Really, what could they say? Nothing would help, I knew this, but their absence only increased my feeling of being alone in my grief, despite having my family around. Ben seemed the only one that I could relate to, his pain strangely parallel to my own.

I got out of bed and went downstairs, just as Larissa emerged from her room. She followed me down to the kitchen.

"Mom, guess what?" She looked rested, though I knew this crisis had to be difficult for her to process as well.

"What, sweetie? You okay?"

"Yep, I had a dream of Uncle Jax last night."

"Really? What happened?" For Larissa's entire life she'd displayed a much higher sense of intuition than others

190

around her. She'd often known things were going to happen before they did. The night her great-grandmother passed, Larissa had seen her in a dream. And her Nona on the day she died as well. I believed they had both come to say goodbye. I was curious about last night's dream.

"He came to you? Did he say anything?"

"No, I just saw him, and he was on a plane."

"A plane? Where was he going?"

"Costa Rica, and when he got there he was partying with all the people in that plane restaurant—you know that one?"

The one near Manuel Antonio National Park. "Yes, the bugger, of course he'd be partying, while we're stuck here in this horror."

Larissa laughed.

"Was he scared?" I asked tentatively.

"That would be Uncle Jax for sure." She walked over to a chair and sat down. "He was sort of, at first, when he was on the plane—well, not really scared, I guess, more excited with anticipation, like you would be if you were going on a holiday—but not now."

We had been to Costa Rica in the winters of 2010 and 2012. It was my brother's favourite vacation place, and mine too. I was comforted by my daughter's dream. I needed to find comfort where I could.

Stu and I got ready to head to RVH. Ben texted and said he was there with his pastor, so at least I knew Jax wasn't alone. Good. He hated being alone.

Mom and Bart would meet us there. Dad couldn't bring himself to go. That irritated me. Larissa wouldn't come; she didn't want to remember her Uncle Jax like that. I understood. Fredrik had found a ride and would be there before the neurologist, along with a couple of Jax's and his friends.

At the hospital, Stu let me out and parked the car while I hurried toward the entrance. It was another depressing day, but with a strange bright grey and white sky. The kind that you need sunglasses for, although the sun isn't visible. It hadn't peeked through all morning. The wind pushed my hair into my mouth and eyes. I had to turn around as I walked and let the wind blow it back into place.

In the lobby I waited impatiently for Stu. I wanted to get to Jax. I had to ask at the information desk how to find the ICU.

"Follow the green line on the floor; it will lead you there," said the volunteer.

Coloured lines led off in all directions, and once Stu returned from parking the car, we followed the green one, making our way down a series of hallways and around corners—we thought that line would never end—until we finally saw ICU. Large double doors led to a small waiting room. On the wall was a button with a note that read, *Please press to enter*. I did.

A female voice said, "Who are you here to see?"

"My brother, Jax Vanbeermen," I said, and she buzzed us through.

A nurse greeted us, and we trailed her to his room. Noticing Ben leaning against the wall, I ran up and hugged him. I was surprised to see that his pastor had already left, but I didn't want to ask why. I didn't see anyone else there yet. Stu followed.

"Hi," said Ben, struggling to smile. "I don't see a change, although I did notice his blood pressure rise again when I held his hand and told him I was here."

"Do you think…?"

"I want to think that he does, but…" He stepped away from the wall and straightened his back. But then he wobbled slightly and placed his hand on the wall to steady himself.

Looking past Ben, I could see through large glass windows into Jax's room. His feet tented the sheets.

"I had my pastor talk with him, and we prayed for Jax to come back."

"Aw, Ben, that's beautiful."

"He said that even if he doesn't, he's asked Jesus to take his hand and guide him. I feel better now, knowing that he won't be alone." He still had his back to Jax.

"Larissa had a dream about him last night, that he was in Costa Rica partying," I said to change the subject. I didn't want to think about Jesus and Jax. If in her dream Jax was partying in Costa Rica, maybe he'd already left his body.

"Could that mean his soul has already left? I wish your pastor was still here—maybe he'd know."

"It was just a dream. I'm sure Jax is still very much with us."

I saw resignation in his face.

Something inside me knew then Jax wasn't coming back. I tamped down that thought, forcing it into the ache that had returned to my stomach.

"How about we go in." I entered the large room, leaving Stu outside. He was being supportive but was staying out of the way. If I needed him, I knew he was never far. I couldn't worry about him right now, and I knew he didn't want me to.

Jax's bed was centered in the room with the ventilator machine behind him, next to his IV. Along the back was a line of windows that let in some natural light. The walls were beige, trim and all. There was a smell in the room, a mild iodine scent.

Jax was still hooked up to both the IV and the ventilator. His colour was the same, and his chest still rose and fell at a different pace than that of the ventilator. On his side table sat yellow roses. Ben saw me look over at them.

"I brought those. I hope that's okay. Yellow roses were Jax's favourite."

I was moved. "They are beautiful—thank you so much for bringing them. I never knew." How could I not have known his favourite colour of roses? But it made me feel good knowing that Ben did.

I bent down to smell their fragrance, and as I closed my eyes, I saw all the years flashing past. Papa's farm, the fields, wheat swaying in the wind as we'd run through it giggling without a care in the world. The smell of pig manure filling our noses and mucking up our boots. Jax as a child running around chasing Tom and me —and whoever was lucky enough to join us——with the zapper for the pigs, pressing it into our skin and giving us shocks, exclaiming, "Does this hurt? Does it?" Jax as a teenager, the life of every party he arranged. And all the times in between the crazy episodes, when he was the kindest soul you'd ever meet. He had a way of making you feel like you were the most important person in the room. Everyone who met him was drawn to him, male or female. When Jax loved you, you knew it, and it was forever. He'd have your back in any

Angie Vancise

situation and support you through your toughest times with a gentle compassionate nature unique to him.

He'd have known *my* favourite flower.

Some time must have passed, because when I turned away from Jax, everyone was there—about 20 of us crammed into the airless room. All his close friends from the city, Uncle Arthur and Tom. Katie too. The new arrivals weren't talking; they were just staring at Jax with white faces. I felt their disbelief in all of this, their desire to make it all go away.

I crawled up onto the bed and lay beside Jax. Wrapped my arm around his chest and rested my head on the pillow next to his. I heard my stepsister Wendy say, "Come on, everyone, let's give her time to be alone with him." She was Norma's daughter from a previous marriage, and she worked as a nurse at RVH. Odd that both of my step-sisters were nurses.

I lifted my head. "No, please don't leave. I'm gathering strength from all of you. Seeing the love inside this room helps fill the hole in my heart. He meant so much to all of you too. Please don't go. He'd want us all around him."

And so they stayed. Telling stories of Jax, laughing, crying. Sitting, standing. pacing, coming and going. Their eyes telling me everything I needed to know about their helplessness, their grief.

I just kept holding on.

It was seven o'clock when the neurologist finally showed up. By then we had been at the hospital for eight long hours.

Jax's regular ICU doctor, Dr. Robins, had been in earlier and apologized for the miscommunication we'd received from the Collingwood hospital. First, he'd moved all of us out of Jax's room into the small waiting room around the corner. I felt that was respectful of Jax, just in case he could hear and understand what was being said. He was a young doctor with dark curly hair cut short around his ears. He hadn't said much more than the apology and that it was best to wait for the neurologist for further results and that Jax was comfortable and in no pain. He spoke from his heart, but with no sugar coating.

The neurologist, Dr. Naza, was a tall skinny man with wiry, salt and pepper hair. He looked like Albert Einstein. All gathered in the yellow room, we listened.

"Well, upon doing my tests"—he spoke in a monotone— "I found that when I put pressure on Jax's chest, his left arm raised, and that's a good sign. When I preformed the eye test, which consisted of putting water safely into his eyes, he had no reaction. I poked the bottom of his feet with my pen, but he didn't move. No reaction when I put cold water on his chest. He has zero voice response and doesn't seem to respond to loud noises—these aren't good signs." Rolling my eyes, I looked at my mom. "So, in my examination I found some response, but not a lot. Now you don't have to decide quickly or…you can, but there is definitely no hurry." *Decide what?* "The fact that Jax lifted his left arm was a great sign, it showed pain response, but as I said before he didn't respond to anything else so…"

I leaned in and whispered to my mom, "This is Dad's neurologist."

"Oh, well, that explains a lot," she whispered back.

By the time he was done babbling, we were more confused than ever.

The consensus was that we would wait until the next day. The neurologist would be back to perform those same tests again, and we'd see if there were any changes for the better or worse.

I looked around the room and noticed that Ben wasn't there. I went looking and found Bart just outside Jax's room, pacing the hall.

"Bart, have you seen Ben?"

"Yeah, uh, he told me to tell you that he left for the day, and he'd text you later."

"Oh, okay, thanks." It bothered me that Ben hadn't said he was leaving. Maybe he just needed to be alone.

Leaving Bart to his pacing, I returned to Jax's room and sat next to his bed. Fredrik, and Maxine, a longtime friend, stood across from me. Maxine was taller than Fredrik and in her late forties. She and Jax had had a love–hate relationship. They adored each other, but Jax sometimes saw her as micromanaging, and he couldn't stand someone getting in his business.

A few of his friends from the city had gone, but most remained. I scanned their faces and saw the familiar horror on all of them. Fredrik and Jax's roommate, Judy, couldn't bring herself to enter his room, so she stood out in the hall, eventually taking up pacing with Bart.

A few people remained in the little yellow room down the hall, but I wasn't sure who all was in there. I assumed my mom was, because she wasn't in Jax's room.

Sitting next to Jax, I willed his eyes to open, flutter, anything. Still nothing. Fredrik had Jax's phone resting on the bed beside him, shuffling through his playlist. Now playing was Adele's "Rolling in the Deep."

Flapping my arms like a chicken, I said, "Do you guys like this song? Isn't it a great song? Tell me, do you like this song? Have you heard it? Wanna hear it again?" I spoke over the lump in my throat. I was trying to lighten the mood. This was what Jax would always say when his new favourite song came on. Then he'd flap his arms like a chicken, just the way I had. We'd all be forced to endure hearing it a few hundred times before we could finally move on. Tonight, there was no laughter, but there were a few smiles at least.

Angie Vancise

"Amelia?" My dark-haired stepsister Wendy was so tall her frame almost filled the doorway to Jax's room. "Your mom needs you in the waiting room. You, too, Fredrik."

"Okay." I got up, grabbed Fredrik's hand, and we headed down the hall.

As we entered the yellow room, I saw a petite, middle-aged woman with a clipboard leaning against the wall across from us. Her blonde bob was perfectly combed. It was Maggie Thompson from Trillium, there to explain organ donation. We'd already been filled in from both sets of doctors here and in Collingwood, so we would keep this visit short and sweet.

"So, now how do we all feel about donation? Is it too soon to tell?"

I just wanted to put off this decision for as long as I could. Besides, until after tomorrow's tests, we wouldn't know exactly what was going on with Jax.

"I think we should wait for tomorrow and decide then." Fredrik looked exhausted, but there was conviction in his tone. "I'm staying here tonight, right next to Jax. I'm not leaving."

"I'm staying with you," Maxine piped up. "I'm not leaving you here alone, Fredrik."

And so, it was decided. Fredrik and Maxine stayed. The rest of us left for the night. I couldn't speak for the others, but I was unsure what I wished tomorrow might bring. All I knew was that I wanted my brother back.

200

16

BEN

My hope was dwindling. I had been praying that Jax might come back to us, but seeing no change in him, I began to feel despair.

Staying as long as I could at the hospital, I suspected that the neurologist's findings would only confirm my fears. I wanted to be there for Amelia, I truly did, but I felt awkward; it really wasn't my place, and besides, I wasn't strong enough. I was barely able to be there for myself.

The ride home felt long. Long and lonely. It was dark, the kind of dark that hides everything around the ditches and fields, and the only thing you see is the light from your headlights shining on the road directly in front of you. I hated the ride. The dark space only reminded me of my life without Jax. I tried listening to the radio to distract me, but it seemed to play nothing but songs that reminded me of him.

The reality that my future might never include him was impossible to absorb. I could hardly understand the past two days—*Has it really only been two days?* What had seemed so clear and important to me before Jax's stroke seemed insignificant now. It left me feeling disappointed over the choices I'd made back then. I wished I'd been stronger.

In moments of excruciating honesty, I knew I had failed him, had failed myself too. I had failed even my kids, depriving them of this man, a good, honest, fun man who had made them laugh. My kids had loved him. I had loved him.

Thinking about that had me remembering the conversation with Amelia about Christmas. Jax really had always found the perfect gifts.

*

It was Christmas Eve, our second one together, and I had stuffed the turkey and placed it into the oven. I wanted to make it special for the kids. Michelle would be picking them up in the morning to go to her place.

I heard the front door open. Soph, Josh, and Caroline bolted from the living room. Caroline was only five, but Soph and Josh had her excited for Christmas. It was all they talked about these days.

"Guys, easy, go slow, so you don't fall."

"But, Daddy, Jax is here with our gifts." Sophie, being the oldest, spoke for all three of them.

"Hi, guys! Whatcha doin?" Jax placed a few bags on the floor while he took off his boots.

Not much snow had fallen yet, but it was cold. I could feel the draft as the door closed. Caroline put her hands in the air for Jax to lift her up.

"Hang on, wee one, I have to take off my coat first." He hung it on the peg behind him, turned, and swept her up in his arms.

"Are these all for us?"

"Sophie, don't be rude," I said.

"I'm not."

"Yes, they are all for you," said Jax. "There might be one in there for your daddy too." He set Caroline down. "Here, you guys can help me bring them into the living room." They each grabbed a bag and moved to the living room. They placed the gifts in the middle of the room and sat around them on the floor.

"Can we open them now, Daddy?"

"Yeah, can we open them now?" Jax seemed as excited as the kids.

"What do you say?" I asked.

"Please?"

"Yes, please?" said Josh.

He hardly ever spoke. He had been slow learning to speak. He'd used his own made-up sign language until last year. He'd point and grunt at whatever it was that he wanted. I'd stopped giving him things that he would sign for, waiting till he named them. It worked. He knew the words, but he just wouldn't say them. He was getting better, and Jax has been really great in helping him. He made it fun, playing word games with him like Hangman. I looked over at Jax. He was nodding rapidly.

"Okay, sure. Dinner won't be for a while anyway."

The three of them leaped onto Jax's lap, and he passed them each one present.

Sophie ripped the paper off hers first. "A kitten Beanie Baby! Look, Daddy. I really, really wanted one of these."

"What do you say to Jax?"

"Thanks, Jax."

"You're welcome." His smile grew.

She brought it under her chin and cuddled it.

Jax then helped Caroline open hers. It was a Tickle Me Elmo.

"How in the world did you find one of those? I looked all over for one, but they were sold out everywhere."

"It's my little secret." He grinned broadly.

I couldn't believe he'd found one. Knowing Jax, he probably drove to the States to get it.

"Dad, look! A Nintendo 64!" Josh said.

"You didn't. You shouldn't have. This is too much. And how in the world did you find that? I thought they were sold out too!"

Each of the gifts was perfect. Especially mine, he had Amelia paint a picture. She's an artist and a damn good one at that. She'd painted the large stone flowerpot structures on Flowerpot island, highlighted by the dark blue water in the background. An osprey soaring in the clouds above. Bugger, he'd made me cry.

"It's nothing. They're such great kids. They deserve it. Now where can we plug this in?" he asked, picking up the Nintendo and four controllers.

They headed for the basement and hooked up the Nintendo. I hung my painting in the living room over the fireplace. Caroline wouldn't stop making Elmo giggle. *Maybe that toy isn't such a great idea.* The other three played Donkey Kong. Sophie and Josh played the two characters in it but would ask Jax to help when they couldn't get past a challenge. Meanwhile, I went back up into the kitchen to check on dinner. All I could hear, coming from the basement, was laughter.

He played right along with them for hours, before and after the meal. I'd never seen four people eat so fast; they couldn't wait to return to Donkey Kong. To them, Jax was the "fun guy." I wanted it that way. I was the disciplinarian. Don't get me wrong; I had fun with them too, but didn't want Jax to take on that role. I suppose I tried to protect him, to avoid any negativity—god knows my family exhibited enough of that on their own. I wanted my three beautiful kids to love him like I did. And thankfully, they did.

*

The sound of the truck shutting off had me back in my driveway. I was filled with a sense of helplessness, knowing I had no say in any choices or decisions that had to be made, being just his ex.

I floundered my way into the house. There was nothing in the fridge that made me want to eat. I wasn't quite sure what to do with my time. I kept looking at my phone, half expecting Jax to text.

I had only ever lost my dad. My grandparents, too, of course, but I don't recall really missing them. I was either too young or just not close enough to them.

Later in his life Dad had had Alzheimer's, and by the end, he no longer knew me. I'd visit him often, and he would look at me as if I were a stranger. His face was so familiar, but he was somewhere I couldn't reach him. By the time he died five or six years ago, I'd been wishing for it. Finally, he was at peace. With Jax it was so incredibly different. He was much too young. You expect to live without your parents one day. I had never expected to live without Jax. I'd thought we had more time, and I took the time we had for granted. I'd thought we'd get back together one day. Grow old together.

We'd discussed it, but I think each of us had been so hurt over the breakup that we were protecting our hearts. I often wondered if that's why Jax stayed with Fredrik. Did it give him an excuse to stay apart from me? They really hadn't gotten along that well, especially lately. I never completely understood that relationship, except that Fredrik was a lot of fun, and Jax is drawn to fun. Jax shared with me that he'd recently told Fredrik he no longer wanted to be with him and that he wanted a future with me. That it was over between them. I'd never pressured Jax, not ever, but I'd be lying if I said the news hadn't excited me. For twelve years I had secretly waited for him. I'd avoided serious relationships, in case Jax came back. That, and I hadn't found anyone as wonderful as Jax.

I made a promise to myself right then that if Jax did come back to me, I'd never ever let him go.

Leaning on the kitchen island, I heard the door open—*No, no, I don't want any company right now.* It was Mom, of course. I'd felt anger against my family since receiving the news of Jax. Perhaps that didn't make sense, but I really didn't want to talk to her now.

I suspected Caroline had told her what happened, and I just didn't feel like going through it all. I was exhausted.

"Hello?" came her voice.

Peeking around the corner I saw Mom standing at the back door with something in her arms.

207

"I don't mean any disrespect, but I really just want to be alone right now."

She walked as far as the doorway into the kitchen. "Oh now, come in here and sit with your mom for a moment," she said, motioning for me to follow her back to the living room. "I want to show you something."

"Seriously, I really just need to be alone with my thoughts. I'm struggling right now, and I don't feel like talking about it." I stood firm in the doorway.

"That's good then, because I'm not here to talk about anything. I want to show you something."

Eventually giving in, knowing she wouldn't leave until I did, I rounded the corner into the living room to see her standing with an old brown book under her arm. *The last thing I need, the Bible.* She sat down and tapped the cushion beside her. I sat—I was too tired to fight her—and was pleasantly surprised to see it was a photo album.

"Look at this one: a picture of my grandmother at our wedding. She was such a dear person. She was ninety-nine when we were married. You know I didn't think I was going to be able to have icing on our wedding cake. The war had just ended a month before, and sugar was in such short supply. I had to trade food stamps for icing sugar."

I'd heard this story before, and right now I really wasn't in the mood. I felt like telling her to get to the point.

The old photo album had worn edges and smelled slightly musty, though the pages inside were still clean and crisp. With each page she turned there was another story. Each picture was carefully placed in chronological order.

"Oh"—she snickered— "I look so young in this picture, don't you think? There are Chris and Bill on the binder with me on the tractor. They were such cute boys. I did learn to love them so. They both had a very bad home life."

"Oh yeah. Those are the boys you and Dad fostered." I felt as though I had brothers that I didn't really know.

"Yes, what you didn't know is that for ten years Dad and I tried to have children, and it just never worked out. Every time I got pregnant, I'd have a miscarriage. Maybe it was because I worked too hard, like the doctor told me, but I didn't agree." She touched the picture gently, and I could see how much they'd meant to her. I'd only met Chris once, quite a few years ago. Mom said he came a few years again after that, and he didn't look great. He was skinny as a rail, pale and with sores on his face. I'd always believed that he came that day to say goodbye and thank Mom for all that she'd done.

"My body never knew anything but hard work, so I didn't see why that would cause a miscarriage. I believe that God had a plan, and I was to help those children before I could have my own. This was Chris's favourite day, this day"—she pointed again to the picture— "on the back of that tractor. At least that's what he always said."

There was a sort of sparkle when she spoke about Chris. She had grown to love both boys, but I suspected Chris was her favourite. She periodically spoke about him after the foster care took the boys back and gave them to their biological parents, and I wondered why she was bringing him up now. I sometimes felt that she loved him more, maybe he would have been a better son.

"I wanted to share this with you because sometimes God's plan doesn't fit with ours. But you must have faith in it, no matter what. You must trust that He knows best and let Him guide you. I couldn't understand why God kept taking my children until after I fostered Bill and Chris. Without that experience, I wouldn't have known a lot of things. I can tell you that right after they took them back, I found out I was pregnant, and your oldest sister was born, then Beverly—then my boy. I finally got my boy." She patted me on my head.

I still didn't see how this was supposed to help me, but it was a nice distraction.

"Thanks, Mom. Do you know whatever happened to Chris? You said he didn't look well when he came to visit you years ago. Have you seen or spoken to him since?"

"No." She snapped the book closed, got up, and said a quick goodbye before leaving.

I wasn't sure what was going on. Had I upset her somehow? I didn't have the emotional strength to worry about that.

My thoughts drifted back to Jax. I asked myself at what point it went wrong between us. Was it any one thing? Or was it a combination? Was it part of God's plan, like Mom said? Did He believe that homosexuality was okay, and did He accept me and love me? If so, then why didn't His plan include Jax and me? Why did twelve years go by without Jax by my side, and why was he lying in that hospital bed now?

I got up and walked to the corner of the room, turning on my small model train. I still meet with the train club on Monday nights. Trains are and always have been my passion. I returned to the couch and watched as the train circled the track, round and round. My thoughts circled with it. Snippets of my life with Jax played through my mind like a movie—only I couldn't fast forward, rewind, or pause—toward our downfall.

*

It was the May long weekend of 1999. The weather, I remembered, had been exceptional. Clear blue sunny skies, 24 degrees, and we were ready to party. We'd been together for three years. Jax had moved in with me the year after we met.

One of the things that had attracted me to him was his sense of fun. Every weekend that I didn't have my kids, Jax and I would go to Toronto to see our friends, or he would have people up to the farmhouse. It was great at first, but gradually a part of me began to wonder if he was getting bored with me, or maybe he just loved to party that much. Either way, I became increasingly exhausted and annoyed. Jax never seemed to understand how many ways I was being pulled. He would go to work, come home, play Nintendo with the kids, and relax. I had to work, had to get my kids to and from school, make their lunches, make dinner, get them bathed and to bed, et cetera. On our weekends off without the kids, I really just wanted some down time. Nevertheless, I always looked forward to camping at Cedars.

Cedars was a gay and lesbian campground born from an old farm. The highlight of the weekend was a dance held in the old dairy barn. The original wide floor planks had been recovered with thick varnish to create a reinforced floor. The barn still had an earthen ramp up into the hay loft. The interior was rustic, with old beams and upper lofts. A faint smell of hay remained.

We arrived there on Friday night, eager for the weekend to start. It was already dark, because Jax worked until seven, and then we'd had to pack, load up the truck, and drive the two and a half hours to Hamilton. We didn't really care, though, because we were here feeling carefree. We found our campsite (we always reserved the same one), set up our tent, and had a couple of beer before heading off to bed.

We spent the whole next day relaxing by the pool.

At around 6 o'clock, I said, "We'd better head to the showers and get ready for the dance. It starts at 8."

"But it's still so nice out. Why don't you go start, and I'll be up in a while."

"I know you. If I leave you down here, you'll never get ready. Come on, man, let's go."

"No, I'll be up. I love the Saturday night shenanigans. What time is it?"

"Six."

"That's late. Why didn't you tell me?"

I shook my head at him. I should have known he was just trying to get me going. He was always late, and he knew how much that bothered me. *Bugger.*

We headed to the showers, made a quick burger each, and opened a beer. After one more, we left for the dance. By then it was around nine.

While at the dance, the bartender poured as the DJ rocked out the tunes. It seemed he knew just what to play to get a bunch of gay people to fill the floor.

"*I am what I am. I am his own special creation.*" The crowd sang out the lyrics to Gloria Gaynor's song, basically a gay anthem. I swayed my hips back and forth to the beat, looking around. There wasn't a dry T-shirt in the place.

213

Angie Vancise

An hour passed, and after a few more drinks, my home became the dance floor, and that's where I remained for the night. I loved the energy; it was my escape. Jax would dance for a while but then tire or become bored and move to the outer parts of the room, usually landing in "his" corner. He'd talk and laugh and sip his beer and watch the crowd, but mainly he enjoyed watching me have fun. He was the popular one and always had lots of people around him. Guys who wanted him, guys who dated him before me, and all of the in-between. But no matter who was around him, he'd always let me know I was his priority by periodically looking over, popping onto the dance floor for a few bumps and twirls, smiling or blowing a kiss.

After a few more songs, hands were pumping and waving in the air now to the beat of Abba's "Dancing Queen." A bead of sweat trickled down my back and past the waistband of my jeans. I took a swig of my beer, noticing how its effects were finally hitting me. Flinging my head back, I looked up at the large shiny disco ball hanging from the hundred-year-old hand-hewn beam, spinning as if it knew the beat. The reflection of the lights bounced all over the room. When I inhaled, an excess of cologne and sweat filled my nose. I closed my eyes only for a moment, and upon opening them, through the mist of the fog machine, our eyes met. We smiled. I was feeling pretty good out there on that dance floor. Shoulders banged together,

214

hips swayed more. The room was loud and hot and sweaty. He came closer to dance next to me, rubbing up against my hip, and our eyes connected longer than they should have. The bass thumped in my chest like my own heartbeat.

"All right, we are going to slow it down for a moment for all of you lovers out there, so grab your partners and get your gay asses to the dance floor," the DJ said.

A few bars in, I knew the song. Some people left the dance floor with a casual do-si-do, while others weaved their way onto it. Spinning around to look for Jax, I saw him heading toward me, his pointer finger leading the way.

"Hey, sexy boy, can I have this dance?" He flipped his palm over and held out his hand.

I grabbed it, and we pulled together, holding each other's waists.

"This is our song," he said. "We always dance to this one."

We swayed to the rhythm, holding each other tight at times and separating a little at others. I could hear his breathing as we rotated. We'd had a few disagreements as of late, what with me pulling back from the relationship and then jumping back in again, and dealing with the incessant condemnation of my family. Suddenly, though, in this moment, none of that mattered. All I felt was Jax's warm body up against mine. He seemed to know this was exactly what I needed. I felt…free.

Whitney belted out, "*I...will always love you, oh oh, I will always love you. My darling you.*" Jax mouthed the words along with her while staring into my eyes. The saxophone played the notes of the bridge. "*And I wish for you joy...and happiness...but above all this...I wish you... love.*" Somehow in our bliss we missed the parts of the song that spoke of bittersweet memories and *not* being what you need. Perhaps if we had, we might have foreseen our future, and we really weren't ready for that.

The song ended with a kiss and a long embrace.

"I'll get you another beer," Jax said.

It appeared that, as usual, his motive was to get me drunk, and it was working. I was alone again and swallowed up in the crowd. I had lost all track of how many beer Jax had brought me, but judging from the buzz, I guessed it must have been at least half a dozen.

He returned with the beer and passed it to me. "Here's another, have fun." Then he made his way back to his favourite corner. Even though the dance floor wasn't his preferred place to spend the entire night, Jax would never stop me from enjoying it. He loved watching me let loose. He much preferred interacting with other non-dancers. Some we knew, some we didn't but that didn't matter to Jax. He had no problem making new friends. I didn't mind, I could dance all night by myself. I loved to dance. Jax loved watching me have a great time. I sometimes thought that he enjoyed that more than anything else.

The cold beer soothed my dry throat. More sweat ran down my back. Time seemed to be measured in notes and bars as it got closer to last call. We'd been here for about three hours, but it felt like we'd just arrived. I didn't want the night to end.

Behind me, I felt someone rubbing up against my shoulder, and thinking it was Jax, I rubbed back. But I turned around to discover it was the mysterious stranger. A part of me wondered if he was getting close only to get to Jax. That had happened many times before, but this guy seemed different, focused only on me. He was cute and young, with dark hair and blue eyes, and he was a great dancer. His shirt was now off revealing a build similar to mine, tall, slim but fit. We danced facing each other for a while, then I'd turn and do my own thing. I found it odd that a connection could be made on such a crowded dance floor, but the look in his eyes revealed his intentions. I glanced in Jax's direction, but he was standing at the bar with another guy, heavily engaged in one of his drunken philosophical discussions. I had zero intentions with this mystery man, but I'm not going to lie: it did feel good to have his attention. It seemed everywhere we went, Jax got hit on; he was a magnet. But this time the guy had noticed *me.* I took another gulp of beer, spun around, and our eyes met again.

"You are fucking hot!" He mouthed the words to me over the loud music.

I reached out and pressed the cold beer bottle against his nipples. He cringed and pulled away laughing. He came right back and traced with his pointer finger from my neck down to the button on my jeans.

"So are you," I replied.

He waved his hands in the air, exposing soft, lighter hair in his armpits. His arms were well defined. I was sure he worked out.

It felt good to be desired. We danced some more, our torsos finally touching. Feeling the bulge in his pants, I became aroused. We almost frotted right there on the dance floor.

Okay, enough. I was going too far. It was all in fun— but wasn't this crossing the line? I turned to see Jax making his way across the dance floor. *Uh-oh, busted.*

"Looks like you're having a good time with your new dance partner," he shouted.

"It's nothing," I shouted back. I turned Jax toward him and introduced them, somehow thinking that would make it better.

To my surprise, my intriguing stranger seemed quite comfortable with both of us. The three of us bumped and grinded for a while.

"Hey, one of those guys over there has a joint," said Jax. "Wanna go outside and smoke it with us?"

Jax didn't do that often, and neither did I, but the moment and the beer made it seem a great idea.

"Sure. Maybe just a little."

I motioned to the sexy dancer that we'd be right back. After some fresh air, and I use that term loosely, I returned to the dance floor feeling the effects of the joint. The night was coming to an end, and I wanted to dance some more, so I left Jax outside still smoking with the circle of guys. I told him I'd meet him out there in a few minutes.

The THC made the music boom louder and the lights seem brighter. I felt the dark-haired god wrap his hands around my waist, his bulge up against my ass. Inhibitions were drowned out by the beer and THC, so I let him explore my chest with his hands, while I laid my head back onto his shoulder. My back up against his chest. His hot breath on my neck sent tingles down my torso. I turned to face him. He came close in the dark, and our hands explored each other's bodies, slowly working down to the crotch, rubbing, squeezing, exposing a bulge that just wanted to be let out. Reluctantly I stopped.

"It's been really great, man, you are smoking hot, but I need to go now. Thanks for dancing with me."

He held onto my arm. I knew he wanted more.

"Where are you camping?" he asked.

"We're somewhere way down at the back. I'll catch you later."

We hugged. Our sweat mingled, and it felt amazing.

I made my way out of the barn, stumbling.

As soon as the fresh air hit my face, I heard the familiar, "Heeeeey." It was Jax. "Are you ready to go?"

"Man, I'm so wasted, I'm not sure I can walk back to our tent," I sputtered.

"Come on, I'll help you." Jax wrapped his arm around my shoulder.

I started laughing; it was the drunk leading the drunk. We met up with a few people outside. With all our arms wrapped around each other, we laughed and wobbled our way along.

"Shhh," someone said, as we approached a particularly dark part of the path. "This is the whispering forest." More giggles.

"The whispering what?" I slurred.

"The whispering forest. Haven't you heard of it?" came his reply.

"No."

"Well, if you didn't hook up at the dance, you can come here, go into the bushes, and get your dick sucked."

Just then someone coughed from behind the cedar trees, and we all broke into laughter.

"See? That's the sign," someone whispered, and we all laughed again.

"Wanna go in and find out?" Jax teased.

"No, of course not!" I think my eyebrows lifted, but because I couldn't actually feel them, I wasn't sure. "I'd rather have you blow me."

Laughs ensued again.

We finally made it out of the whispering forest. In the clearing, you could see sparkles of orange, yellow, and red lights from the bonfires at many camps. Most of them came from the lesbian camps. There weren't any lesbos—that's what we called them—at the dance, though. It was rumoured that they are too cheap to buy the booze, although my theory was that they just didn't want to be around all that muscle and testosterone. It's no secret, really, that lesbians and gay men often aren't the best of friends. We just don't have anything in common.

Good-night hugs were exchanged along the way, as each member of our group found his campsite. The air smelled of burning wood. Finally approaching our campsite, we were blinded by the flame from our fire.

"You boys have a good night?" asked Tomas, a friend of ours who was tending the flames.

"Yes, but I have to sit down. The world is spinning." I staggered to the log he was sitting on and managed to get to a seated position, while Jax plunked into a camp chair beside me.

"Oh my god, I'm wasted," Jax garbled. He turned to Tomas. "So why did you come back so early?"

"Ugh, I was bored and tired. Also no one interested me."

"Did you go to the whispering forest?" Jax asked.

I chuckled. I was looking over in Tomas's direction to see his response, when a dark shadow appeared behind him. His face became clearer as he approached the glow of the fire. The air was cool, and he wore a hoody, the hood half covering his face, but his eyes and dark hair were unmistakable. *The guy from the dance.* My drunk brain tried hard to process what was going on. How had he found us? *Jax is going to think I told him to come. What does he want?* Was he expecting me? Jax? Both?

"Hey there, what are you up to, man?" I blurted out, looking over at Jax to see his reaction.

"Hi," he said and stepped, without invitation, even closer to the warm fire. He sat down on the log, landing somewhere between me and the chair Jax was sitting in. He stared into the fire. If not for the alcohol, this moment could have been awkward.

"How did you find your way back here alone?" Jax asked.

"It wasn't hard," the stranger replied.

"Sooo, Bently," Tomas butted in. "Who is your friend?" He looked puzzled.

"We were all dancing together tonight." I looked at Jax and then at the guy, saying, "Sorry I didn't catch your name."

"I'm Ryan."

I looked over to Tomas, who rolled his eyes. I could feel his disapproval. I hadn't asked Ryan back, though. He'd just showed up. Like us, he was a horny young man who just wanted sex. That was no surprise, but I had no idea what Jax was thinking. We'd joked about a threesome but had never discussed it seriously, and now, right here, I was faced with making a decision that I didn't want to make.

"Anyone else want another beer?" Jax got up and headed toward the cooler.

"Not me," I replied.

"Sure," Ryan answered, and Jax handed him one.

"How about you, Tomas?"

"Not for me. I'm heading to bed soon."

Jax and Ryan clinked bottles and each took a long gulp. After an hour of some disjointed conversation and awkward silences, I managed to get Jax's attention and mouthed, *Do you want to do this?*

Sure, came the response, along with a shrug of his shoulders.

The reality of having a threesome with this hot guy was hard to process through my drunken, weed-filled brain, but it got me excited.

"Well, I'm getting cold and need to lie down. Wanna stay and join us, Ryan?" I asked.

"You guys are terrible." Tomas shook his head and looked down at the ground, as he stood up and headed toward his tent. "Have a great night."

"Sure," Ryan replied, as if he hadn't even heard Tomas. His blue eyes met mine.

I looked at Jax, who nodded and got up slowly.

"Okay, let's do it." I stood up, too, and turned toward our tent, not knowing that this one decision would change everything.

Jax and Ryan followed.

*

The sound of the train brought me back to my living room. My mind spinning, I shook my head, walked over, and turned it off. That night at Cedars had returned often to haunt me, and it haunted me more now than ever, as I struggled to understand what had happened between us, what had led us to this day.

Jax hadn't moved over in the bed to get closer to me after Ryan left. I recalled asking him if he was okay. His reply was that he'd only done it because he knew that I had wanted to. I knew it had bothered him that Ryan was more into me than him. I told him that I never would have done it if I'd known how he felt...

But something had shifted in our relationship that day, something was lost—an innocence, a trust.

17

❦

AMELIA

The morning light peeked into my bedroom early and woke me. It's funny to think the sun rises every day despite dark clouds hiding its glow. For a blessed moment, I forgot about the last forty-eight hours, but then it all came rushing back. A small part of me wanted to get to the hospital before everyone else, but mostly I just wanted to hide under the blankets. When I heard my phone, my stomach dropped.

My hands were shaking so hard I fumbled the phone, and it took me a few moments to answer. "Hello?" My voice shaky.

"Hey, did you get any sleep?" It was Ben, and I was relieved.

"Sort of. You?"

"Not really. I'm feeling anxious today. I've been thinking about your call last night about Dr. Naza's findings that Jax reacted to pain. That must be good, right? When he comes back today, though, we have to hope that Jax will respond again and maybe to more tests. That's going to be the tough part because that will determine whether we get to keep Jax or…" His voice trailed off.

"Well, let's see what happens. Fredrik and Maxine stayed there with him last night, so I thought I'd take a little longer to get there today, like, actually try to eat some breakfast and have a shower. What time are you planning on going?"

"I'm not really sure. I'm finding it hard to move my legs." His voice sounded weak.

"Yeah, me too. I can barely get out of bed." The light outside remained dull—but another day without the sun seemed fitting.

"Did Jax or I ever tell you about the time in Vegas when I finally told Jax that I knew he was gay? It was in 2001. After you guys broke up and before he'd met Fredrik. Jax was 37. Mom and I went there with Jax and Lily, Jax's old roommate. I was thinking about it in the middle of the night for some reason."

"No, I didn't know if Jax came out to you guys or if you always just knew. Normally gay guys talk about these things, but since I knew that you guys weren't aware of Jax's and my relationship being more than just friends, I figured he hadn't come out yet at that time. I wondered if he had after we broke up."

"He technically never has come out and I'm not sure if he would have had I not forced the issue. It was pretty funny actually."

And I told Ben the story.

I had decided, even before we left, that that trip to the Knights of the Round Table show might be the perfect time to tell him I knew he was gay and that I supported him.

The faux stone walls, dirt floor and dim lighting had created just the right medieval feel. Horse's hooves clipping and clopping. The smell of horse shit and sweat permeating the stadium. Dust flying up onto my table. Sitting next to me, my brother clapped his hands as he watched our mother, who was seated beside him, becoming more nervous with each pounding of hooves. Jax loved every minute.

"I can't wait to see Mom eat her dinner," he said mischievously.

The serving "wench" set our chicken dish down in front of us without utensils. We were, after all, in medieval times, albeit in the middle of a Vegas hotel in the early 2000s. I gulped down the drink that Jax had bought for me. Extra-large and extra boozy, of course, it had me feeling rather giddy. And making me brave. Yes, tonight I would tell him what I knew.

"Look at Mom." He nudged me with his elbow. "Do you think she's having a good time?"

I looked over to see Mom's look of disgust, as the wench placed her chicken in front of her. Mom searched for a knife and fork.

"Jax, how on earth am I supposed to eat this?" she shouted.

His eyes brightened. "With your hands!"

"I don't know why you brought me here." She turned her head away in disapproval.

Jax looked at me and laughed. *Now, right now, is the perfect time*, I thought to myself.

I took in a deep breath, tapped his shoulder, and shouted to be heard over the crowd, "I just want to tell you that I know you're"—before I could get the last word out, the hum of the crowd fell silent— "GAY!"

Feeling myself turn red, I added, "And apparently now everyone else does too."

Jax had the biggest smile on his face.

"Now that's funny," Ben said, bringing me back to the conversation. For a few moments I'd felt like I was back there. I could smell the horse sweat. See Jax's smile.

"I always say the wrong thing."

"Are you kidding? That would have made Jax's night."

Ben was right. I knew he was right.

"It had been important to me to let Jax know that I was okay with him being gay. Though, the idea of AIDS scared me,

229

and I remember telling him to be careful. I think that danger was always in the back of my mind. But his being gay? Non-issue. I can't remember what he'd said. How come I can't remember?"

"I'm sure it meant a lot to him."

"He did say thank you, that I do remember." I paused for a moment. "But I feel guilty for all of the times Jax could have taken something I said or did the wrong way. Like when he attended University of Guelph, he'd invited me down for the homecoming party. We drank so much that night. On our way back to his dorm, I'd spotted two people necking on a park bench. And by necking, I mean it looked like they were actually trying to eat each other." Ben laughed. "I'm all for affection, but this was ridiculous. I remember saying, *that's disgusting*. But a moment later, I realized they were two women. I felt bad, imagining how Jax must have taken that, and because I'm certain there were hundreds of similar examples in our past. So, letting him know that I was comfortable with the idea of same-sex relationships was important to me. In fact, I actually thought it was pretty cool, him being gay."

"He may have taken it that way, but I'm sure he knew exactly what you meant. My sisters on the other hand…they would have meant every word and thrown it in my face. He knows you love him, Amelia—he knew it then and he knows it now."

Ben's response made me feel better. Surely as a gay man, he would know.

Over the phone, Ben and I decided that we would leave around noon to face the decision that we couldn't escape. I offered to drive him, but he wanted to drive alone to be with his thoughts, and I respected that. He'd mentioned feeling irritated with his family and not wanting to be around them right now. I guess in a way he blamed them for the past twelve years. He said he felt especially agitated toward his mom. That her loyalty to God was a major factor in why they broke up.

I was suddenly reminded of something Jax had shared with me about Ben's family. Something he'd never told Ben— and so, neither had I. Hearing how upset he was at them this morning made me wonder whether I should say something. But Jax had never told him because he didn't feel it was his place. I wasn't sure it was mine either.

I finally pulled myself together. Stu drove again, and I was thankful for that. I didn't think my focus was great for driving.

It was one o'clock when we got there. Fredrik and Maxine were still by Jax's side, when I entered the room. I didn't see Ben anywhere yet.

"Hey, guys, any change?" I said quietly and went to the side of the bed. Jax looked paler than the day before, I thought.

"No, not really. It was nice sleeping beside him all night, though." Fredrik was holding Jax's hand on the other side of the bed and had Jax's phone playing music on his chest. Adele again, and I found that comforting. Fredrik had been a rock these past few days. I couldn't imagine what was really going on inside of him although the music playing, him washing Jax's face and leaning in to kiss him showed me his adoration for him. He really did love him.

"I hear that song and expect him to jump up out of that bed and start waving his hands in the air and..." I couldn't finish the sentence.

"He's dancing to it. We just can't see it." Fredrik bent down, placed his chin on Jax's shoulder and stared at him.

I bent down on his opposite side and rested my head on his chest. He was so warm. I grabbed his arm and put it around me, holding it there. I wanted to stay there forever.

"It's comforting, isn't it?" Fredrik lifted himself back to standing pushing the hair off Jax's forehead. He leaned down again, and kissed it.

"What am I going to do without him? Larissa had a dream the other night and he was in Costa Rica partying with the plane people. I think that means that he's already left us." I could feel the tears threatening again.

"If he's left, there isn't anything we can do about it. It's ultimately his choice. Do I like it? Of course not, but even if he left this body, he'll never truly die, you know that. His energy is so strong, he'll always be around us. And you know he wouldn't want to live like this." I saw Fredrik's eyes redden as he spoke, and I wasn't sure if he was trying to convince just me of this.

I knew that should comfort me, but somehow it didn't.

Dr. Robins was on Jax's care again and that settled me. "Dr. Naza, the neurologist, is here again to do his exam on Jax," he said when he entered the room. "Do you mind if I ask you to wait outside while he does it?"

Fredrik, Maxine, and I trudged to the tiny yellow waiting room. There were again about twenty or so of us squished in there, and some were even forced to stand just outside the door. Some had been there since early morning, anticipating the news. None of us knew what to say, so we just stood or sat staring at the ceiling or into our hands or into the narrow spaces between us.

18

❧

BEN

I stood outside Jax's room watching Fredrik and Amelia. Fredrik was brushing the hair off his forehead, and Amelia was hugging Jax. I was envious of Fredrik. He had had Jax by his side for all these years. I felt he hadn't appreciated what he had. But then, who was I to criticize? Like me, did he feel bad now for the way he'd treated Jax? Did he wish he could start again?

The light in his room had a yellow haze. The roses I'd left were still on the side table and in full bloom. The water was clear inside the vase and fuller than I remembered. I was thankful that someone was changing it. On Jax's chest lay his phone. I pictured him picking it up and texting me—how I wished he would.

Out of the corner of my eye I saw John. He was sitting on one of the chairs in the hallway with his husband, Greg, and they were holding each other. I'd met the couple through Jax, who'd known them for years before that. They all were great friends.

John was the one who'd inadvertently ushered in the end of my relationship with Jax.

It was a Sunday morning in early fall, a few months after the irreparable mistake at Cedars. Weekends that I had my kids, Jax had begun spending time away from us. He was partying a lot, and there wasn't much conversation between us. Moments of intimacy were becoming fewer and farther between.

I could hear one of my kids rustling around upstairs, but no one had come down yet. I was busy getting breakfast organized—cracking eggs, putting toast down, pouring orange juice. I knew once breakfast was over I'd had to tie hair up, shine shoes, and iron pretty dresses for the girls, along with slacks for Josh. Then get them dressed and out the door to church.

The day was warm and bright, and I was thankful for that. I wouldn't need to pile on the heavy coats and boots.

Just as I finished buttering the toast, the phone rang, and I answered.

"Hi, it's John. How are you doing?" His voice sounded strangely concerned.

"Hey, man, I'm good—and you?"

"What are you up to?"

Angie Vancise

"Just getting breakfast for the kids and getting ready for church. What's up?"

"I might as well just get straight to the point, hey? I mean, what's the sense in messing around." He sighed. "Last night Greg and I went to a G.L.A.S.S. dance and met your Jax there."

G.L.A.S.S. dances were held once a month in an upstairs hall at the Oro arena. G.L.A.S.S. stood for Gay, Lesbian Association of Simcoe County. They were always well organized and packed. Just like at Cedars, the gay men dominated the dance floor, while the lesbians, who didn't dance much, lined the walls. There was a well-stocked bar, and at midnight usually a buffet. In our area it was law—might still be—that to serve alcohol in a hall, you had to provide food. Jax and I would go as often as we could, but because Michelle worked, I had the kids three weekends a month, I wasn't always free.

We had been drifting apart for a while, both putting up barriers. This didn't come naturally for me: I had to work really hard to push him away. It was against everything that I was feeling inside. But it appeared better to my family, thus shutting them up, at least for a while, and I'd convinced myself that it was better for my kids. Looking back, I suspect Jax's distance was a defence mechanism.

236

Jax had left Friday after work, and I expected him back sometime Sunday night.

"I mean, I know you guys have been going through some stuff lately," John continued, "but there's something that you need to know." He was stammering. "We love both you guys. You are so matched, and it hurts both of us to see you struggling. I'm so upset right now."

"It's okay, just tell me." I suspected what he was about to say.

"Jax... He went home with another guy last night..."

My throat closed up on me. In that moment I couldn't have spoken if I'd wanted to. Jax had never before cheated on me, at least not to my knowledge. I guess it shouldn't have been a surprise to me that he would now, given the problems in our relationship, but somehow it was. I could no longer deny that we were drifting apart: this was proof. Jax had always needed lots of my attention, and he wasn't getting it from me these days. Was this also payback for that threesome back in the summer? Why had I ever gone through with that?

Not that it mattered really, but I had to know. My voice hoarse, I asked, "Who was it? Do you know?"

"I think the guy's name was Brian. I've seen him there before. I want you to know that we tried to stop him, but he wouldn't listen. I didn't sleep all night, I'm so upset. I am so sorry to have to tell you this. I mean, we know Jax better, but we both care about you a lot too."

There was dead air for a few moments. I didn't know how to respond. I mean, I had fully expected this might happen sometime, but now I felt gutted. It occurred to me that I had a legit reason to kick him out, but the sting of that hurt too.

Staring in at him now, I wished I could turn back time, run to Jax when he got home from that infidelity, wrap my arms around him, and tell him that whatever issues we'd had, they were silly. We loved each other, and that's all that should have mattered.

Watching Amelia lying beside her brother and Fredrik rubbing Jax's face, I truly felt bad for both of them, but especially for Amelia.

I was moved by her tenderness with him and remembered all the times that Jax had spoken of her. They had a connection that I'd never had with my sisters. It was beautiful and, in this moment, also terrible.

I felt bad for them, I felt bad for me. And I was angry. Angry at myself, at my family, even at Jax. *How could you leave me?*

None of this was fair.

I felt the beat of my heart in my ears and my face heating. I knew I needed to walk it off.

I took off for the cafeteria and settled there with a cup of hot tea. Watching other people as they got their food and drinks, I wondered who else here was facing tragedy over a loved one. No one looked as lost as I felt.

My phone beeped—it was a text from Amelia. The neurologist had arrived. The others were heading to the yellow room to wait.

I couldn't, just couldn't.

Angie Vancise

19

❧

AMELIA

It seemed like hours that the neurologist was with Jax, although it was probably only ten minutes. The air in the yellow room was stale. The silence…loud.

A couple of friends paced back and forth across the small floor; a few stood outside the room, while Mom, Fredrik, and I sat. Katie stood against the wall beside Mom. My head felt heavy. I rested it in my hands, my elbows on my knees. Stu was rubbing my back. Whatever happened next depended on Jax.

Again, Dad had stayed home. I'm not sure whether his illness was making him too weak to travel, or whether the thought of watching his son lie motionless, close to death, was unbearable. A part of me was disappointed, but I wasn't surprised. I'd come to expect it. Never in my life had he been a support for us when difficult decisions had to be made. I had hoped that this time he'd be here, if not for Jax then at least for me and Mom. I got that he was sick and all, but sometimes you have to give your head a shake, dust yourself off, and suck it up. This was one of those times. *Does he think any of us really want to be here?* At least Uncle Arthur was here, and Tom. Uncle Arthur always had been and always would be there for me. Since the first moments in the hospital, he'd never been far from my side with a reassuring smile or hug.

I looked over at Mom sitting across from me, her expression closed. I wondered what she was thinking. Was she disappointed in Dad too? Or, like me, had she become accustomed to his absences? Maybe she was in shock. No doubt we all were.

Every time a message came in, my cell made the sound of a monkey, a soft *ee, ee, ee.* I'd chosen that notification when we were in Costa Rica. The sound seemed amplified in this silent room, so I clicked "Do not disturb." I appreciated everyone's kind thoughts and prayers, but I could read those later, when I was alone. Still, the monkey sound made me smile.

On our first trip to Costa Rica, we set out one morning on an adventure that would forever remain one of my favourites: Jax, Fredrik, myself, Larissa, Stu, and our friends Kyle and Ritchie were all there. While in the Jeeps we'd rented (we had two for all of us), my brother got a text; his sound was a *bing bing* like a timer to tell you your bagels were done. It was our dad asking how we were all doing. Dad contacted us repeatedly that day, only because of a glitch. He'd sent the text

241

once, but it kept resending. *Bing Bing, bing bing, bing bing.* Jax thought this was hilarious. He'd say, "I wonder who that's from? Who do you think is texting me? Oh, look, it's Dad, and he's wondering how we're doing." Some people in that situation would have turned their phones off, but not him; he'd laugh harder every time it binged. Finally, Stu asked him to turn it off, claiming he didn't care about the noise but was worried about our father getting charged each time a message came through. Reluctantly he turned it off, but later, when he turned it back on again, texts and corresponding bings flooded in—at least a hundred of them. Jax was clearly delighted.

This went on for a few days, with Jax waiting until the most inappropriate time to check his messages, resulting in the rush of bings. His Cheshire-cat smile would be followed by a deep grunting laugh and "Who could that be?"

It occurred to me now that the things that drive you the maddest about those you love are sometimes the things you'll miss the most.

I heard the door squeak open and looked up to see Dr. Robins and Dr. Naza entering. A couple of friends got up off the small couch and motioned for them to sit. They did. My stomach tightened. I looked around for Ben. I'd texted him to let him know the neurologist was here. Where was he?

I wasn't ready for the news I was sure was coming.

Dr. Naza, got straight to the point. He had performed the same tests as the day before, only this time Jax had zero response. He didn't lift his arm when they applied pressure to his sternum. Jax was declining on his own.

After explaining his test results, the neurologist left the room. Jax's physician stayed behind.

"Jax has suffered severe damage to his brain," Dr. Robins said. "The only part of Jax's brain still functioning is the primitive part at the back of the head, the part that controls breathing and heartbeat. Nothing else." He leaned forward in the chair. "If Jax were to ever wake up, and there is only a one percent chance of that happening, he wouldn't see, he couldn't speak, he'd never walk again, and he wouldn't even know you were in the room."

In other words, Jax would be on life support forever. The MRIs, CAT scans and x-rays all showed the same results. The neurologist from Sunnybrook, over the past two days, had also viewed and confirmed these findings.

There was nothing they could do for my brother.

His words had cut off the blood supply to my heart. I was afraid any movement would cause me to pass out. The room had fallen silent. My eyes met my mom's. Her lip shivered. Her shoulders rounded, and she lowered her chin to her chest. Scanning the room, I saw shock on the faces of each one of our family members and friends. My gaze landed on

Fredrik. He was still staring at the doctor with his jaw slack. The colour had left his face. Then he closed his lips and sat up straighter. He shook his head like he was trying to clear it, to calm himself. My heart was breaking for him. I knew he'd been angry with Jax over his constant anxiety. He'd lost his patience more often than he'd wanted to. We all did—but would the guilt break him? He loved Jax despite all of that and had been by his side for ten years. We both had in common our families relying on us for strength. I would tell him that he didn't have to be strong this time. I would have to tell myself that too and that I'd always be there for him.

Out of the corner of my eye, I saw Ben with his hand up against the frame of the door as if that's all that was holding him up. I knew that I should go to him, but I couldn't make my legs move.

We had our answer. It was now time for me to prepare myself for the worst possible outcome—but how? How could I prepare to lose my best friend, confidant, and soul mate?

Dr. Robins continued, "I'm sorry this wasn't better news." He explained that we had time to make the decision, although he'd seen families hang on too long, causing the patient severe bed sores and even pneumonia. We certainly didn't want that for Jax. He brought up a point I hadn't thought of, that seeing a loved one in an unresponsive state over a prolonged period causes stress on the family too.

"I have to say in all the years I've worked at this hospital and in the ICU, I have never seen this many people surround a loved one. It speaks volumes about the kind of guy Jax must have been."

I know doctors have to say certain things to make you feel better, but I sensed in his tone and demeanour that he meant every word. Jax was touching this stranger, even in his unresponsive state, in the same way he'd always touched people. The doctor placed his hand on my mom's shoulder and whispered that he was sorry. She brought her hand up to meet his and gave it a squeeze, but said nothing.

He again mentioned organ donation. I saw Ben quickly turn and walk away.

"First I want to make it perfectly clear that at no point will Jax feel any pain. We will have a team there to ensure that. We start by taking the tubes out and administering morphine. If at any time we see Jax in distress, we up the dose. Because of the breathing tube being removed, his body will be deprived of oxygen and his heart will go into cardiac arrest. Once that happens and he passes, we then escort you out of the operating room and proceed with the donation, provided it's within two hours. If that's the route you want to take. If not, then we just let him go as peacefully as possible, with the same procedure, in his room."

The room was silent.

Gathering himself and showing why his family feels he's the strongest, Fredrik was the first to speak. "Thank you, Doctor. So, you are positive that he will feel no pain? Jax was so afraid of having a heart attack and dying. His only fear, really." Fredrik leaned forward in his chair.

Not seeing him cry through any of this had me worried for him. And his tone... It was almost as if he were talking about a stranger. His questions more like confirmations than concerns.

"I can assure you that he will feel no pain." The doctor's expression softened.

"Then I guess we have a couple of decisions to make." Fredrik looked around the room. "Did Jax ever talk to any of you about organ donation? I for one don't think he'd want to do it."

This was all just too much for me. I could barely breathe, let alone speak.

Maxine piped up. "I remember having a conversation once with Jax, and I was saying how I wanted to donate my organs, and Jax's reply was, 'Well, why wouldn't you?' So, I'm throwing it out there that I think he'd want to despite his fears."

Ben reappeared in the doorway. There was an added strain on his face that I'd never seen before. Was it because he didn't like the thought of donation and felt he couldn't say

Cry of an Osprey

anything? He came over to let me know that he was leaving to be with Jax. I nodded and squeezed his forearm.

Katie remained against the wall not saying anything. Looking over at her to see if I could read her thoughts, I realized that she didn't feel it was her place. She was glancing down at the floor biting her lip.

I turned to Maxine. "Are you sure? Did he mean why wouldn't you as in *you,* or as in why wouldn't you as *everyone*? I know my brother, and I don't know if this is something he'd want. Maybe just like we did yesterday by letting him decide about turning the machines off, we can let him decide this. I mean if we all say yes, and they take him to the operating table, he will decide by either letting go in time or not. What do you think? Mom? Fredrik?"

They both nodded.

"So, you will go ahead with the organ donation?" the doctor asked.

"I guess I'll speak for everyone and say… yes." My voice didn't sound like my own. I looked around the room to see if anyone had objections, almost hoping they did.

The doctor said he'd send Maggie from Trillium in to speak with us again and to have us sign the donation papers. He'd check to see when the operating room would be available.

"I think we should let him go sooner rather than later," Fredrik said.

247

I looked at Mom. "What do you think?"

"Do you have his ring, Fredrik?" she asked. My mom had bought Jax a ring when he was a teenager, probably for his grade thirteen graduation. I remember him spinning it on his finger and playing with it. He once dropped it during a movie in our local movie theatre, and it went rolling several rows down, under the seats in front of us. There was Jax saying *excuse me*, *excuse me* to people in every row, hunting in the dark, until he found it.

"I have it. I'll give it to you." He placed his hand on my mom's leg, tapped it a couple of times, then brought it back to his own lap. "I think we should have it done tomorrow if the operating room is available. I really hate seeing him like this, and I feel we need to let him go. That's just his body in there anyway. He's already left."

"He had a living will." Mom's voice was shaky. "In it he said that if he was ever on life support, he wanted to be let go. I know this because I typed it up for him. I agree with Fredrik."

Those had to be the most difficult words she'd ever spoken. I thought of all the times she'd given that advice to clients when preparing their wills, never guessing her own words would have to be used on her son. The light reflected a shiny stream down Mom's cheek. I'd only seen her cry a few times in my forty-four years, and it usually involved my dad.

She was a strong woman who'd been through so much. This just wasn't fair to her. It wasn't fair to any of us. Least of all to Jax.

She opened her purse, grabbed a tissue, and blew her nose.

I'd never have another brother, and she'd never have another son. There would be no turning back. I had to be sure we could live with the decision for the rest of our lives. But the alternative wasn't any better either. I hated this.

"Amelia," said my uncle, sensing my reluctance, "I feel Jax wouldn't want to live like this. I know it's hard, but think of him." He came over and knelt in front of me, rubbing my arms. "I'm not going anywhere. I'll get you through it, I promise."

I loved him so much. I knew he was right. I knew Mom was right. I just didn't want to believe it. And there, yet again my uncle came to my rescue. There supporting me. A large part of me was frustrated that Dad hadn't come to help with this devastation. You'd think after all this time he'd have learned. It wasn't the first time I'd felt that way and it probably wouldn't be my last. Knowing that he was struggling with his own health issues I tried to sympathize but he always had excuses. Having enough to deal with and like always, I pushed it aside and accepted it for what is was, history had taught me that.

"As much as I hate the thought of never seeing my brother again, I do see your point. If there's a time it can be done tomorrow, I agree that we should let him go. I don't want to watch him suffering, and if he declined that much overnight, I'm sure he will continue to go downhill."

"I just don't see the point in letting him lie there for weeks getting worse and worse. It's not really even him. Getting pneumonia and bedsores, for what? He's not going to get better." Fredrik tilted his head, something he sometimes did when making a point.

I nodded.

It was decided. Tomorrow would be the day that I would watch my brother die.

20

BEN

I wanted to be a part of the donation discussion, but didn't feel it was my place. I strongly disagreed with it, because I didn't think Jax would want it. Of course, I couldn't say that. None of the decisions included me, nor should they have. I was nothing in this narrative. Not his partner, his husband, his brother—and that realization killed me. I had had to leave that yellow room. It became unbearable to be there any longer.

Alone, I went to Jax's room, where he lay in the same position as before, his head propped up slightly on a pillow. His arms by his sides. Tubes ran to his mouth and nose, the IV dripping, one second at a time. I don't know why, but every time I entered his room I expected him to be sitting up, huge smile on his face saying, "Hey, Ben." And every time he wasn't, I felt the same despair.

The roses that I'd brought still brightened the nightstand. There was a spot of blood on the sheets beside the

IV site. I panicked, until I realized that the nurse had taken blood earlier.

I walked over to the window and stared out. Behind the hospital were a few houses in a small subdivision—dorms for Georgian College, I thought. The college was only a couple kilometres away. On one side of the street a guy was walking with his girlfriend. They appeared to be in their early thirties. Roughly the same age as us when we were a couple. They were holding hands. I wanted to scream out to them to never take what they had for granted. They looked happy and in love, just like we once were. On the other side of the road, a few doors down, another guy was walking his dog. I hated the sight of these people walking around doing normal everyday things, while I was in this room watching the love of my life dying. How I wished for their normal.

I walked back to Jax's bedside. His skin, when I touched it, was warm, and everything about him looked familiar.

"How can you leave me?" I grabbed his hand and squeezed it so hard it hurt my own. My jaw clenched. As I lifted his hand to my cheek, I broke down. I thought I could feel life leaving me. The life he had given me each and every day, the life that we'd promised to each other, my life, his life, gone, just like that. And I couldn't stop it.

Amelia came into the room and ran over and held me. She didn't know everything; didn't know how much I'd screwed up. I would tell her in time. When I did, I wondered, would she still hold me? Or would she be as disgusted with me as I was with myself? She had been so caring. Worrying about me even through her own grief. The thought of losing her, too, was unbearable. She wasn't just my last connection to Jax; she'd become very important to me in the past three days. My lifeline.

She looked up at me. Her eyes were red and swollen. "We've decided to let him go tomorrow. We're just waiting on his doctor, so we can find out if there's a time available. Fredrik said it was probably better sooner than later, because watching him like this is too hard." She looked over at Jax. "I know he's right, but how do I leave here today knowing that tomorrow is the last time I'll ever see him?"

She returned to the bed and crawled up beside her brother. I could see her back convulsing in small spasms. She sobbed in silence, rubbing his chest with her fingers, then wrapping her arms around him and squeezing him, sighing. I wondered how she would get through this. I wondered how any of us would. Desperation rushed back in, and as much as I wanted to stay, I had to go. I knew she needed this time with Jax, and I couldn't stand by and watch the unfairness of Jax being stolen from all of us.

Angie Vancise

When I walked over to her and whispered that I had to go, she nodded. I kissed her cheek, then Jax's, and after one last look at him, I turned and walked out.

I heard the tiny stones popping under the tires as I finally pulled into my driveway. How I'd come to hate that forty-five-minute drive. I parked the truck in the usual spot by the shop. As I opened the door to step out, I wasn't sure my legs would hold me. Jax would never walk, talk, or play games again, I thought. He'd never annoy, shock or tease anyone. No party would ever be quite the same without him. All of this was too much to accept. The worst part was that he'd never know how I felt.

Halfway up the stairs I saw my mom at her sliding glass door, about to open it. *Nope, don't want to see you, don't want to see anyone.* I turned right back around and got into my truck and drove off. I knew exactly where I needed to go.

It was still early afternoon, so I'd have enough light. The beach wasn't far, maybe twenty minutes and I'd be there.

I headed east onto Mosley and kept right on River Road, over the new bridge. I turned onto Powerline Road and pulled over once I saw the small shoulder by the wooden fence. I put the truck in park and sat quietly for a moment before opening my door and stepping out. I'd been here tons of times, but this time felt different. I put my keys in my pocket and headed into the bush.

254

The clouds were thick, making the bush darker than usual. That didn't matter to me. I knew this trail like the back of my hand.

Pausing at the top of the large sandbank, I stood there looking down the seventy-foot sand cliff. For a moment, I thought how easy it would be to jump, to just end all the pain right now. But then I thought of Amelia and all that she was facing. I couldn't do that to her or to my kids either. I knew Jax would want me to help her get through this. I followed the path around the top of the bank.

The chickadees chirped, while the red squirrels darted back and forth in front of me, gathering all they could for the winter. The chickadees reminded me of Flowerpot Island. Jax had mentioned them that first day there. They were so much like him: social, positive, cheerful, flexible, and courageous. Remembering that had me stop and bend over to breathe feeling like someone had punched me. But I had to keep going.

Most of the leaves had dropped to the ground, creating a brown cushion, soggy after the rain, to walk on. The smell of the wet leaves filled the air, a sweet earthy smell, like on the day we had canoed here. I kicked the leaves and punched the trees as I passed. It didn't help. I kept going, memories of Jax filling my head.

The second year we were together, I'd decided to try to make his birthday special. Jax always said he didn't need anything other than my attention, that my one-on-one time was what he longed for. I spoke to Michelle and begged her to keep the kids that weekend. It was almost September 15, Jax's birthday, and to my surprise, Michelle agreed.

I booked us on the steamship RMS *Seguin* out of Gravenhurst. I had been once before and really enjoyed it. I loved anything steam and spending time with Jax. Jax loved spending time with me, so it was the perfect combination. Truthfully, I didn't have to take Jax anywhere; he'd have been happy as long as we were together. But I wanted to treat him this time.

Jax hadn't known where I was taking him, so when the whistle sounded departure time he didn't noticed.

"Come on!" I shouted. Grabbing his hand, I ran to the ship.

He was confused, until we stepped on board. Then he gave a huge smile.

The *Lady of the Lakes* was off. She had sailed these waters for over a century and knew them well. I had booked the later dinner cruise, so we could enjoy the sunset. We stood side by side on the bow looking into the dark Muskoka water. The keel sliced through the water like a knife through watermelon, ripples running away from the hull. It was a perfect evening, apart from our having to conceal holding hands. We passed huge waterfront mansions and joked about buying one someday.

The autumn colours had just begun, casting a pale-yellow shoreline with a slight haze of red. The sun setting set the horizon ablaze with a velvety purple red. We clinked bottles and enjoyed our beer until it was time for dinner.

They seated us in the period dining lounge at a table for two at a window. Our server was pleasant, and in no time Jax had her laughing. Her suggestion of wine was from a private stock specifically labelled for the ship. Jax, of course, said yes to that. He also said he'd pay for it, as I had paid for the cruise.

Throughout the dinner our server seemed to spend more time with us, but I wasn't surprised. Jax had a smile and a charisma that charmed everyone. The suggested wine was fantastic and paired so perfectly with our cordon bleu that I recommended we buy a bottle to take home. When I mentioned it to our server she explained that it was only to be served and consumed on the ship. Well, now Jax had a challenge.

He smiled impishly, as though he knew something neither the waitress nor I did. "Just wait, I'll get you one," he said to me.

He continued with the chatter and jokes and smiled broadly as only he could do, dropping hint after hint of larger tips to our server. I sat and watched him in action, and he enjoyed every minute of it. I knew that convincing our server to break the rules was like a quest to him. No wonder he made such a great salesman.

About halfway through our cheesecake dessert, the server came over to our table carrying a brown paper bag. Like many, she had succumbed to his charms. She leaned over, handed it to Jax, and whispered,

"Please don't let anyone see you take this off the ship, and tell no one, or else I'll be in deep trouble, probably fired."

Jax lit up when he peeked inside. He thanked her over and over again, and as promised left a huge tip.

Crying so hard I could hardly see to walk. The night of the cruise was only one of many memories of a guy who would have given me the world if he could have bribed God to help.

I had to stop. Placing my hand on a tree, I bent over for a few minutes, then stood and screamed. I screamed so loud I thought I saw a bird fall from a tree. I punched the big old maple tree that stood in front of me, making my knuckles bleed, but that pain wasn't even close to the pain in my heart. I wiped my eyes and started to run. I ran down the path not really knowing why I was running passing by some of the riverbanks from that day so long ago. I saw the dragonfly, I saw Jax paddling, and his shirt blowing out behind him. Us capsizing the canoe. I came up to where that poor fisherman stood watching as I received the best blowjob I'd ever known. I yearned for that day again. Given a second chance, I'd do so much differently.

I caught sight of something from the corner of my eye. It was an etching in a tree on the other side of the path, near where the fisherman had stood all those years before. It was too far away for me to read it, so I went closer. It had faded, but up close the letters were still legible. *AIDS IS A CURE FOR FAGGOTS*. I blinked a couple of times, wiped my eyes, and stared, thinking the tears had made me misread it, but they hadn't. *Someone really did this?* I was stunned for a moment, until it sank in. Heat began at my toes and shot up through my body, all the way to my cheeks. I felt the burn of anger. All of the ridicule, the racist slurs, the hurtful comments my family had said came rushing into my head, like bubbling lava.

Those words of hate reminded me of another time long ago when someone wrote on the Zellers bathroom stall, *Jax Vanbeermen sucks Ben Olsen's cock*. It surprised me for many reasons but the main being that we tried to keep our relationship a secret. I'd always suspected a jealous ex of mine was behind it. Ben had noticed it and stormed out of the bathroom, rightfully upset. He spoke to the manager and asked that they paint over it, but a week later, they hadn't. The next day he bought orange spray paint and had me stand guard while he redecorated the bathroom. "There," he said when he was done. "They will have to paint it now."

I glared at words carved into the tree. *Why the fuck won't they leave us alone?* I felt defeated, lost, alone. I wished

I'd never been born. Jax had always helped me through these feelings, although I'd never seen him as upset as that day in Zellers. The thought of how many people had seen this vile message through the years sickened me.

I picked up a rock and banged it against the tree as hard as I could. One hit for the bathroom message, one for my mom and each of my sisters for every hurtful shame they had instilled in me, one for me listening to it, one for kicking Jax out, one for never letting him know how I really felt, one for the fear of who I was and the fear of losing Jax. Twelve more for each year that I'd wasted. More still for my lost happily-ever-after.

I pounded and pounded, but the message stayed like a bad tattoo. I turned the rock to the pointed side and scratched instead for all that I'd not done, all that I wouldn't get to do, and all the hateful thoughts I held onto. I scratched for Jax. By the time I was done, my shirt was full of sweat, and it looked like a beaver had chewed a wedge into the tree, but I didn't care, the message was gone.

I chucked the rock, not knowing where it landed, and took the few steps forward up the small hill, where I could stand and see Montgomery rapids.

Across from where I stood was the corner where the canoe had capsized. The small island where Jax and I had had lunch that day looked barren. There were no leaves left on the tree, which was larger now than it had been back then. I felt another wash of heartache and despair, and I fell to the ground and started hyperventilating.

Deep breaths, Ben, deep breaths. My heart gradually slowed its beat. *That's it, breathe.* I knew I had to calm down. The sharp pain in my chest had returned. *In slowly, out slowly.* As I leaned against the tree I could feel its strength, its sturdiness, and I was thankful for that. I wanted to steal its energy for myself. I knew that somehow, I needed to stand tall like that tree.

I glanced from one side of the rapids to the other. At this time of year there wasn't much water. It was calm. My mind calmed.

Spotting the tree where we saw the osprey that day, I silently searched for it with no success. I remembered that in October they fly to Mexico for the winter. And just like Jax, it wouldn't be there. Remembering seeing it a few times back then I became angered again. *What the fuck had it meant? What had it been trying to tell me?*

It occurred to me that throughout my lifetime, and despite all stressors, the only time I'd ever truly felt free was with Jax and I threw him away.

21

❦

AMELIA

October 24, 2012. The date that would be engraved on my brother's tombstone.

I had hardly slept. I hadn't wanted to leave the hospital. I'd wanted to spend every last moment with Jax, but I couldn't hog all the time; others were grieving too. Fredrik and Maxine had needed their chance to say goodbye to him.

Plus, I had a daughter of my own who needed my attention. She still hadn't opened up about how she was feeling. I had found these past four days difficult, trying to juggle my roles as grieving sister, mother, wife. I felt bad that I hadn't been around more for Larissa, but she seemed to understand that I just couldn't be. Was she taking this harder than she was letting on?

When we arrived home the night before, Larissa had been sitting on the couch playing Skyrim, a game that I will never understand.

"Hi, sweetie. Can we talk for a moment?"

"Sure."

I went to sit next to her, and Stu followed. I knew he'd let me do the talking but would jump in if needed. "Uncle Jax didn't respond to anything the neurologist did today. He's declining on his own."

"I'm sorry, Mom. I know you were hoping for more."

"Thanks, hon. We have decided to let him go tomorrow. I don't need to give you the details of how, unless of course you want to know," I said, trying to keep my voice even, keep myself together.

"I'm good." She shuffled in her seat as she clicked the buttons on the game controller. Her eyes remained on the television screen.

"Are you, Sweetie? Good, I mean? Do you want to talk about it at all?"

"I'm okay. I just see death differently than anyone else. We don't really ever die. Uncle Jax will still be with us, and I know we will see him again one day. I just feel bad for you, because he's your best friend."

Was she staying strong for me? She'd lost her Nona, and two great-grandmothers, but that was a while ago when she was little. This was the first big one for her, and I couldn't believe her strength through it all. I was relieved. I wasn't sure I could have helped her if she *weren't* okay.

Angie Vancise

My friends still hadn't come around. They'd sent texts here and there, but I hadn't seen them. It hurt. Maybe they were dealing with too much of their own pain to help me. Maybe seeing me would tear them apart. After all, Jax and I look like twins. It is was it is, I decided. At least I had been updating them over the past four days and posting to Facebook. So many messages of condolence had come through there that I couldn't keep up. I found these comforting and would sometimes read them to occupy my mind during the long hours at the hospital.

Getting out of bed, I had to turn the light on to see. I pushed the button on my phone: 6:50 a.m. It was early, but I needed to get to the hospital. The doctor had confirmed that the 4 p.m. slot was open in the operating room, so barring any unforeseen emergencies with other patients, that would be Jax's time. Stu had slept in the basement due to his roaring snoring, but he entered my room as I turned back toward the bed. He reached out and pulled me close to him. Together we sobbed.

I couldn't remember the last time I'd showered—was it yesterday? Letting go of Stu, I walked in a daze to the bathroom and turned the water on, waited for it to heat up. Stu said he was going down to put the coffee on. In the shower, the cascade of water mixed with tears slid down my face. I crumped to the tile floor and sobbed. My stomach felt sick—there would be no breakfast. I sat there for a long time under the running stream, willing myself to get up and make it through this day.

Ben had texted shortly after I arrived home the night before. He'd mentioned that last night he'd gone home, but then had left again to avoid talking to his mom. He couldn't even look at her. I almost told him what Jax had witnessed years ago. I really felt that he should know, but even if it *was* my place to tell him, it didn't feel like the right time. Maybe the opportunity would present itself. Maybe it would help him to understand her more.

I'd also spoken to my mom on the phone the night before, after I'd chatted with Larissa.

"I wish I'd gotten up and checked on Jax. Maybe then this wouldn't be happening." Her voice sounded softer and weaker than usual.

"You did get up, and you helped him back to bed after he used the washroom at 6, you told me."

"But I never checked on him again. I wonder how soon after that it happened? Do you think I could have gotten him to the doctor on time and saved him?"

"Mom. You can't do that to yourself. I've been going through the what if's too, and it only makes it worse. This whole thing sucks. I don't know that there was anything more we could have done."

"Do you think that weird thing that happened to him in the car was a small stroke? Maybe we should have taken him back to the hospital. I just feel..." Her voice cracked, and I could hear small short gasps into the phone.

My nose started to run, and the back of my throat hurt. More tears. I tried to reassure her that she was an amazing mom and had done everything she could. I knew her next words would be that she felt she'd let him down. She'd said that often. Despite giving up her social life, her entire life, for us kids, she somehow always felt she should have done better. Dad's infidelity had bruised more than just her ego; it had taken away her confidence as a woman, and a parent. A part of me would always hate him for that.

"He kept complaining about his eyes, the pressure in the back of his head. How did I not see it? Remember at the kiki? He wasn't his usual party self."

Back in August, Jax had arranged what he called a "country kiki" at Ben's farm. He'd always wanted a country party and knew Ben's was the best place for it. Mom was right: he hadn't been his usual crazy self. Yet I remembered him kicking it up a notch.

The country music that played—after he'd replayed Dolly Parton a hundred times—was boring him, so he replaced Ben's phone with his and blasted his new favourite song, "Let's Have a Kiki," by the Scissor Sisters. His chicken arms appeared just before he'd thrown his hands in the air and danced around, encouraging others to do the same. He loved the bit in the beginning of the song when she's talking on the phone and says *motherfucker*. Any song that included the word *fuck* instantly became Jax's favourite. He loved to get a reaction, especially from Mom. She hated that word.

Just before I left the party, I'd seen him go over to Ben. They shared an extra-long embrace. It warmed my heart, but something about it also frightened me. Maybe the way Jax looked at Ben, or the way he hadn't wanted to let go.

My heart flipped as it dawned on me. There would be no more kikis.

I finally got out of the shower and dressed, then called Mom back again to let her know we were leaving for the hospital. She sounded shaken—but weren't we all? We were just hours away from having to say goodbye to her boy.

The day was grey…again, and cold, only six degrees.

I couldn't remember if all Octobers had been this gloomy.

Stu drove, while I spoke to Jax's therapist on the way. Jax had really liked him, and I felt he should know what was happening. He told me I needed to ride the many waves that would be coming. To let them come. I must grieve, and within that grief would be anger, sadness, confusion, isolation, guilt, but I must remember that it's all normal and okay. He was very kind. In time I thought that what he said might help, but right now, nothing did.

267

I had so much guilt surrounding my grief. I'd let Jax down. He hadn't just been anxious—he'd been really sick. All those texts and phone calls where I'd taken my frustration out on him—

I urged Stu to pull over and got out by the side of the road, retching, but heaved up nothing. More retching. Still nothing. I grabbed a napkin from the glovebox, blew my nose, and got back into the car. I sat silently. Stu, not really knowing what to say, stayed silent too.

He had sent me a text the night before. In the silence of the car I grabbed my phone and read it again. It comforted me. I had responded with a simple, *Thank you, I love you.* It seemed all I had to give. His said:

I witness your grief and what you are going through and I feel helpless. Tomorrow will be the worst day of your life and I wish I could somehow make it better for you but in this I am helpless and have failed you. Just know that as your husband I am here to hold you and kiss all of your tears away.

I looked over at him. His face was gaunt. I placed my left hand on his arm, and when he looked at me, I said, "It's your strength I need right now. Without it I couldn't do this, so thank you. I sometimes forget that you are losing someone too."

He reached for my hand and squeezed it. "I'm just so sorry that you have to do any of this."

When he let go, I placed my phone back in the cup holder. As Stu pulled back onto the road, memories filled my mind. The past year, Jax's first trip to the hospital, second, third, and fourth, his anxiety, his many texts... *Will I ever be okay?*

A couple of days before Jax's stroke, I had gone to his place in Toronto to pick him up, because he didn't want to be alone. I was angry and disgusted by that and his not wanting to drive. I didn't show him that, though—thank god. I felt a bit sorry for him. I drove the two hours to his house. When I entered, I saw him sitting on the couch with his two small Chinese-crested dogs cuddled on his lap. He was petting them with tears in his eyes. After his last two shepherds died, he didn't have any animals until he moved in with Fredrik. Fredrik's favourite dogs had always been hairless Chinese crested. Jax loved them like he loved all dogs.

"Hi."

"Hi, Amelia." He didn't look up and his voice was quiet.

"How are you feeling?"

"Not so good—something is really wrong with me. Why can't I just be more like you and calm down?"

He was pale, I thought. I looked down at his fingers, afraid of what I might see. Something I'd noticed with all the people I'd lost was that their fingers turned white from the second knuckle down to their fingertips. I didn't know if that was a thing or not, but still, I checked. *Good, not white.*

"Are your eyes still bothering you?"

"Yes, I can't see. There would be no way I could drive. I still have that jiggly thing going on, and now there are blacked-out spots." He looked over at me trying to focus his eyes.

"Blacked-out spots? Have you been breathing? I know when you get really anxious, you don't breathe properly. Like when you passed out at Katie's wedding."

"I'm trying. I'm just afraid..." He broke off and bent down to rest his chin on the dog's head.

"When do you want to get going?" I said, ignoring his unfinished sentence.

"I guess...anytime."

We left about half an hour later, and as I was backing out of his driveway, I noticed he'd started crying again. I was starting to feel irritated.

"What's wrong? You okay?"

"I—I... It's just my dogs. I'm worried I'll never see them again." He was staring back at the house.

"For Christ sake, Jax, do you really think you're going to die? That's the stupidest thing I've ever heard. You *aren't* going to die."

I'd heard that just before some people die, they seem to know it's coming. They tie up loose ends. They call family or friends that they hadn't seen in years, get all their banking in order, all sorts of things. It sickened me now to know that I hadn't taken Jax seriously that day. He knew something was wrong. He *knew*.

And he never did see those dogs again.

We arrived at RVH at 9:10 a.m. Stu parked the car, and I walked to the ICU. I couldn't believe how many of Jax's Toronto friends were there already; the place was packed. Not just his room and the yellow room, but the hallways too. All of his friends from Toronto and Collingwood shuffled in, one by one. I felt bad for the other patients. He was still gathering people together, still the centre, though this wasn't a party any of us wanted to attend.

I'd text Ben to let him know that I was there. He'd be here soon.

Maxine and Fredrik were there in Jax's room when I entered. Maxine was pacing by the window, and Fredrik was lying beside Jax. The roses had opened up.

My brother now needed the ventilator to breathe. His chest was synchronized to the mechanical puffing. This seemed to confirm our decision to let him go.

I went to the side of his bed and gazed at his face, trying to imprint it in my mind. In less than seven hours we'd be

Angie Vancise

wheeling him into the operating room and saying goodbye one final time.

"I definitely don't think he's there anymore," Fredrik said. "I slept next to him all night, and I think his soul has already left. This is just his shell."

I knew Fredrik was trying to help, but it wasn't working. "Today sucks, it really, really sucks."

"It does. We have to be strong for him, though. Now that you are here, Maxine and I will run to the cafeteria. Do you mind?"

"No, not at all, go ahead. I'll stay with him. I want to be right here for every minute of this day...until I can't be."

"I know." He walked over and hugged me.

After they left, I crawled up to be next to Jax.

"I'm really going to miss you. I need you to help me get through this. I know a part of me should be angry at you for leaving me, and maybe one day that will happen, but today, I'm just sad. Who is going to push me like you do to get out there and live? Please don't leave me. Wake up right now and make this your biggest *gotcha* yet. Please, Jax, please just wake up."

His friends began gathering in his room to say their goodbyes. I was glad they didn't mind me being there, because I wasn't leaving. It did help to know that I wasn't the only one feeling this dreadful loss.

Katie and Mark arrived came over and stood on either side of the bed. Katie was crying as she hovered over both of us. She turned and walked out unable to speak.

Ben arrived around eleven. By then Fredrik and Maxine had returned from grabbing a coffee. I don't think any of us could eat.

Now Maxine was standing next to Jax, rubbing his hair and humming. She had a great voice, and Jax would often ask her to sing to him.

"I sure am going to miss you. You are a bugger for leaving us here." Then she hummed some more. I didn't recognize the song.

She grabbed Jax's phone from the side table and called Fredrik to find his music on it and play him a song.

Ben was there. He looked drawn, and years older than he had a couple of days ago. Jax wasn't even gone yet, and Ben was already falling apart. I kissed Jax's cheek and crawled out of the bed.

"You want to cuddle him now?" I asked Maxine.

She nodded and came closer, and I walked over to Ben. He was still leaning against the wall with hands clasped. His gaze was fixed on Jax.

"Have you eaten yet?"

"I can't. I just can't stomach anything."

273

"I understand. Me either. Want to go get a tea with me?"

"Sure. Although I really don't want to leave him."

"I know, but we should get a little something. Hey, have you seen my mom yet?"

"Yes, she's in the yellow room. Will she be okay?"

"I hope so." I was worried about her. The call from last night was the most she'd really said. She and Jax had had a strong relationship. In fact, I'd always blamed her for picking favourites. When I was a kid growing up, she'd leave notes for duties around the house, only they were all left for me, none for Jax. He could do no wrong in her eyes. I knew she loved us both, but Jax being her first born and being a boy, he seemed extra special to her somehow. Losing Jax, I feared, would start her on a downward spiral. I'd do my best to be there for her, but I knew I couldn't take his place.

I grabbed Ben's hand and pulled him along.

In the cafeteria, I got him seated at a spot by the long window and bought us both a peppermint tea from Tim Hortons. From the window I could see that it hadn't gotten any brighter outside, not that that surprised me.

"How are you really doing?" I asked once we were seated. Ben kept telling me he was okay. I knew that was a lie.

His eyes were intense and fixed on my face. "I'm falling apart, man. There is so much you need to know, and I'm not sure how or where to start even." He bit his upper lip.

"You can tell me, Ben. Take a deep breath, and take your time."

Ben nodded, took a sip of his tea, then spoke. "Jax and I had a lot of wonderful times together, and over the past few days I've been thinking about all of it, good and bad, you know?" I nodded knowing exactly what he'd meant. I'd been doing the same thing. "But the bad have been coming more, and I know it's all my fault that we weren't together. It's my family's fault really. I haven't even told them what is going on. They were so mean to Jax, and a part of me doesn't want them to have the opportunity to feel bad. They don't deserve to feel bad. I don't want to hear anything they have to say." He ran his hand through his hair, and a strand stayed out of place. He smoothed it out.

His knuckles were scabbed with dried blood. Recent. I wondered what he'd punched.

He saw where I was looking. "I was trying to relieve some of my anger on a tree when I went on a hike yesterday. Don't worry, I didn't punch anyone, although I might like to."

He had no one to comfort him. I knew his family wouldn't be there for him, after all, he had to hide his relationship with Jax way back then. He had one good

275

childhood friend that I knew of, but I hadn't seen him at the hospital at all. Knowing the little about Ben that I did, I wondered if he'd even told his friend about Jax being in the hospital and what he was going through. Ben mostly kept to himself.

He continued. "Nothing seems to help it. I don't feel guilty about keeping this from my family. They weren't there for me then, so why should they be there now? I just wish I'd known something was wrong with Jax—I would have been there. Jax was always there for me. And I threw *him* out. How messed up is that?" He gasped twice and placed his hands on his head then let go clasping them in his lap. He swayed slightly forward and back then placed his clasped hands on the table. "The one person in my life who loved me unconditionally, who gave me the world, and I tossed him out like the trash. He accepted me without judgement or ridicule. I cried and cried the day I made him leave. He never knew that. I threw him out not because I didn't love him but because I thought I didn't have any other choice. Now, looking back, I should have thrown my family out."

I reached across the table and placed my hands atop of his clasped hands. Tried to stop him from swaying. My heart broke for him; it broke for my brother too. He would never know or see how much this man loved him. And Ben was right. It's all that Jax ever wanted.

He pulled his hands from underneath mine and placed them on top squeezing them. "You know, over the past year, he and I spoke about reconnecting. I always respected his relationship with Fredrik and would never have interfered, and I told Jax that. He knew that I wouldn't cross that boundary. Well, maybe a few other boundaries." He managed a small smile. "But I wasn't going to be the reason they broke up, you know?" He'd been gazing out the window, and now he looked back at me.

"Did you know that just before all of this, Jax told Fredrik he didn't want to be with him anymore?" he asked, letting go of my hands. He picked up his cup and wrapped his fingers around it, as if warming them, though it wasn't cold in the room.

"No," I said, "although I sensed that maybe there was more tension than normal. Jax never talked to me much about him and Fredrik. Actually, now that you mention it, I do remember someone saying that they broke up or were breaking up." Who the hell was that? I couldn't remember. Why couldn't I remember? I took a sip of my tea.

"It was true. Jax told him he couldn't do it anymore and that he wanted to be with me. It was happening, man—we were finally planning our future. We had decided to live at your dad's farm, because Josh would soon want mine."

"So…that's why Jax had reacted so badly to Dad selling the farm. I thought it was only because he'd wanted it for so many years." Dad had sold the family farm to our cousins that past summer due to his poor health, and Jax had seemed really hurt by that. I figured it was because Dad did things like that all the time; he'd made false promises our entire lives and then reneged on them. Money always came first for him. He'd promised the farm to Jax; it was even in his will. But then he got sick and panicked and sold out of desperation.

"We were so close, man, you have no idea. We'd finally made our way back to each other. It was going to happen. My future was with Jax. But now …"

I touched his hand again, not really knowing what else to do. I almost told him what I knew, but today was about Jax. The right time would reveal itself.

"I can't, I just can't." He wiped his nose with the napkin. "Why? Why is he being taken from me again?"

In a strange way, his pain helped me. I didn't feel so alone, knowing that Ben was hurting as much as I was.

"I'm sorry. I wish I knew the answer to that. It's unfair and shitty and so desperately sad. Please know that I'll be right here, always. I'm not going anywhere. Together, maybe we can get through this." I got up from my seat, went closer, and stood with my arms stretched wide. I needed a hug, and my guess was he did too.

Wrapping his arms tightly around me he said, "I can't do this without you Amelia." And he sobbed into my shoulder.

We stood for a few minutes embracing in silence. It was just what we both needed. I suspected there would be many more of these moments to come.

"You want to get back to him?" I wasn't sure how long we'd been talking, but it felt like time was slipping away on this, Jax's last day.

Ben nodded, and together we made our way back to the ICU. I told Ben to go be with Jax, because I wanted to check on my mom. It was now 2 o'clock. *Only two more hours.*

She was sitting in her usual chair in the yellow waiting room. Bart was sitting next to her mumbling to himself. There were a couple more of Jax's friends embracing at the opposite end of the room. I wondered if they'd just come from Jax's room. Where was everyone else?.

This room had become our home away from home in the past four days. I found myself wondering how many other families had sat in that room, making the same horrific decisions that we had. My mind went to the organ donation. I pictured a family desperate for hope, gathered just like this, waiting to hear if they would get my brother's lungs, kidney, eyes, or liver. Pacing back and forth, not knowing if their loved one would live or die. For a moment it upset me to think that they would live while my brother wouldn't. Then I realized that

279

there was no guarantee for them either. I mean, if Jax didn't die before the two hours, his organs would be oxygen-deprived for too long, rendering them useless for transplant. And no matter what the outcome, his heart wouldn't be available. How sad. No one should have to experience this, no one.

"You okay?" Mom asked me.

She looked beautiful. How could she look so beautiful? And how could she be worried about me, when her first born was lying in a room less than fifty feet away, living out his last few hours? I knew the answer. It was the kind of mom she'd always been. Caring and nurturing, always putting us before her, putting anyone she loved before her, really. She may not have been a physically affectionate person, but she didn't have to be for you to know she loved you.

"Are you?"

"I'm doing okay, I guess. But...I don't want to go in there."

"Where? Jax's room?"

"Well, that too, but I mean in the operating room, when they take him down there. I don't want to be in there. I... just..." She cleared her throat and tried again. "I just want to see him one last time without the tubes, so when they take them out I'd like to go in, but then leave."

"Are you sure? I mean, just on the way here I called Jax's therapist and said that I didn't want to be in there and watch him die. He told me to picture a month from now. Would I look back and wish I had, as hard as it would be today? Would I regret not being in there? The answer for me is a resounding yes. So, I'll ask you the same thing, just to be sure."

She paused, and I saw her think about it for a minute. Her eyes filled with unshed tears. She shifted in her chair.

"I only want to see my son one more time as he was. I won't be in there. I can't be in there." Her voice bold and loud.

She had given him life; how could she watch someone else take it? "Okay, I totally understand. I'm sorry." I wasn't sure if I should hug her, but I did anyway. She stayed seated in the chair, but as my arms wrapped around her, her body collapsed toward me.

I worried what this might do to her. Would she survive? I pushed that thought from my mind. I was emotionally exhausted and couldn't even imagine losing her too. I just couldn't.

Not sure of what else to say to Mom, I gave her shoulder a slight squeeze. I wanted to say something, anything to comfort her, but those words just didn't exist.

Finally, I headed back to Jax's room, where I found Fredrik, Ben, and Bobby around his bed. Jax had dated Bobby briefly just before he met Fredrik. I think maybe Bobby had found Jax and Fredrik together. I wasn't sure and never asked.

"I think it's so sweet that all three of us can be here, by his side together. We all loved him in our own way," Bobby said.

I stood and watched as three people who should hate each other held hands and cried together. I walked over and wrapped my arms around them. Their faces were blurry through my tears. We didn't speak, just cried and held one another.

Then my stepsister Wendy bolted into the room. "They're only going to allow two of us in when they turn off Jax's machines."

"What? That's not fair! How do we choose only two people? Can you speak to anyone?" There was no way that was possible. I started counting—me, Ben, Katie, Mark, Fredrik... I was already at five.

"I know. I tried to explain that to them. I'll go talk to the doctor again and explain that that just won't do."

"Why would they only allow two people?"

"It's got something to do with the size of the operating room versus all of the team they need in there on standby, should Jax..." Wendy's voice trailed off. She blinked away tears as she looked over at him. Her nurse voice kicked in. "Should he pass within the two hours, they have to have everyone they need there to perform the operation and get the organs to where they need to be. Anyway, I'm going to go let them know that two is not acceptable."

282

With that she rushed out again. Fredrik and Bobby followed.

"You know I'm going to fight for you to be in there, don't you?" I grabbed Ben's arm. "You have every right to be there." I searched his face. "Well, that's if you want to be in there." I knew that even if he wanted to be, he'd never ask.

He looked surprised, then confused. "I don't know what to say. I appreciate you fighting for me, but I'm not sure I should be in there. I don't want to take someone else's spot."

"Ben, do you want to be in there or not? Put all the shit aside. The day after tomorrow, next week, hell, next year, are you going to wish you had been in there?" I demanded.

He bowed his head. "I'm...I'm not sure."

"Okay, well, let me put it this way then. I know Jax would want you there, and based on what you told me downstairs, I don't think he'll go until you *are* with him." I knew my eyes were imploring him. "Besides, I need you in there."

He looked away from me, considering, and then back into my eyes. "If it means that much to you, then yes."

"Okay, it's settled then. Thank you." Now the only question was whether Wendy would have success appealing to the doctor to allow more of us in with Jax.

"And what did you all decide about donation?"

"Oh god, I didn't tell you? I'm so sorry. We decided that we would go ahead with it but leave it in Jax's hands."

He nodded, then asked, "How do you feel about it? Do you think Jax would want that?"

"No, I really don't think he would, but for me, I need to make some sense out of his death, and this makes me feel better, like his death is for a reason."

"Funny you say that. I had a dream last night—well, it wasn't a dream really. I think Jax came to me."

"Really? What did he say?"

"I was standing on a porch at a small wooden house with a yellow porch light. It was in the middle of a forest, in the middle of nowhere. It was really restricted with guards and barbwire. Just off the porch was a fence I knew I couldn't cross. Like a chain-link fence. It looked kind of like an airport security place or something. I wondered why I was there, and then I saw Jax walking toward me on the other side of the fence. He looked so good, younger, like when we first met. Anyway, he approached the fence and smiled his huge smile. He then said— and this is where it gets broken—that when it first happened, he was fighting hard to stay here. He didn't want to go and leave us all behind, but then he got there and was shown why and what he had to do. He said he couldn't tell me much more, but that once he saw what it was that he had to do there, he knew he had no choice, and that whatever it was involved protecting all of us."

I was silent for a few moments, taking it all in. "Wait! Do you remember when I mentioned the dream that Larissa had?"

"The one where Jax was partying in Costa Rica?"

"Yes, that one. I have goosebumps." I looked down at my arm. "I never told you the entire dream. Before that, Larissa saw him sitting on a plane. He was excited, like you would be when heading somewhere on vacation. When I asked her where he was going, she didn't know. She thought maybe Costa Rica. You said where he was standing looked like airport security, right?"

"Yes, wow, Amelia."

I was speechless.

Wendy entered Jax's room looking quite smug. She said that she had got the number up to four.

I looked around the room, full of family and friends, and frowned.

"Um, thank you for your efforts, Wendy, but that's still not near enough." I didn't really want her in there, and I knew Jax would feel that way too. Although I couldn't say that, and she'd need to be one of the people going in. I mean, how could she not be, when our other stepsister Katie would be? And since she was negotiating for more people, how could we restrict her? Both Jax and I had had a better relationship with Katie.

Shortly after finding that letter in Mom's closet, we'd also learned about Norma's marriage to Wendy's dad dissolving. After Mom divorced Dad, he had invited us to Norma's—it was his house too by then, though he didn't tell us that—for dinner. She was having her family over. Upon our arrival, Dad greeted us at the door and stepped outside. I think it was fall. Hers was a small house in a place called Innisfil Beach close to Barrie. The house was grey and white brick with a white door, and I remember the top part of the door had oval glass with an iron floral design.

"I just want to let you two know that Norma's daughter Wendy calls me Dad. I'm not really sure why, but I didn't want that to be a surprise."

A surprise? She calls you Dad? *What?* I was barely able to call him Dad for his lack of presence at the time. Boy, he must have been around a while for her to feel comfortable enough to do that. Anyway, we went in, and soon it was dinner time.

The dining room had been set up like something out of a magazine. I think the curtains were even pressed. Although they were pretty, it didn't impress my fourteen-year-old brain too much. I just wanted to leave. Hearing all about their Christmases together on Boxing Day. *Boxing Day?* Jax and I had looked at each other. See, every year for pretty much our entire lives, our father had told us that he had to work on Boxing Day. He would pack up and leave either Christmas night or Boxing Day morning. We finally knew the real reason. To say the evening was becoming uncomfortable was an understatement. I wanted to crawl out of my skin and slither away. I also felt bad for our mom. She'd pretended to be happy that we were going, but I knew this was hurting her. That alone was enough to make me want to walk out.

Once dinner was ready, Norma set the kitchen table for two and told us, my brother and me, that we would be sitting there. The kitchen wasn't terribly close to the dining room. In fact, it was down a small hall and a right turn from them. We couldn't even see the other guests while seated there. Jax and I ate our dinner and talked under our breath about how rude we felt this was—how could our dad allow it? Jax said we might as well eat before we left, so we gulped down our dinner and hightailed it out of there.

"Please, Wendy, you have to get more allowed."

"Well, who do you want in there? Or who all wants to go? Maybe if I go back with a number, that would help."

"Okay, there is me, Fredrik, Katie and her husband, I'm assuming you, Tom, Ben…"

"Your mom." She was counting on her fingers.

"No, actually Mom said she only wants to come in after the tubes have been removed, to see him one last time. So not Mom. But there are nine of us." I added them up again in my head. "Oh, and Fredrik, do you mind if Ben is there? I really think Jax would want him there."

"I agree. You know Jax—he'd want everyone in there." He gave a quick unbridled laugh.

"I want to be in there," Maxine blurted out of nowhere. "Someone needs to be in there for Fredrik."

"We will all be there for him," Wendy said.

"I really want to be in there. I have to be in there," Maxine insisted.

"Okay, I'll do my best. So that is ten, then, correct? Maybe I won't count because I'm a nurse. I'll push for that."

Fredrik piped up, "I'll go with you. Patsy will get the job done. We will have all ten of us in there." Patsy was the name Jax had given to Fredrik when he would get angry and freak out. A sort of alter ego. Jax always had liked seeing Patsy surface.

Yep, Patsy would get the job done. I had zero doubt. That poor doctor, I thought.

"Well, tell them we will stay out of the way as much as we can. Jax wouldn't want to be away from us all." Desperation fuelled my voice. I felt like saying if they wanted his organs, they'd better let us all in.

"I'm on it," said Fredrik, and he followed Wendy out.

When they returned five minutes later, it was with good news. Not only would the doctor let all ten of us in, but he'd escort my mom in personally. Patsy had done her job.

Angie Vancise

22

❦

BEN

It was three o'clock. Time was running out.

I sat in the empty chair against the wall in Jax's room holding the roses. And just as a song can play over and over in your head, so too did the meaning of the osprey. Yesterday, after my frustration and confusion about its appearance and meaning, I'd realized that I'd never looked it up. Just before bed I'd grabbed the Animal Speak book and read:

> The osprey is a god of communication and messenger of Heaven. Osprey appears to tell us to dive into our emotions opening us up to new relationships, opening the heart spaces and a willingness to take greater risks for the greater good. While you lose your wishes, your needs, your hopes, and your will, you will find out later how much you've gained. You will learn how to love yourself, so you can give others the love they need.

In a rare moment now, I was all alone with Jax. It occurred to me, looking over at him, that the osprey had been no coincidence back then. I stood up and placed the roses on the side table. Grabbing his hand, I brought it to my chest right over my heart.

Leaning in, I whispered, "Thank you for showing me not only how to live but to live freely. You gave me the feathers that allowed me to fly and I now have to learn how to soar without you. I'm not sure how. It's too late for us now, but I do promise to love myself and others the way you did. I love you, Jax, I always will." Kissing his cheek, I placed his hand back down by his side. When I heard some people approaching from the hall I retreated back to the chair.

I knew some of my close friends were worrying about me. I'd been quiet all day. They'd texted, but I hadn't replied. I'd told no one about Jax. I just couldn't find the words. But they deserved something. I looked down at my phone. A group reply text might be best. I typed,

Hey, guys, it's been a tough week here. Some sad news. Jax Vanbeermen suffered a massive stroke on Sunday past. I've been at RVH with him and his family since Mon. There is no hope of recovery and they have decided to take him off life support tonight and donate his organs. Sorry for the text, just been struggling with talking to people. Didn't realize how much I cared for him still. I'll be in touch soon, Ben.

Angie Vancise

Even as I typed the words, I could hardly believe this was happening.

I'd lost this man once, and now I was about to lose him again, and forever.

I felt a sharp pain in my left side. The rhythm of my heart pumped into my ears and the back of my head. I felt panic, until I remembered that I'd had this feeling before. I'd had it when Michelle was taking me to court. I had it every time my mom came over and told me how awful I was to be living with a man and exposing my children to such sin. I had it that time after my Pastor called me out in church in front of everyone.

I'd had it the day I kicked Jax out.

I'd woken that night at 3 a.m. to heart palpitations and what felt like my heart skipping a beat. I'd breathe in, only to have pain cut off my breath.

Although not the smartest thing, I'd rushed myself into Emerg.

"There, is that better?" the hospital doctor had asked, massaging my neck. "Do you drink a lot of caffeine?"

"No, I don't drink any," I said.

"Well, the only other thing that could cause this is stress. Are you experiencing a great deal of stress?"

That question hit hard. Where would I begin?

I had had a lot going on at that time. Messy divorce, three little kids, a family that seemed to dictate how my life

292

should go. A sales job that demanded too much from me, and a relationship that my family rudely ignored or ridiculed—there was no in-between.

She continued to massage the left side of my neck. I was hooked up to a monitor, and it showed a steady decline in my heart rate. Finally, it read normal.

"How did you do that?" a nurse asked.

"It's my little miracle of the night." The doctor grinned. "Okay, your body is clearly giving you signals that you have way too much stress in your life." She started removing the monitors. "There is a sensor point in your neck that can influence your heart rate. By massaging that point I was able to lower it; however, if you do not reduce your stress levels, you will eventually have serious health problems, if not a heart attack." She went on to suggest some counselling and relaxation techniques.

Half an hour later I left the hospital. It was still dark. On my drive home, I pondered on what the doctor had said. Somehow it hadn't surprised me.

At that time, my career was insurance sales, and I wasn't a natural salesman. The pressure of making my quotas weighed on me.

Then the divorce. As much as I tried to block all the nagging in my mind, it won. According to my ex, I could do nothing right. Her demands, the accusations, the threats were all a constant worry. I had recently received more papers from her lawyer asking for further ridiculous compensation. In the middle of all that were my three kids. They were unaware of the turmoil surrounding them, but they had daily needs that I had to keep up with too. I would do anything for them. They were my reason for living; they had to be a priority. Along with Jax and his needs as a partner.

Then there was my family, another set of dynamics. Sure, they rallied around me as a single parent, but it came with a cost. They were simply unable to accept me as I was. I was loved as long as I behaved according to their laws, their beliefs. The fact that I had Jax as a partner was too much for them. They just pretended he didn't exist, which hurt and angered me. And they treated him poorly. They thought I was damaged from a youth sexual experience. They also thought they could pray the gay away.

As I pulled back into my driveway, I turned the car lights off. I didn't want to wake Jax. Inside, I tiptoed up the stairs, undressed quietly, and snuck back into bed.

"Is everything okay?" he whispered.

"Yeah, I'll fill you in in the morning."

He moved closer and put his arm on my chest. It felt so good. Every time I'd get upset, he'd hold me tight. How would he ever understand? We had been together four and a half years. Despite the divorce, the sales job, my nagging family, and the demands of being a single dad, these last four years had been the happiest I'd ever been. We'd made love, travelled, made lots of friends, laughed, cried, gotten angry, laughed again. Eaten countless dinners together with and without the kids. Sleigh rides, wagon rides. Slept in this bed next to each other since Jax moved in.

Of course, it wasn't always easy. Relationships never are. Jax required a lot of my attention. I was his sole focus, but he was only one of the people I felt responsibility to. I had to find a way to balance it all. In the last while I'd felt myself purposely pulling away from Jax, and lying here now, I knew why; it was suddenly, abundantly clear. I had been preparing both him and me for this moment. Subconsciously I must have known it was inevitable.

Just last month, I'd suggested going to Puerto Vallarta. A last-ditch effort to save us, perhaps? We'd been three times in the four years we'd been together, and each time it had brought us closer. I thought the time away would do us good. We could reconnect and be alone without the stresses of life. We were drifting further and further apart. Jax was going out more. I'd push him away when he was around. I was at a loss as to how to fix it all, but hoped this trip might be the answer. During past trips, the tensions of daily life had melted away.

Not this last time.

Each time we'd gone there had been this twenty-something local guy that came onto me. Jax nicknamed him Fast Eddie. In the years prior, we would just laugh about it. Jax was able to let it go, but I suppose our tension of late didn't allow it to be funny anymore. He loved it when people flirted with him, but when it was with me, he'd get jealous.

One-night mid-week, we'd gone out dancing at our favourite club. It was a bar on one of the main streets known to local gay guys. We'd stumbled, quite literally, on it the second year we were there. Jax heard dance music faintly from the street, and we went in to check it out. Flashy lights, dancing on the bar and bar stools, and body shots. Jax was hooked.

It seemed every time we'd go each year, Fast Eddie was there like a fly on honey. This time was no exception. He followed me around like a duckling. Jax grew increasingly annoyed. Eventually we went outside to get some air, and Fast Eddie followed.

"Ben, what are you doing now?" he asked.

"You know he has three small kids, don't you?" Jax interrupted.

"Yes, I do, and they are my world." I shot Jax a disgusted look, turned, and walked away.

I'd had enough. I couldn't believe Jax had used my kids against me. I told him never to do that again. I'm still angry about it when I think about it. That was out of line.

The rest of our trip we spent mostly apart, seeing each other only back in the hotel room.

There'd been no improvement since we got home. And now, after hearing the doctor's words, I realized the solution to my health issue was staring me right in the face. My kids would always come first. Jax both knew and accepted that. My family, although they placed guilt on me, had been a support. Also, with my parents living right next door, I couldn't move really, and I couldn't ask them to either. I was stuck with them. Mom had helped me tremendously with the kids. How could I not be thankful for that? If I died of a heart attack, that left my kids vulnerable to the whims of my ex.

I knew what I had to do.

Hating myself, I rubbed his arm where it lay on my chest. I tamped down the tears that threatened. I knew I would get no sleep tonight. Morning would come too soon. I held Jax for what would be the last time.

The light must have shone into the room as it had many mornings we were together, yet somehow in my memory, it's dark. Jax was still holding me when his eyes opened.

"Good morning, beautiful." He rolled over, groaned, and stretched. "What happened last night? Did you leave? Where did you go?" He sat up and leaned against the headboard.

Angie Vancise

I couldn't look at him. "I had to go to Emerg." I remained on my back, staring at the ceiling.

"Emerg! Are you okay?" He leaned forward and scanned my body.

"That's what I have to talk to you about."

"Uh-oh, that doesn't sound good. You don't seem yourself, like something is really, really wrong. Should I be worried? Do you have—No, it can't be—You don't have HIV, do you?"

"No, man, it's nothing like that." I shifted to a seated position. I had more chest pain, and my heartbeat was uneven again. I had to tell him. "I went to Emerg last night, because I thought I was having a heart attack."

"A heart attack! Ben, jeez, why didn't you wake me? You shouldn't have been driving! But...you're home—So... it wasn't a heart attack? Then what—?" He looked so scared. I hadn't told him I'd been having it for a few months. I thought it was heartburn.

I knew this was going to be hard.

"You know how stressed out I've been lately. The doctor told me I have to reduce my stress, that it's causing the pain. If I don't, I'll actually develop serious health issues and probably have a heart attack."

"Pain? When...?"

298

I cut him off. "Please let me just get through this—let me finish, okay?" He nodded, his gaze intense, waiting for my response. The ache I felt was etched in his expression. "I've gone over in my mind the only two ways I can think of to reduce my stress. One is to quit my job, and the other..." I could hardly get the words out. "The other—Well, you know we've been struggling lately. And...I just don't see how this can work. I think..." I cleared my throat. "I think it would be best...if you left."

Jax didn't speak. He just sat there on the bed. He looked at me, then away. He did this several times. Finally, turning away from me and using both arms, he pushed himself to the edge of the bed. He looked at me again.

"Did you... Are you breaking up with me?" He got out of the bed and stood beside it. He looked confused. "You mean you want me to move out? But we will still be together...right?"

I couldn't look at him. I shifted my gaze to the floor. "No, Jax. What would be the point to that? I mean if we couldn't live together, what future would we have?"

His expression changed from confusion to anger. "Seriously? This is your solution? I thought you loved me. I thought that you were happy. That we were happy."

"Too many things are going against us lately. We both know we haven't been getting along. Even Mexico didn't work.

And besides, I have to focus on my kids and on my health."
This was even harder than I'd imagined.

Without another word, he grabbed the clothes he'd
worn the night before and got dressed. Then he stomped around
the room gathering up his things. He emptied the drawers of
some of his clothes, jamming them under his left arm. He went
over to the nightstand, took his watch and ring out of the
drawer, and put them on. Then he threw what was under his arm
onto the bed right next to me. He left for a few minutes, and
returned with his suitcase from the closet in the spare room. He
tossed everything from the bed in, squished it down, and
zippered the case. All the while saying nothing. His face was an
angry red. Grabbing the handle, he headed toward the stairs.

I finally got out of the bed and went out into the hall. I
wanted to stop him. I wanted to tell him that I'd made a
mistake, but the pain in my chest had returned, reminding me
that I couldn't. He stopped at the top of the stairs and looked
back at me.

"I can't believe you're kicking me out. The best thing
that has ever happened to you... Your words, by the way." He
turned away and stormed down the stairs. "This will do for now.
I'll come back for the rest tomorrow." Standing by the front
door, he turned again and said, "I hope you're happy." His
expression was furious, but underneath I could see the hurt I'd
caused him. I'd hurt myself too.

"I am not…not at all." I watched as he walked out the door, slamming it behind him.

Choking on a sob, I ran down the stairs so fast that I missed a few and almost fell. I looked out the window of the door, watched as he threw the suitcase into his truck. He looked back at me. I wanted to run after him and tell him I'd made a huge mistake. I reached for the door handle and turned it just slightly, but then he raised his hand in an abrupt farewell. He climbed into his truck, slammed the door, and peeled away, turning up gravel.

Opening the door, I ran out and down the driveway to the road. There I bent over, placing my hands on my knees to catch my breath. I watched as he drove straight down the road. His truck getting smaller and smaller until it finally disappeared.

Slowly I trudged back up my driveway into the house. In the living room, I collapsed on the sofa and cried so hard I almost hyperventilated. I couldn't believe what I'd just done. Had I made a mistake? I brought my sleeve up to wipe the tears. I pushed my nose into the fabric. All I could smell was the scent of him. I couldn't stand it, I had to wash it away. I ran up to take a shower.

*

I had replayed that awful day over and over in my mind, wishing I'd jumped into my truck and chased after him.

Angie Vancise

I'd had twelve years to run after his truck, but I didn't. I couldn't back then, and by the time my kids were older and maturity and wisdom had me caring less of what my family thought, Jax was with Fredrik.

And now…it was too late.

23

AMELIA

Four o'clock.

I'd wished for time to stop. It hadn't.

My eyes scoured every inch of Jax's body as if embossing it forever in my mind. He had two tattoos, one around his left biceps and the other around his right ankle. They were both Celtic rings. He'd gotten them in his thirties.

I stared at the one around his ankle. A variety of vines intertwined with leaves scrolled into beautiful detail. It had turned that green shade of a faded tattoo. I thought how sad it was that I'd never see it again. Jax would be cremated, such artistry ending up in a pile of ashes.

Then I focused on his feet. Feet that had walked many miles in many countries. Feet that had bungee-jumped from the tops of bridges in New Zealand, that had chased me around the farm, that had landed in hay as we jumped from the rafters. It seemed implausible that they'd never walk again.

Angie Vancise

The nurse came into Jax's room, checked his vitals, and emptied his urine bag for what I realized would be the last time. That familiar ache returned from the first day.

She explained to the nine of us that we'd have to put on booties, caps, and blue gowns before entering the operating room. It was a sterile environment, and they had to keep it that way. She placed the nine sets of caps, gowns, and booties on one of the chairs in Jax's room.

We all walked over and grabbed a set. I was shaking so hard I could barely stand on one foot to place the bootie over my shoe. Trying to unfold the gown I somehow ended up twisting it into a tangled ball. Fredrik helped me, and I finally got it on. After he'd placed the cap on my head, he put on his own garb.

The nurse wheeled Jax's bed toward the doorway. The ache now unbearable. I had to force my legs to walk forward. I wanted to yell, *No, I've changed my mind, don't let him go*! But as I gazed at my beloved brother, I realized that if we didn't go through with it, this would be his life—this bed, this machine, this unresponsive state. We had no choice.

The nine of us and Wendy, side by side, formed a small line behind Jax and the nurse who was guiding his bed toward the hall. Ben beside me. We all walked slowly.

No one spoke.

My senses heightened. The brightness of the overhead lights got to me. There was a yellow haze, and a hum from the fluorescents that grated like nails on a chalkboard. Everything seemed to be happening in slow motion. I felt weak.

We rounded a few corners. There were no patients in these halls, and I wondered vaguely what lay behind the few doors along the way. Deceased patients? Supply rooms? My focus shifted back to Jax.

These were his last moments. But there would be no last words.

Would it have been any easier if we'd known he was going to die, and had a chance to say goodbye, to hear his last words?

Did Jax know what was about to happen? Was he afraid?

Was he even still with us, inside the shell of the man we saw before us, or was he hovering above, looking down at all of us? I glanced up but saw only the speckled ceiling.

We finally stopped at an elevator with huge dark green doors, and the nurse pushed the down button. When the doors opened, she wheeled Jax in. We all followed.

Everyone stood silent and still in that enclosed space, staring at Jax.

The ding of the elevator startled me, and I jumped. Ben looked over at me then closed his eyes. A tear rolled down his face as he swallowed then exhaled. Fredrik was rubbing Jax's hand. The door opened onto a white cement hall with more bright fluorescent lighting. Frigid air hit my face taking my breath away. It felt cold in every way imaginable.

At the end of the hall was a double steel door—Operating Room 5.

24

❧❧

BEN

Four o'clock.

Wiping my eyes as we exited the elevator, I thought of all the people that had come and gone from Jax's room all day, saying their final goodbyes. Picturing the roses beside his bed, I decided that I'd give them to the nurses when Jax was…when Jax would… I would just take them the roses after.

The country kiki entered my mind. He'd been so sick; how did I not see it? I'd had no idea at that party that in less than two months he'd be here. We'd all be…here. Looking over at Jax, I found it hard to believe that he wouldn't be planning another party for next August—any August. Our conversation, the day of the kiki, as we were setting up, stung my heart.

"You'd like me better now. I like me better. I've changed a lot," he said, as we banged the folding tables together by accident. He'd mentioned this a few times in the past few months.

"I always liked you, Jax. You must know that."

"I know," he replied, "but I'm even helping you get ready for the party. It used to drive you mad when I'd invite everyone but leave you to the preparations. Amelia always got mad at me for that too, but someone has to get everyone here."

I smiled. He was right about all of that. "I do appreciate you coming early to help."

Jax and I had both changed. The struggles from the past that we'd gone through both individually and in our relationship were ending.

That first party, to me, was a kind of coming-out party. All of our gay friends under one roof. My roof. A place I'd never let anyone gay come to, other than Jax. I had wanted to show him that I was ready to not only reveal the real me but to live it too. Imagine feeling your whole life that you are mortally flawed and can't fix it. You think everyone can see it and despises you for it, even though it's not your fault. Jax never looked at me that way. Nor did Amelia. And despite his own insecurities, he'd lived life.

My journey had been about to begin—but now this.

The large steel doors to Operating Room 5 opened inward, as they pushed him through. They made a loud bang when they hit the stoppers behind them.

The room stank of antiseptic. It was cold, really cold, and white. So much white. Sterile. I hated it. Jax would hate it.

What wasn't white was steel, cold hard steel. How could I spend the next two hours in here? But I was relieved that Wendy had gotten us all in here. Jax would not have wanted to be in this room alone.

They wheeled him to the centre of the room, transferred him onto a horrible, flat stainless-steel bed. We all stood to one side, while they got him positioned. Then they wheeled his bed over to the back wall, out of the way, motioning us to go to him. We circled his bed. I wondered how many others had died in this room. How many were saved? My body tingled, and I wasn't sure my legs would hold me for the duration.

Would Jax die right away? I knew that would be better for the organ recipients. Maybe better for him too.

I watched as ten or so interns lined up in a semicircle around the doctor. They were to be educated on the removal of the ventilator. They looked eager—not sad, not devastated. They weren't losing someone. They were here, not only to learn about the removal, but about organ donation and how to detach organs quickly without damaging them. This whole thing was a training session for them.

Glancing around at the faces of our group—I'd been afraid to look at them till now—I saw the same fear and anticipation I was feeling. The same grief. My gaze went to Amelia standing next to me, hers was at her brother. The strain on her face was hidden behind a softness and a sibling love I'd never known.

I heard the suction of the tube being removed.

I squeezed Amelia's hand.

25

AMELIA

The next morning, after not much sleep, I got out of bed and went downstairs. Stu and Larissa weren't up yet. I'd spoken to her on the way home from the hospital. She'd said Uncle Jax was in a better place now. She again explained how she saw death differently. She knew only his physical body was gone and that he was very much still around and always would be. She reassured me over and over we'd be together again someday. I wished I could see it that way. By the time we got home, she was in bed.

We were told before we'd left the hospital that an autopsy would be performed in Toronto; then Jax would be cremated and returned to us.

The autopsy would reveal the cause of Jax's stroke. Loose plaque on one of the major veins at the base of his neck had lodged in the V where that vein met another, and the blockage had limited blood flow to his brain. The loose and shifting plaque had caused the symptoms Jax had complained about in the year before his death—high blood pressure, vision problems, even anxiety. If his condition had been diagnosed earlier, Ben asked, could anything have been done to save him? The answer was no.

It was better, I thought, that Jax didn't know.

My mind kept replaying every moment of his last two hours as if it were happening again right in front of me. The cold sterile operating room, all white and steel. The smell of rubbing alcohol and disinfectant so pungently offensive. Jax lying on that hard, cold metal table. The sound of the tube as it exited his mouth. All the interns waiting to witness organ donation, possibly for the first time in their careers. Maggie from Trillium running back and forth writing notes on charts and speaking quietly on the phone. The nurses and doctors checking the monitor constantly, then injecting the IV site with more morphine.

Jax hanging on.

The doctor escorted Mom in himself, as promised. She held onto his arm, as he led her to Jax. When he stepped away and gave her space, she placed her hand on top of Jax's.

"Goodbye, Jax." She leaned down and kissed him on his forehead. Her lips trembled, and tears fell. She patted the top of his hand, then turned and walked away.

As I watched, a pain went straight to my heart. No mother should ever have to do what she was doing.

Jax was still alive after two hours. Still fighting to breathe. The constant strain on his face for that entire two hours had me questioning our choices. Had he not wanted to donate? Had we made the right choice? Should we have just let him go not bothering with the donation? Would he not fought as hard and just let go sooner? It wasn't until they wheeled him back upstairs, and he was surrounded by the rest of his family and friends that he finally let go.

That didn't surprise me.

All of us circled his bed. I watched as each of his friends leaned down to kiss his cheek or tap his hand, saying: I'm going to miss you, God speed and Rest in peace, Jax. Then turning and waking away, tears falling. Some arm in arm as they left.

Fredrik giving Jax one last kiss, rubbing his face as he whispered, I love you.

Eventually everyone had filtered out including Fredrik, leaving Ben and me alone in the room. I was next to Jax; Ben was in his usual place across from me, up against the wall, shaking uncontrollably, his hands in his pockets. His eyes looking away from the man he loved.

I crawled up beside Jax one last time, wrapped my arms around him, put my face against his and whispered, "You were the best brother I could have ever asked for. Goodbye, Jax. I love you more than you'll ever know." After one more hug, I got out of the bed, went to Ben, and together, arms around each other, we left.

It was 8:30 a.m. now, and I was thankful that we hadn't had any guests staying with us. We had decided not to hold the celebration of life right away. Because Jax was being cremated, we'd have time. We were thinking around November 3, giving more guests time to make their arrangements to be here knowing there would be many.

Ben was coming over around eleven, and we were to meet Mom and Bart at the funeral home. Fredrik didn't have a ride from the city, so I said we'd FaceTime. That way he could be with us too. Predictably Dad didn't want anything to do with the planning. "I think you will make it wonderful, my darling daughter," he'd said over the phone. I'd never heard him cry so much.

A friend of Jax's that worked at the funeral home had messaged me early this morning and said he'd be taking him around Toronto's gay village for one last drive before going to the crematorium. Last drive. Nausea set in. My insides actually felt like they were shaking. I don't think I'd ever felt that before. My life as I knew it was gone. I had to sit down. I closed my eyes, wishing I never had to open them again.

I needed Ben there with me, despite his thinking he didn't belong. We had talked on the phone more after we got home from the hospital. He was the one person who knew how I felt. We cried together. We recalled times with Jax that made us laugh, and we cried some more. We agreed that a part of us had died with him. He told me that he'd need me in the coming months, that he didn't feel he could get through this without me. I felt the same. Somehow being near him made me feel close to Jax.

Jax would want a celebration of life. Not some stuffy, religious funeral. He wasn't like that. He'd want it to be the biggest and best party of our lives, with all of us laughing and talking about the crazy things he'd done. He'd want us to dance, waving our hands in the air just like he would. I had to honour that. Mom, Fredrik and Ben agreed. The problem was finding somewhere large enough to fit all those who knew and loved him.

I walked to the bathroom to get a tissue. My eyes had cried so many tears. Looking in the mirror, I could see they were puffy and sore-looking. The centre of my forehead hurt. It reminded me of that first day, five days ago, when I'd looked at myself in the mirror at the hospital. How had it been only five days? I struggled to breathe through my stuffed-up nose. I wandered into the kitchen, but my stomach couldn't handle any food; even the glass of water I poured was hard to swallow.

The silence was too loud, so I turned on the television, putting a music station on for background noise. I looked out the living room window. To the left, Blue Mountain was

Angie Vancise

enveloped in its signature blue haze. Sunbeams shining from the east bounced on the slopes. All the leaves had dropped, leaving only the evergreens with colour. For the first time in days, the sun was shining. Strangely, though, while the sky to the northwest, over the mountain, was a bright, robin's-egg blue, to the northeast, over the water, it was an ominous grey.

And then it appeared. The most striking rainbow, a full arc. All the colours visible. I stood there, mesmerized. I thought again about the last few days and how grey they'd been. And now, here was this rainbow, radiating colour, like someone had painted it for me. Could it be? It seemed so close I felt I could almost touch it, and for just a moment, I felt better—but it didn't last. As the rainbow faded, disappearing into a dark sky, so did my will.

I stood there, unable to move. Not knowing how I'd make it through the rest of the day, and the rest of my life without Jax. I really didn't want to. Life felt too long, stretching out before me. I'd relied on my big brother for everything. I didn't even know who I was without him. I had Stu and Larissa, and I loved them both so much, but in that moment, it didn't seem enough. I needed Jax. I needed him to get through this. He was the one person who truly knew me, had always known me. My thoughts took a dark turn. How easy it would be to end it all. To be with him again.

Cry of an Osprey

I heard Stu come up from downstairs. He must have sensed something, and asked how I was doing. I didn't feel much like talking, couldn't tell him what I was really feeling. Lying, I said I was okay. He knew I wasn't. He held me tight. I knew he wanted to take away my pain, but he couldn't. No one could. I felt bad that I wasn't able let him help me. I also felt bad because I knew he must be grieving too. We let go of each other, and I stepped into the living room. Stu sat down at the kitchen table to read the newspaper and drink his coffee. He was just a few feet away, where I could see him, and that was a comfort.

How could I make sense now of my forty-four years? All those years merged into a moment. And what did they mean? The next forty-four years without Jax seemed impossible.

How would I ever laugh again when he wouldn't?

The song playing on the television suddenly sounded louder, as if someone had turned it up. The lyrics said something about travelling down an unfamiliar road and holding on to him as we go. And then something about demons.

"Wow, Stu, are you hearing this? Who sings this song?"

He didn't know, so I checked the TV. It was "Home" by Phillip Phillips.

317

When American Idol was on TV, Jax would often text and ask who my favourite contestant was. That year it was Phillip Phillips. Jax said he didn't like Phillips, said that in every song, he sounded the same. But I really loved him. I felt that his passion for music showed every time he sang. We continued to bring it up, each of us trying to convince the other. Phillips actually won that season, so I teased Jax that I was right.

What were the odds that it would play just now??

Suddenly I didn't feel alone. Somewhere deep inside, I knew I would survive, because my brother would be right by my side. Maybe Larissa was right. With all my heart, I wanted to believe she was. That Jax would be just like the sun: although you couldn't always see him, he would always be there.

I could almost hear him telling me that I was stronger than I thought. He certainly wouldn't want me to kill myself, and he wouldn't want his memory to sadden me. He would want me to live my life as he had—to take chances, to embrace all that life had to offer, to jump in with both feet. To go after my dreams and write that book.

Perhaps I'd just have to close my eyes to see the world he sees.

I knew I'd continue to grieve, and it wasn't going to be easy, but I would move forward, one foot in front of the other. And I'd throw Jax the best celebration of life anyone ever had.

I'd have to live for both of us now.

26

❧ ❧

BEN

July 2013

The blue heron took flight and disappeared around the curve of the island. Feeling the morning coolness of the rock underneath me—its strength and tenacity—gave me comfort. So many things were different, yet this place would remain the same.

It had been nine months since I'd lost Jax. Nine months of no texts, no dinners, nothing. I missed his zany personality and our long talks. Going to the movies and spending time with my kids. Nintendo. His smile. I'd never forget it and the way he looked at me, the delicate way he'd run his fingers through my hair or touch my face.

That last day in the hospital would be forever imprinted in my mind. Seeing the life leave his body. I wondered if the pain would ever fade. Would those dark images ever be completely replaced by those of the fun times, when we were

319

younger and in love? Or even later, 12 years later, when we were moving toward love again? Would my heart ever heal?

That was the hardest thing I'd ever had to go through. Watching Amelia lose her brother and best friend, her mom lose her son, and all the other people who loved him lose him too. Even watching Fredrik lose him was hard. And after it was all over, Jax's mom had wanted to ride home with me, because she was worried for me.

There had been so much love in that room.

I thought by now that I'd be sleeping better, eating more. I wasn't. I hadn't expected that I'd still be thinking of him constantly, but I was.

The poplar seeds had showered us like stars from Heaven on that first date in the canoe, showing us who we were from birth. I could never un-live it or relive it.

Was this as good as it would get?

I wondered if Amelia was up yet. If so, she'd wonder where I was. I'd brought her to the island because she'd decided to write a book about Jax—the brother she'd loved—and because I wanted to share this special place with her. She was the sister I'd always wished mine could be—supportive and loving. I couldn't have gotten this far without her. We'd become so close. Relying on each other for support every step of this journey.

Placing my hand on the infinity symbol dangling from its chain around my neck I held it. Tight. His ashes inside were never far from my heart. Amelia had surprised me with the pendant. She was so much like her brother. She'd said it would help, and surprisingly, it had. It wasn't the infinity I thought I'd have with Jax. That would have to wait.

Amelia had given me another unexpected gift. Shortly after Jax passed, she and I met for lunch. She told me something he had confided in her.

After Jax moved in with me, bringing Nikko and Girdy, we had built a dog pen that happened to be right outside Mom's bedroom window. One day when Jax went out to clean it, he'd heard my mom crying and praying to God to keep me safe. Jax knew he shouldn't listen, but he couldn't help himself. If God could love me, Mom had prayed, so could she, but she was petrified of losing me. She'd lost her foster child Chris to AIDS, and she couldn't bear to lose me too.

Amelia said Jax had struggled over whether or not to tell me, and concluded that it wasn't his place. But he'd shared this story with her. I'm not sure why Mom couldn't just tell me her fears herself. All those lost years of misunderstanding... But I was happy that Amelia finally had.

Mom didn't know that I knew. I'd decided to keep it that way.

Angie Vancise

Looking out over the rock formations, the Aboriginal figure and the monkey—the elephant, my heart sank. I thought of the egg salad spilling onto Jax's shirt. I took a deep breath in, bowed my head and closing my eyes, whispered I love you. The smell of Cedar had returned. I blinked back tears while seeing myself slumped over with my legs dangling off the edge. My head in my hands, that first time, on this very day sixteen years ago when we came here. How Jax had lifted my chin and made me look at him. I thought of all the kind words he'd said to make me feel like less of a freak and accept myself as a human being. Who would do that now? I would have to do it for myself.

My hand still trembled resting on the knapsack. I could feel the tiny keepsake urn Amelia had given me in the front pocket. I reached in, pulled it out, and set it beside me up against my thigh wanting Jax here with me for a while longer. I would keep my promise to embrace the person I was and live the life he'd always wanted for me. To do anything else would dishonour him—dishonour our love. The view was just as it had been that first day, so clear you could see for miles. The clouds had lifted and the sun rose further creating pinks, yellows and purples that melted into the same shades on the water. The horizon was hard to see. The waves smashing up against the rocks below no longer sounded soothing. They sounded insistent, demanding. Were they trying to tell me something?

I grabbed the urn with my left hand and brought it to my lips, kissed it softly.

A large bird soared in front of me. I thought at first that the blue heron had returned, but as this bird flew closer, I squinted.

The osprey.

Thank you.

Carefully I removed the top of the urn and tilted it, spilling a thin stream of ashes into my palm. As I watched, they fell through my fingers, and then were swept up by the wind and sent swirling out beyond the cliff, beyond the waves, into the morning light.

Angie Vancise

Epilogue

August 2014

The sun was shining when Stu parked the car along the wooden fence near the farmhouse around five o'clock p.m. I got out and retrieved from the back my platter of devilled eggs, then rose looking at the property. Jax had been right about this being the best spot for a barn party. In front of me stood Ben's house, more than a century old, its entrance flanked by white columns. Directly behind the house was the red and white livestock barn, currently unoccupied. To the left of that was Ben's workshop.

As I walked toward the newer barn, I heard Adele's voice, growing louder as I got closer. Stu followed with the cooler. A gust of wind almost blew off my cowboy hat. Ben had insisted that we all dress up western style, just like last year—though that hadn't been part of the original kiki. Who said you couldn't make a good thing better? At least it was a warm late August wind. Throughout the day, the sky had shifted from grey thick clouds to blue and back to grey. The sun had finally won the battle.

Cry of an Osprey

To the right of the barn stood the old steam engine. It was as if a locomotive and a tractor had a baby. The large black iron spoked wheels on the back and smaller ones on the front allowed it to drive. Steam blasted from the smoke stack upfront. A sweet whiff of cooked corn on the cob filled my nostrils. I remembered Jax standing in the doorway of that barn telling me all about how he and Ben had built it together. He was so proud of how it looked, and rightfully so—it was stunning. Ben always told me, "Jax makes sure it gets done, and I make sure it gets done right!"

The entrance was two barn doors wide, and it opened up to a vast space, the barn boards separated just enough to let the setting sun laser through. A hefty oak to the left of the entrance welcomed us, its outsized branches hanging close enough to sit on.

Immense fields and rolling hills, a Sound of Music view but without the Alps, spread wide behind the barn. It made me want to twirl and dance like Julie Andrews. Hopscotch patterns of gold and many shades of green led your eye straight to Blue Mountain, far off in the distance.

This morning on the phone, Ben had asked, "Are you still bringing the devilled eggs? Yours are the best."

"Yep. And did you make a gazillion pies?"

Ben laughed. "Of course. I thought of making a coconut one, but I figured Jax's ghost would just knock it on the floor."

325

Angie Vancise

"He really didn't like coconut, did he?" Remembering that made me sad, which seemed silly—but even now, two years later, the smallest memories of Jax would tear at my heart.

This would be the second country kiki without him. It had been Ben's idea, and a wonderful one, to carry on Jax's legacy.

As I walked into the barn, I saw some of Jax's friends from the city talking and laughing, sipping their drinks. I didn't count how many, but Ben had said at least thirty people would be coming. Overwhelming happiness filled my heart. Jax was still gathering people.

Greg and John were here, and Kyle and Ritchie, Bobby, Judy, Maxine, Mom and Bart, as well as a few people I hadn't met—all assembled here for Jax. As I placed the devilled eggs on the counter against the side wall, one by one they came over to hug me.

After the hugs, I headed back toward Ben's house to use the washroom inside. I spotted the painting Jax had me paint for Ben years ago hanging in the main living room. It was Ben's Christmas present from him. Ben took me to see Flowerpot the summer after Jax passed. I stood in almost that exact spot in the painting. The Osprey soaring in the back ground stood out more than before. Jax had insisted one be in the painting.

Starring at it had me remembering something that happened in Mexico this past winter. I hadn't really thought much about it until now—other than it being pretty cool. Stu and I had gone with some friends and while playing volleyball on Mexico's day of the dead, a large bird hovered above our heads then moved closer to the water, dove down scooping up a fish in its talons then flew off. I'd been so distracted by it, I missed the volleyball completely. When I asked Rene—the entertainment guy—about it he said it was a sea hawk otherwise known as an osprey. They nest by their resort he'd said.

While turning away to head back outside and to the barn, I decided that I needed to ask Ben why Jax had insisted on it being in the painting. Did it mean something?

Ben had some highlights planned for the night, including a steam-engine sparks show, a hay ride through the woods on the property, and a bonfire.

Even my friends were here. Turns out they had been frozen in their own grief and shock at the suddenness of Jax's crisis. During those four dreadful days we spent in the hospital, they weren't sure how to deal with their own reactions, let alone how to try to help me. I understood that more than they knew. But in the past two years they'd more than made up for it.

Along the back wall was a woodpile, and on it rested a 20 x 30-inch framed black and white photo of Jax—the one we'd used for his celebration of life. I'd later given it to Ben. I had snapped the picture just months before Jax died, as a business portrait. It captured his essence. And it was as close to life-sized as we could get. There he sat, with his huge smile, smack dab in the middle of it all. Right where he'd want to be.

My dad hadn't felt well enough to come this year. His health had declined rapidly in the last two years. So had Mom's. It seemed to me they had both begun dying the day Jax did. No wonder. Life wasn't supposed to happen that way.

Since Mom had had a pacemaker put in last March, she didn't remember things as well as she once did. And she looked frail. But here she was, laughing and hugging, swaying to the music.

Larissa would arrive soon with her boyfriend. This was one of her favourite parties.

Fredrik and his brother were standing just outside the entrance to the barn, next to the barbeques. Beside Fredrik was his new partner, Hans, a German. They'd met only a couple of months after Jax passed. Everyone had given Fredrik a hard time. You're moving too fast... It's rebound... That sort of thing. I felt sorry for Fredrik, but I can't lie: it was hard for me too, to see him move on. But we'd all grown to love Hans, and he'd become an important member of our pack and he made Fredrik really happy.

Decorations were my responsibility. Ben had decided that each year there would be a different theme. Last year it was

Mexican ranch style. This year was North American cowboy style, so I'd purchased some large decals from a local party store and placed them around the barn earlier that afternoon: saloon doors, saddles, bull horns, and such. The folding tables hadn't been out at that time, so I now began placing the tablecloths on them. Cleaning up the barn and getting it ready for the party had been Ben's responsibility. And the pies, of course. He'd prepared several flavours, most of them different from last year, except the apple. Apple pie seemed to hold some significance for him, some connection to Jax, but I didn't know what.

I saw Ben standing by the entrance talking to someone he and Jax had met in Puerto Vallarta. Dolly Parton's version of "I Will Always Love You" started playing. It was a song we'd chosen for the slideshow for Jax's celebration of life. Ben had told me it was their song. What a celebration it had been, with over six hundred people attending. Four decades of Jax's friends in pockets around the Weider Room at Blue Mountain— the only place large enough. Friends from public school, high school, university and beyond. Customers of his from ten years at the dealership and his Toronto friends all there to celebrate Jax. He'd touched each and every one of them in his own way.

Ben turned and I could see him searching the room. His eyes met mine as he walked toward me, grabbed my hand and led me to the dance floor.

As he approached I couldn't help but notice how handsome he was in his cowboy hat and overalls. And such a kind man. I understood how Jax had loved him the way that he had. I loved him too. He'd been my savior in these past two years. The only good thing to come out of Jax's death. He was family—I suppose, looking back, he always had been, ever since Jax brought him to us, and even all those years the two had been apart. Once someone's in the family circle, we don't easily let them go. Our healing was happening together. We hurt together, cried together, laughed at old stories of Jax together, and through it all we had found an everlasting friendship.

Looking around the room as we danced, I realized how lucky I was. Jax had brought all of these wonderful people into my life. He'd introduced me to a world that otherwise would have been nonexistent for me. I was thankful for him, for the time I had had with him, but most of all for the love he'd gathered in this room.

When the song ended, Ben whispered in my ear, "Thank you for loving me." I gave him an extra-long hug and said, "That was the easy part."

I watched as Amelia placed tablecloths over the four tables. The blue and white looked familiar. Then it came to me. They were larger versions of the one Jax had spread out that day on the small island while setting up our little lunch. They were so alike, those two. Amelia wasn't as wild as Jax, but her heart and her smile were just as large. She looked so beautiful in her red and black plaid shirt and cowboy boots. Her hair hung in two braids from under her cowboy hat. She looked so much like Jax, sometimes it took my breath away. I'd planned a surprise for her tonight.

I scanned the barn, which was fast filling with Jax's family and friends. The original party had been his idea, and even though he'd been sick at the time, he'd planned it perfectly. It had been so much fun. So Jax.

After his death, I had planned last year's through the numbness of grief. This year was only slightly better, but I prayed it would get a little easier with time.

In the two years since his death, Amelia and I had grown closer. Now we spoke almost every day. Just like she and Jax used to do. I know I can't replace him for her, but I can love her the best way I know how. She'd helped not only with my grief but with my acceptance of myself. She replaced my birth sisters and gave me a new faith in family.

Hearing a familiar song intro, I headed over to Amelia and dragged her onto the dance floor. We danced to Jax's and my song, "I will always love you."

On one wall of the barn hung antique tools and pitchforks. Jax knew how much I loved anything with a history.

Angie Vancise

Admiring them wistfully as we twirled to the music, I remembered we'd spent countless hours at antiques shows, and he'd surprise me with something every time. The collection hanging on that wall was a sort of shrine to him. In the opposite corner stood the old sleigh to which we'd hooked up Bud and Jake all those years ago. Those were some of the best times of my life. When the song was over Amelia went back to the tables and I went back to hosting.

The barbeque was fired up now. Stu had offered to do the cooking. Amelia was setting out an array of covered dishes—appetizers, salads, desserts—that guests had brought along. We would eat—then, my surprise.

My daughter Caroline, now nineteen, approached me. "Dad, Willy keeps pointing to Jax's photo. Do you mind if I set him beside it?"

Caroline had given birth to Willy after Jax passed. I wished he could have met the little guy. "Of course, Sweetie, go ahead."

She walked back and placed her son on the woodpile next to Jax. Willy leaned in to give the image a kiss. Then reached out and touched Jax's face. He must have kissed it three or four times before Judy, Amelia, Elizabeth and some more of our friends took notice and wandered over. We all watched for a minute in silence, dumbfounded.

Amelia turned around, and our eyes met. When she came over and stood close with her back to me, I placed my hands around her shoulders. Together we watched in wonder as my grandson expressed some sort of connection for this man he'd never met. Caroline's face was wet with tears as she picked him up and carried him away. Willy screamed and looked back, arms outstretched, as if he didn't want to leave Jax.

I knew that feeling.

Later, after everyone had eaten, I walked over to my phone and chose the song, "Home" by Phillip Phillips. It was time for my surprise. I heard Amelia sniffling at the opening refrain. This isn't going to be easy.

I corralled everyone in the middle of the barn and passed out the shots of maple liquor that I'd prepared. Then I motioned for Amelia to join me. About thirty people stood there, solemn, waiting expectantly.

As the music played in the background, I said, "You are all gathered here today because of a man we all loved." I gestured to the picture. Amelia was wiping her eyes. I couldn't look; I had to get through this. "The first one Jax planned. He wanted it to be successful and to continue, to be bigger and better every year." I cleared my throat and swallowed back the tears, but it didn't work. I had to take a moment. Amelia hugged me, which didn't help. Moments later, a little more composed, I continued, "I loved this man with all of my heart. It hasn't been easy being without him, and I know you all feel it too. Please all raise your glasses."

I turned toward his photo, looked right into those soulful eyes of his, and held my glass high. "Here's to bigger and better every year, and here's to you Jax." Amelia and I clinked glasses. Hearing clinks behind me, I turned toward the crowd of Jax's family and friends. There wasn't a dry eye. He'd had a lasting effect on so many people, and knowing that somehow helped me.

In the years without Jax, both before and after his death, I had tried to date, I really had, but no one had ever compared to him—yet. He'd been right—he was my Wolfie, my mate for life. But I knew I would have to try to rewrite my story, this time with a happier ending. I looked over at Adam, a man I'd just met, unsure yet if he'd be my happier ending but glad to have him here tonight. And even if he wasn't, I was content with the knowledge that no matter what happened with my future, I'd had the most beautiful love. Feeling truly grateful that I'd been fortunate to have experienced what most people never would.

As if on cue, Fredrik marched over to my phone, unplugged it, and plugged his in. The song he'd chosen was one I knew on the first beat, "Let's Have a Kiki." He turned toward us, grinned, and broke out into Jax's signature move—the chicken arms. Family and friends joined in, doing the same. Laughing, I grabbed Amelia's hand and pulled her onto the dance floor.

Angie Vancise

Acknowledgements

First and foremost, I want to thank my brother for his unconditional love throughout my forty-four years with him. He taught me how to love, how to live and how to laugh. I will miss you for the rest of my days.

I want to thank Deborah Johnson for without her this book would have still been just an idea I hid from everyone.

My editor, Allyson, who has become so much more than that. Out of billions of people in this world I was lucky enough to have met her. Her dedication and compassion for this book went above and beyond and I will be forever grateful.

My uncle, for teaching me how to love all animals and everything nature. For always believing in me and having my back. Having you as a second father was truly the best gift.

My cousin for always being there right by my side. Another journey has begun but know that I'll always be home for lunch.

To my dad for teaching me a business mind and pushing me to go after my dreams. And to my mom for her love, her support and hard work, her 'get up and dust yourself off' attitude has made me stronger than I knew I was. I miss you both so much.

To my husband and daughter for the countless hours I spent ignoring them while I typed these words over and over and over again.

Katie for always knowing how to decipher the medical garble and getting us through the tough times.

To all of my friends who have more than stepped in as family.

And Fredrik, especially Fredrik, for understanding the direction this story went and for never giving up on me.

And finally, to Ben, for helping me each and every step of the way! I couldn't have done it without you.

And to YOU reading this right now. Out of all of the books in the world you chose this one. My heart is full of gratitude. Thank you so much and I hope that you enjoyed it.

Cheers,

Angie

Manufactured by Amazon.ca
Bolton, ON